The Fallen Crown

Book 10 in the Anarchy Series

By

Griff Hosker

The Fallen Crown

Published by Sword Books Ltd 2016

Copyright © Griff Hosker First Edition

A CIP catalogue record for this title is available from the British Library.
Cover by Design for Writers
Thanks to Simon Walpole for the Artwork.

The Fallen Crown

Dedicated to all my New Zealand fans, especially Dave and
Cathy.

Contents

Prologue

Stockton Castle - January 1140

It had taken us two weeks to travel north to our home on the Tees from the lands of the west controlled by Empress Matilda and her half brother, Earl Robert of Gloucester. It had been a frozen land that became increasingly covered with a blanket of snow the further north we went. It was a journey fraught with potential danger. There were still supporters of the Empress in the land through which we passed but most of the knights, lords and magnates were her enemies. We chose the castles in which we stayed wisely. We passed through old trails and forest as we avoided the scrutiny of Stephen the Usurper's supporters. Had there been any brave enough then we might have encountered bandits for we carried back the fruits of our victory. We had horses, weapons, mail and coin. The war in which we had fought had given us knights for ransom as well as the goods and horses of the dead we had slain. However, my banner was well known and any bandit knew that an attack on the Warlord of the North would result in but one thing, death. We rode north and were unmolested.

The journey back afforded me the time to reflect on the last months of the old year. I had advised the Empress that I would stay away from her court in Gloucester. She had not wished me to do so but I did not want any hint of scandal associated with the Empress. Her brother suspected that I was the father of young Henry Fitz Empress, her son. We could not have that suspicion. The Empress' husband, Geoffrey of Anjou, still prosecuted the war on her behalf in

Normandy. A hint of scandal might tear our fragile alliance apart. The Empress' forces would consolidate the land around Worcester and Gloucester. I would stay in my northern fortress. True I was surrounded by enemies, but none frightened me. I had beaten them all. If they came again then I would defeat them. I had a small retinue but all of my men were renowned fighters and they fought for me. Each was worth five I might hire in the markets.

When I had reached my castle and our goods had been stored, I realised that I was alone. My son and my grandson were in Normandy and the woman I loved was separated from me by my enemies. I had my men and I had my land but, as I looked out on a frozen River Tees, I felt my isolation more acutely than ever. I had my men at arms and they were like brothers to me and I had my squires but I still had to rule the land of the Tees for my Empress alone. I had no one with whom I could consult. If I made the wrong decisions and we lost it then the flood gates would be opened. The Scots would pour across the river and devastate the land. Had we not held them at Northallerton, at the battle they called the Standard, barely two years ago then this land would now be Scottish. The effect of that last invasion was still clear for all to see. Ruined castles had still to be rebuilt. There were manors without lords and without the people to work the fields. I had parlous few lords I could appoint to do so and the lack of a lord meant a lack of revenue. This war cost money. The Palatinate of Durham was ruled by the Scottish puppet, William Cumin, and Prince Henry, the son of King David of Scotland, was now Earl of Northumbria and he ruled the land north of mine.

I roused myself. I had been taught by my father not to waste time worrying about what I could not do. I had money now and I would use it. I would summon my steward and my mason. We would rebuild the north, one castle at a time.

Chapter 1

Theland of the Warlord

The land of the Warlord

That winter seemed to last forever. In some ways that
helped us for although we could do nothing about my
castles, the smiths in my towns were able to produce more
mail and armour for my men. We used the spare labour we
had to help my smith, Alf, and his men at their forges. It took
skill to forge a sword but only muscle was needed to work
the bellows. My squires now had full hauberks. All of my
men at arms wore mail and had fine helmets. The armouries
had swords and spears aplenty. My fletchers produced the
hundreds of arrows my archers needed and we bred more
horses. My men at arms, and the men of my manor, trained.
When I went to war it was the burghers of Stockton and my
small garrison which would defend my walls. I had used an
idea from the east where I had been brought up. Instead of a
mighty wall running all the way around my land, I had a ring
of castles and fortified manors. Each could be defended
against a smaller enemy but if we were invaded then they
would garrison the jewel in the crown, Stockton. It was one
of a handful of powerful castles which could withstand a
prolonged siege. Durham, Bamburgh, Barnard Castle and
York were the others.

The ice and the snow did not stop me from venturing to
Norton where Erre guarded my northern frontier, nor
Normanby in the east. Barnard Castle and Hugh of Gainford
protected the west and in the south lay Sir Richard of Yarm.
With Hartburn, Thornaby and Elton close by we felt safe. I
knew that could not last. The Scots had been quiet for over a
year and soon they would make another attempt to enlarge
their land at our expense.

When the first grass was seen after the snows and the ice,
I summoned my knights to my hall. I had sent Captain
William and my ship, *'Adela'* to Anjou. My son had his own
manor now; he was Baron of Ouistreham but Sir Leofric was
the constable of my manor of La Flèche. It was a rich manor
in Anjou and the riches we had collected would allow us to
buy that which we could not produce. It also provided men at
arms for us. We were not reliant on those who had been

8

brought up in England. When I saw the new grass it meant we could think about going to war once more.

My knights arrived for my council of war. This was the first time they had all been together since we had returned from our campaign in the west. Not all had been with me. I had left most at home guarding my land and they were full of questions for each other. I did not mind the noise and banter. I sat back with a goblet of Angevin red and enjoyed it. Whilst apart they were bastions and held the line. When they were together they were a force to be reckoned with. We had a combination of superb archers and doughty men at arms. Wielded wisely and well we were an unstoppable force. Our enemies had discovered that. Even when we were outnumbered, we emerged victorious. My detractors said it was because I was lucky. They were wrong. I thought about warfare more deeply than they did. I had studied at the Emperor's school in Constantinople and I had read of leaders from the past. I knew how Alexander, Hannibal and Caesar had fought. I had seen Justinian's walls and spoken to those who kept many times their numbers of barbarians at bay with well-armed and well-led soldiers. I tried to copy that. The only one of my enemies who came close to thinking as I did was my nemesis, the usurper Stephen of Blois. He was a clever general and he was popular with his men. He also had more honour than Prince Henry of Scotland. That made him harder to defeat.

I was aware that the noise had stopped and they were all staring at me. Dick, formerly the captain of my archers and now titled Sir Richard, looked concerned and said, "My lord, does something bother you? You have a frown on your brow."

I realised that I had been deep in thought. That was the problem with being alone so much. It made a man brood. I stood and smiled, "Forgive me, my friends. I keep alone too much. Now that we are all joined then nothing worries me. John, have Alice bring in the food. Please sit. Choose your own places, you know we are not precious about that!"

I knew that some Earls, such as Richard of Gloucester, liked to reward their men by allowing them to sit closer to them. That was not my way. We were all equals and they chose their companions. Erre, Wulfric and Dick sat together with Edward. They had all been lowly men until I had elevated them and made them knights. Tristan, Hugh, Harold, John and my squires sat together; they were the young bloods and Sir Richard of Yarm sat between me and his son. I had invited Father Henry, the priest of my manor, too, and he chose to sit on the other side of me.

Aiden and his two hawkers, Edward and Edgar, had been hunting and we had a fine deer. Along with the other delicacies which Alice had procured we ate well. My lands in Anjou ensured that we had better wine than any in England. The feast was convivial. When the plates had been cleared and we nibbled on the sweetmeats served by Alice, talk turned to the civil war which raged.

"So, my lord, do we head south to join with the Empress and the Earl? Do we drive Stephen back to Blois?" Wulfric was blunt. He spoke the way he fought, directly.

"Would that it were that easy, my friend. Twixt here and Gloucester lie a sea of enemies. I promised the Empress that I would await her commands and, as yet, she has not sent me word. The day will come when we join forces but for the moment she and the Earl consolidate what we won in the autumn and winter."

Sir Edward of Thornaby was a wise warrior. "Do not be so ready to leave this valley, Wulfric. The Scots look for weakness."

Sir Hugh of Gainford who was the constable at Barnard Castle nodded, "My men have caught and hanged four Scottish spies this winter. They probe and they watch. Balliol wishes his castle to be returned to him."

"I know and that is why you are my rock in the west."

"Then we just wait, lord?"

Wulfric craved action. For him, a castle was somewhere warm to spend the winter. Now it was getting on for spring and he was keen to fight. "Do not worry, Wulfric, if you have a stout garrison and constable then, when we do go to war, you shall be on my right hand, as ever."

His grin showed me that I had pleased him. "I will have men to garrison by the time *'Adela'* returns, my lord."

Sir Harold had his own manor of Hartburn but in these uncertain times, his family lived with me in my castle for he just had a hall. I liked the arrangement. His wife and children made me remember my family when they were growing up. Sir Tristan's family did the same at Yarm. Elton and Hartburn did not have castles and the fortified halls were not strong enough to defend with the Scots on the rampage. It was these who looked at each other and then Harold spoke for them both. "We, too, would come to war with you, lord. We know our families are safe here."

I nodded. "Sir Edward?"

Laughing, he said, "I am not too old to go to war, lord. Besides, you will need someone to keep this wild berserker in check."

He nudged Wulfric in the ribs. Wulfric feigned innocence. "Just because I am fearless in battle there is no need to insult me!"

We all joined in the laughter for when Wulfric had the smell of battle in his nostrils, there was no holding him back. He would charge into any number of enemies wielding his war axe. His squires did not last long.

"Then I have my conroi. I would Sir Hugh Manningham was with me for he is a doughty warrior but he is the only knight who is north of here on whom I can rely."

Philip of Selby said, "Then will I be with you and Sir Richard? We are your mounted archers."

"You are. You have proved time and again how you can turn a battle when all seems lost and to that end, I have an errand for the two of you." They both leaned forward expectantly. "Philip, I would have you visit with your uncle, the Archbishop. It is some time since we spoke. I would have you gauge the mood of York."

"Aye, lord. It will be good to see the old man again."

"Dick, I need you to risk the high country and visit with the Empress. I will not trust my plans to letters; they can be intercepted. She knows you and can trust your words. I will give you a message for her."

11

Sir Edward asked, "Not her brother, lord?"

"The Earl has yet to commit fully to our cause and he has little love for me at the moment. The Empress commands the army and it is her orders I shall obey."

"And when do we leave, lord?"

"Tomorrow. That will give us a month to prepare for a campaign. A word of warning, Dick. Steer clear of the land around Chester. That treacherous Earl changes sides every time the wind blows."

"I will."

With our plans made my knights spoke of horses and castles. They talked of men at arms they had trained. Sir Edward's son was now a squire and he, too, was full of the promise his son betokened. His words were fulsome and proud as he spoke of his family. "I was a man at arms, lord. Had you not elevated me, I would be one yet but my son is the son of a noble." He hesitated. "When I fall, will he have the manor?"

"If it is in my power then aye. That may be in hands other than mine." He nodded. If we lost this civil war then all of my knights might lose their manors. Choosing the wrong side could be disastrous.

Father Henry took his leave after the last of the sweetmeats had gone. He had listened more than he spoke. "Pray to stay, Father."

"No, my lord. Your men are warriors and would talk of war. I do not mind that but I fear they would be inhibited by my presence. Besides, I have to be up early in the morning for matins."

"As you wish. Thank you for coming."

He nodded, "Despite what your enemies say about you, lord, you are a good man. I see that in your deeds around the manor, not on the battlefield. I know not who is right in the matter: the King or the Empress. I know that this anarchy is bad for the country but I am happy that I live here on this island of peace. The people prosper and they are happy. I am their shepherd and they are my flock. That is all a priest can ask."

"And you are a good man."

"I try. Our church prospers. Each year, William the Mason makes some improvement. The avenue of yew trees we planted has lasted well this winter. It will be some time before your men can make bows from their branches but they are a fine avenue and help to shade the graveyard."

"You are the shepherd of men, father. You watch over their souls. I plan for the future. My son and my grandson will be here long after I am gone. They will thank me for the yew trees and the bows they produce."

He smiled sadly, "They will thank you for much more than that, lord. Pray, do not give us the memory too soon."

After he had gone I reflected on his words. He was right. I had challenged Stephen to single combat. I was the Empress' champion but he had refused. He was a good knight at the tourney but he knew I had never been beaten. Had I had a lesser reputation, we might have settled this conflict with no loss to the people. They were the losers. Bands of knights and vagabonds roamed the land raiding, raping and stealing either in the name of Stephen or Matilda. In truth, they served neither. Knights like Sir Miles Fitz Walter, Sir Pain, Sir Brian Fitz Count and Sir Geoffrey Talbot were true knights. They served the Empress well. As for others...

The wine flowed freely and my knights were replete. None ventured forth and they slept where they could. The company had put me in good humour. The morbid black humour of January had gone. Perhaps it was winter that made me feel that way. I had a grandson I had never seen and a son who had grown up and become a man without me knowing. My other son I could never acknowledge. One day he would be King of England and I would bow my knee to him. I knew his mother would never tell him that I was his father. The fate of England, Normandy and Anjou lay in his hands. We would have to take that secret to our graves. My head and my heart were filled with secrets. I saw them each night when I closed my eyes. They weighed heavily upon me.

After they had gone I sent for my two squires. Gilles was the son of one of my archers who had died in Normandy and Richard had been the squire of Sir Ralph Buxton whom I had slain. They had both proved to me that they would make fine knights but that day was some way off. They were still learning. Both had killed men but they were not yet ready to be in the line which charged. They needed more muscle to carry the armour that they would need. However, they both needed a better sword. I took them to see Alf. He was the smith in the town and along with Ethelred, the merchant was one of the most important men in the manor. He was also the most loyal. A fierce warrior with an axe, he would fight alongside my Frisians to defend my town if enemies came.

The clang of his hammer told me that he was working. His smithy was close to the river. He needed water to temper the steel and it needed to be away from other buildings. The danger of fire was too great. One of his many sons ran to fetch him as we approached. He stepped from his smithy red and sweating. Even though the days were still cool, his furnace was, as ever, red hot.

"Yes, my lord?"

"I would have you make a good sword for my two squires. They both have one but they need one made by Alf of Stockton."

He bowed at the compliment. He pointed at some shafts of iron that were laid on a table just outside the smithy. "They are sword blanks. I pray you each lift them. When you find one that is just a little too heavy to lift over your head with your right hand then fetch it to me."

As they went I said, "Too heavy?"

"Yes, lord. They will become stronger, for they are young men. They will grow into their swords. If they were fully grown then I would not use this method. When I have fitted the guard and the pommel, each weapon will be better balanced."

They both came back with their pieces of iron. Alf nodded and took a piece of rag. He tore it in three. He tied one piece to Richard's blank and two pieces to Gilles. "You, young masters should come here at the end of each day to see the progress of your blades."

Richard, who was the youngest asked, "How long will they take?"

"As long as they need. You do not hurry a sword. His lordship's sword has never let him down. Each smith puts part of himself in every sword he makes. For those who serve the Earl of Cleveland, it must be the best. You will have to be patient." He pointed to swords in various stages of manufacture. "The blade has to be hammered and tempered. It must be balanced. See those, they are almost ready for their point and these for sharpening. Finally, they have the pommel and the guard fitted. You, young masters, will help in that process. These swords are for sale in the markets of Anjou and Normandy."

As we headed back to my castle Gilles asked, "Did your former lord not have a sword made for you, Richard?"

Richard shook his head, "I was the one who fetched and carried for the others. The sword I offered to the Earl was one I took from the field."

I remembered that day. I had made a good decision to spare his life and accept the offer of his sword. "And when you are full-grown then we shall visit with Alf again and have your mail made. For the present, that which you wear will have to do. Now go and tend to Rolf and your horses. We ride at the end of the week. I would see how my people fare. Make sure that all is well. Check every piece of leather and groom all the horses well."

"Aye, lord."

I sought John, my Steward. He was less parsimonious since the last attack by the Scots. He had realised that the coins I had used on weapons, mail and the castle were well spent. Some men built fine castles to make a statement. They told the world that they were important. My castle was not like that. It served one purpose: to protect the Tees valley and my people.

"When the *'Adela'* docks I want her turned around as quickly as we can, John. We need more men from Anjou." The Normans and the French were not as good natural bowmen as those we had in Wales and in England. Griff of Gwent attempted to reverse that by training any likely archers. There were many good men at arms and Brian and Padraig made sure that any they sent were good warriors.

15

"Aye, lord. And I have a list of things which we need. We will need to build a larger bread oven. The one we have cannot keep up with the demand."

I pointed to the outer bailey. "There is room aplenty by the river wall. It is safer there too."

"I will get the men to build it immediately. And there is something else, lord. The mill is not producing as much flour as we need."

The mill was by the manor of Norton. It was inconvenient having to transport it by cart along the greenway. "Any suggestions?"

"Father Henry said he had seen a mill at an abbey he visited. They had dug a leat from the river so that they could divert the river to power the mill. It saved them having a millpond." He pointed upstream. "There would seem to be a good place."

"Ask for the Father's advice. I think it is a good idea. If we are besieged again, it will save us being cut off from our mill. And we have goods aplenty to send and sell in Anjou?"

"We have. The tanners have produced much leather and the women are adept at making many things from it. The wool we produce too is much sought after. The potters are getting better and one day we can sell our own pots and tiles made from the clay of Stockton."

"Good. I shall visit my manors this week. I will hold sessions the week after. Have all the cases I need to hear ready for then and be ready to collect the taxes." He nodded. Those tasks brought in an income. He liked them. "Next month I expect to take a conroi south. I wish everything to be ready. Servants, tents, horses, weapons and food. I rely on you, John."

"I know, sir, and I will not let you down."

"On the morrow, I will take a tour of my land."

He already knew that I was leaving a healthy garrison. He had no fears there. My chores were done and I retired to my solar. I had had a busy morning. Alice would have placed my jug of wine, bread, cheese and ham there already. She knew my habits. I enjoyed looking south and west from my window. I felt I could see all the way to Gloucester and

Matilda. My lady and I knew we were fated never to be together but it did not stop me from dreaming. As with all such fantasies, it led me to try to come up with a strategy to defeat Stephen once and for all. Had the Earl of Gloucester not been so arrogant, we might have joined forces after we captured Lincoln and defeated Stephen of Blois. He had been weak then. The moment had slipped away and now we were having to claw back land lost in his campaign. The defection of the Earl of Chester had changed everything.

I left my castle before either Philip of Selby or Dick returned. I was not worried. Both were clever men and would not be caught. Better that they take their time and gain valuable intelligence than come back too soon with ill-founded news. I took just my squires and ten men at arms. I was not travelling far but with the bandits and brigands who abounded once I left my valley, it was as well to be prepared.

I would travel to Gainford and thence to Barnard Castle. Sir Hugh had a castellan at his manor. He held Barnard Castle for the Empress and one day he would return to Gainford. He had had William my mason build him a fine gatehouse and barbican. He still had a castle with wooden palisades but little by little he was improving it.

Spring in England, especially the north, was unpredictable. When we set out it was as though winter had returned. A chill wind hurtled in from the north and was in our faces for the first few miles. It was only when we turned, just before Yarm, that we managed to get a little respite. The wind made conversation impossible. That was probably just as well for I had much on my mind. Sir Hugh was a fine knight but I had given him a task which was almost impossible. His nearest aid, should he be attacked, would come from his small garrison at Gainford. It would take a rider almost half a day to reach my castle and even if we left straight away, he would have to hold off an enemy for at least a day. His castle was well built and had a curve in the river for protection but he did not have a large number of men to defend the walls. I hated leaving him alone while I went to fight for the Empress.

After halting for some refreshments and a warm at the fire in Gainford Castle, we pushed on to Barnard Castle. The approach from the east was deceiving. The castle seemed to have no natural defences. It was only when you tried to get around the castle that you saw how formidable they really were. That was Hugh's problem. The river could be forded or even bridged and once he was besieged then an enemy could overwhelm him.

He greeted us at his gate. His men had spied my banners coming from some distance away. "Good to see you again, lord. I will have rooms prepared for you and your squires."

"Thank you. I thought Stockton was cold but here it is even colder and I am sure I felt a few flecks of snow!"

He laughed, "You did, lord."

I turned to my squires, "See to the horses and then join me in the Great Hall." As squires, the care of the horses was second only to their duty to protect me.

His wife bobbed a curtsy, "It is good to see you, my lord. I have had mulled wine prepared and there will be hot food soon. I will go and hurry the servants."

I smiled, "Not on my account, dear lady. I need little in the way of comfort these days."

She smiled, "Nonetheless, lord, I would not be showing you the proper respect if I did not."

We sat before his roaring fire. "How goes the work on your defences, Sir Hugh?"

"I have made devices to pour oil and boiling water from my walls. We have laid in great supplies of pig fat. I know that is the best deterrent."

"And how will you keep them from your walls?"

"I am loath to improve a castle which may well be returned to that traitor Balliol. I will not give him a drawbridge but we now pull in the bridge each night. I keep scouts and hunters in my woods. If Scots or strangers are seen then we pull up the bridges straight away."

"Good. But remember, I am but a day away. It seems to me that you are in a good position to hold off an enemy for a few days at least."

He hesitated.

"Speak, Sir. Hugh. You know me better than that."

"When you are away, lord, as I know you must, then who will come to my aid?"

It was a good point. "Sir Erre and Sir Richard are both well placed to come to your aid. If the enemy was the Scottish army then all would retire to my castle anyway. I would say send to Durham but I fear that is full of enemies too."

"I will have to pray that Sir Richard and Sir Erre can reach me in time then." He sounded resigned to his fate.

I drank some of the mulled wine. It tasted good. I came to a decision. "I will also leave Philip of Selby and his archers. They are well mounted and if they reached you before an attacker then I am confident you could hold off the Scots. Do not forget the men who live in this valley have no love for the Scots. Their lord, Balliol, might but not his people. Use them on your walls. We have shown before that doughty folk using slings and bows can defeat mailed warriors."

My squires returned and we spoke of other things. "Think you that this is the year the tide will turn for the Empress, lord?"

"I hope so but I confess that I do not have enough knights to force the issue. The Empress and I are dependent on the Earl of Gloucester."

"Why does he not support the Empress more than he does?"

That was a very good question. "I am not certain but in my dealings with him, over the years, I have seen that he sees himself as his father's son. He can never be king but he seeks power. He seeks a throne. He has one now. It is in the west of England. He has conquered large parts of Wales yet that is a poor country." I shook my head for I could not understand the strategy. "If he conquered more of the south and the east then he would have even greater revenue!"

I realised I had become heated. My squires looked fearful but Sir Hugh smiled, "Fear not, Gilles and Rich. Your lord is a passionate man. He fights for this country and has a greater vision than any other I have met. It is why we all serve him."

The doors of the hall swung open and servants appeared with trays laden with food. "Your men are eating with the men at arms, my lord. They have fine fare too."

"Thank you, mistress, now pray come and sit by me. I would hear about your children!" I was regaled with tales of their young family and it made me think about the young family I had never seen, my son's.

I decided to head home through Durham and we left before dawn. I had not seen Geoffrey Rufus for some time nor had I heard from him. He had not been the Bishop his appointment had promised. Most of that was the fault of William Cumin, his secretary. He was in the pay of the Scots. It meant that the Bishop neither supported nor opposed the Empress. He had to tread a fine line between appeasing the Scots and upsetting me. If I was going away then I needed him to guard my northern borders or at least warn me of Scottish incursions.

We passed through empty villages as we headed east. In some lay bodies, decayed and eaten by animals, in open view. It was desolate. Where we did see life, on distant farms, the sight of my horsemen drove the people within to bar their doors. Had I had time then I would have investigated but time was pressing. The days were still short. The city of Durham had always been prosperous. It was the jewel in the northern crown and yet, as we headed through the outskirts, I saw few people and those I did see were fearful and scurried away as we passed. As we neared the walls I said, "Richard, unfurl the banner."

My ten men at arms were led by Wilfred. As we neared the walls he said, quietly, "I like this not, my lord. Is this safe?"

"I know not, Wilfred, and, like you, I am cautious. Keep your eyes open. I shall just take Gilles with me. If we are admitted then I will speak with the Bishop. If we are not admitted then that tells us much. I do not intend to stay long. Keep your eyes and ears open."

"We will, my lord."

The gates were closed. That was not a surprise. The land was on a war footing. A face appeared at the battlements. I had taken off my helmet and my hands were not close to my weapons. I came in peace, "I am the Earl of Cleveland and I would speak with the Bishop."

The two guards looked at each other. Their heads disappeared and then reappeared. One shouted, "The Bishop is not a well man. It is said he is close to death."

"Then all the more reason that I speak with him."

There was a hurried conference and the two men left.

I turned to Wilfred. "Watch for treachery."

My men were the finest men at arms in the land. Each was equipped as a knight. All had a full mail hauberk, good swords and the best of helmets. More than that, they could think for themselves. There were just ten of them but I would back them against fifty others.

"Aye, lord." He turned to Richard, "And you, Master Richard, you keep tight hold of that banner and if I say move then stick closer to me than my horse's saddle!"

Wilfred was a rough and ancient soldier. He had lost teeth and had scars. I saw Richard nodding fearfully, "Aye, Wilfred!"

Eventually, the doors groaned open. The two men we had seen waved us through. I saw a knot of men at arms waiting by the keep. I saw no priests. I glanced around the walls. They were manned but not heavily. Where was the garrison? If this was all that the Bishop had to defend his walls then the Scots could walk in any time they chose. We stopped and I handed my reins to Oswald and my helmet to Richard. My shield hung from Rolf's side.

A sergeant at arms gave a slight bow, "I command the garrison, lord. I am Ralph of Rothbury."

I had not met the man before but he was a powerful looking warrior. Rothbury had been English and was now Scottish. This man could have allegiances on either side.

"I hear the Bishop is ill?"

He nodded, "The priests are with him."

"Then take me to him."

He hesitated, "I am not certain that is a good thing, my lord."

21

I looked him in the eyes. "Know you that I am the Warlord of the North?" He nodded. "I led the armies of the north when we defeated King David at Northallerton and I have a warrant from Empress Matilda to rule in her stead. Would you disobey me?" He looked around. Someone else was making decisions here. He quailed. "He is in the chapter house."

"I know where that is!" I did not add that I had recaptured this castle from enemies before. "Wilfred, watch the horses. Come, Gilles!" As we strode across the green to the chapter house I said, quietly, "I rely on you to watch my back!"

"Aye, lord." His hand went to his sword.

I entered the chapter house and surprised a young priest who turned around with a startled expression on his face. "I am the Earl of Cleveland. Where is the Bishop?"

Unlike the sergeant at arms, the priest looked happier to see me when he heard my name. "Come with me, my lord. It is good that you have come."

As he led me through a corridor I asked, "Trouble?"

"The Dean will tell you all." He shrugged, "I am but a novice, my lord. You need to know facts and not what a young priest has gleaned."

I smiled, I liked this young and earnest man. "What is your name, priest?"

"I am Brother Thomas, sir, from Leyburn."

"You are an honest man. My castle always welcomes such men." He nodded. I knew we were close to the Bishop's quarters when I began to smell death. It hung in the air and lay like a fog in the tees valley. If the Bishop was not already dead then he would be before too long.

An older priest stood as we entered the chamber.

I turned to my squire, "Gilles, go back to the chapterhouse door and keep watch." He glanced around the room and I smiled, "I am safe here. These are men of God and we can trust them." He left.

The Dean said, "Not all men of God are to be trusted, my lord. I am William of Arundel, the Dean of Durham."

I looked at Geoffrey Rufus. He lay still and white looking like a piece of marble. "How is the Bishop?

"He clings on to life by a thread."

"What is the illness?" The young priest and the Dean looked at each other. "Speak!"

The Dean said, "I think he was poisoned. He was hale and he was hearty a week since and then he woke one morning vomiting. We gave him purgatives and water but I think the deed was done by then."

"Has he woken?"

"Sometimes he opens his eyes but we have heard no words these last three days."

I went to the bed and touched the Bishop's hand. It was still warm but only just. I could feel his heart beating in his wrist but it was painfully slow. As I held it I said, "I saw empty villages and dead bodies. Was this the Scots?"

I heard the Dean say, "The Scots have not visited their wrath on us these last two years; not since the battle." I took that in as I looked down at the man on whom King Henry had placed such faith. "And the garrison; it seems a little smaller than it used to." His words were guarded.

"They are riding abroad."

"And who leads them?"

There was another pause and before the Dean could answer the Bishop's eyes opened, "My lord, you have come. God has answered my prayers." His voice was weak but I saw the spark of life in his eyes.

"I have come."

His claw-like fingers gripped my hand as though he was clinging on to life. He pulled my arm down towards him. I lowered my head. "I have not long for this world. I am at peace and I have no more sins for I have confessed." I did not know if he was talking to me or to God. "I have been poisoned. It is Cumin. You were right in your suspicions he is in the pay of the Scots."

The effort of speaking was too much and he sank back into the bed. His hand fell to his side.

I turned, "Where is Cumin?"

The Dean said, "In the Great Hall. He commands here now."

"And his men?"

"They are led by his nephew, Osbert."

"And they lay waste to this land?" The Dean looked helplessly at me and nodded.

I felt the Bishop's fingers as they tapped on my arm. He did not open his eyes but he whispered, "Take care of my people, lord."

Just then Gilles burst in. "Lord, armed men are heading this way from the keep!"

I turned to the Dean. "Stockton will always welcome those who cared for this man. I will have to leave now. I have few men with me but I shall return."

The Dean nodded, "I know, lord. That has always been a comfort but we are bound to the Bishop. So long as he lives we stay. I pray you to hurry. They mean to trap you."

I was drawing my sword even as I hurried down the corridor. "Gilles, stay close behind me. We must get to the horses!"

As we burst from the door, I saw the eight men at arms led by Ralph of Rothbury. They were forty paces from us and hurried towards us in a column of twos. Wilfred had seen the danger and he and four of my men rode towards us. They were on the other side of the bailey. I pulled my sword back and ran at the eight men. They had shields and we did not. As Ralph of Rothbury swung his sword at me, I grabbed his right wrist and punched him in the side of the head with the hilt of my sword. He was not expecting it and he fell to the ground. The man behind had not expected that and when I swung my sword sideways the blade ripped open his cheek and jaw.

I felt a blow to my back but my mail was well made. I whipped my sword around me in an arc. As I turned, I saw that my sword had bitten into the neck of Ralph of Rothbury who had attempted to strike my unprotected back. Gilles was pulling his sword from the stomach of another as Wilfred and my men bundled their horses into the backs of the others. Their swords made short work of them. The alarm bell was ringing. I saw Raymond of Le Mans and Richard galloping towards us as my men finished off the men at arms. The walls were filling with men.

As I mounted Rolf I shouted, "The sally port! The gate will be guarded." I pointed to the small postern gate which lay close to the Cathedral.

Wilfred nodded. We had used the sally port to gain entry. He waved his arm and the last of my men galloped towards us. I donned my helmet and hefted my shield. Cumin was a cunning man and he would know about the sally port. It would be guarded but not as well as the main gate. I spurred Rolf towards the small gate in the curtain wall. As I had expected, he had men on the walls and four crossbowmen at the gate. Other men were flooding from the keep where they had been hiding. I led and that drew the bolts. The four all aimed at me. I held my shield across my chest. One pinged off the side of my helmet and two struck the shield. Cumin was no soldier. If he had been, he would have used archers. It took too long to reload a crossbow. Rolf was fast and my sword hacked into the neck of one of those with a crossbow as Gilles slashed a second across his back. Wilfred sent two men up the ladders to clear the ramparts while the rest slew the remaining crossbowmen.

Oswald leapt from his horse to open the door. We would have to lead our horses through and we needed to buy some time. "Gurth, Leopold of Durstein, with me! The rest of you get through the gate. Gilles, hold the gate for us!"

We did the unexpected. We charged the gaggle of men at arms who raced towards us. Leaderless now that Ralph of Rothbury was dead, they came like a rabble. Rolf had enough space to open his legs. With my shield protecting both my left side and my middle, I leaned forward to scythe sideways at the men at arms. They were already trying to get away from Rolf's slobbering jaws and his mighty hooves. The last thing they were watching for was my sword as it hacked through necks, backs and arms. My quick hands struck four blows so quickly that my blade was a blur. I reined him around. It took all of my strength to do so. My two men at arms had carved a similar path and we rode back through the maimed and wounded. The ones who could fled before us. Behind me, from the top of the round keep, I heard William Cumin, screaming, "Kill them! Kill them all!"

25

Cumin was not a soldier. Had he been, he would have led his men. With their captain dead, his men were reluctant to risk the wrath of the warlord. They were tardy in their advance. We slowed our horses down, to calm them, and walked them to the sally port. Gilles stood, as I had asked, holding the door open. We dismounted and walked our horses through. On the other side, my men waited on the narrow path which circumnavigated the walls. I had no doubt that the men on the walls would try to shower us with crossbow bolts but we had our shields. We made the Stockton road with just one injury. A bolt had managed to penetrate the links on the hauberk of Stephen the Grim. It had barely nicked his leg. We rode home and I realised that we now had no allies whatsoever north of Barnard Castle and Norton. We were alone.

Chapter 2

As we headed south, my wounded man at arms was the butt of my men's humour. "I see the bolt did not make you smile then, Stephen the Grim!"

"Repairing your mail will cost you a coin or two!"

"I saw the crossbowman if you wish to go back and get him!"

He shook his head. It was true he never smiled. He had been wounded in the face and for some reason, he had lost the ability to do so. He had a good sense of humour and gave as good as he got. "Fear not, Leopold, I have coin enough. I, unlike you, know how to choose rich knights to fight!"

Wilfred rode next to me as they bantered. "I am sorry I was so slow reaching you, lord."

"I wondered at the delay. What happened?"

"I see now the ploy. They sent out food and ale. We were distracted."

I suddenly turned, "You did not partake of either, did you?"

"No, lord, for we saw the men at arms moving towards you. Why?"

"In all likelihood, it was poisoned! The Bishop is dying and he believes that Cumin poisoned him."

"Curse him for a dissembler and a villain!" He turned and looked back at the walled city. "Does this mean that Durham is now a stronghold of the Scots?"

"Not yet. He is not Bishop. Until he is then he cannot ally with Scotland but one of his nephews, Osbert, serves Prince Henry and leads the savages who raid and pillage. Once we reach my home and before we join the Empress, we will rid the Palatinate of this scourge."

"Then Sir Hugh is on his own?"

"I fear so. We will have to leave a stronger garrison in Stockton. This land is more dangerous now than when we set off."

We reached my home well before dark. After warning John that I would need to take a conroi north, I sought Aiden and his falconers. The two youths were now almost men and Aiden was training them well. "I need you to find this band which rides through the Palatinate. They murder and they destroy. Their trail should be easy to find."

"And yet you ask for the best scout in the Tees, my lord."

I nodded, "You are, Aiden, and you are wise. I do not wish you to be seen. If we fright this prey, they will run to Durham and I have no desire to try to winkle them from that stronghold."

"They will probably use that as their home, lord. It is central. Did you see where they had been already?"

"They have laid waste to the land around Barnard and the upper Tees. Gainford is safe; for the moment."

He nodded, "There lies your problem, lord, for if I were this robber baron then I would strike at the richer settlements along the Tees. There are but two castles to stop them; this one and Sir Hugh's."

Harold and Tristan rode in from a day's hunting. I told them my news. "I will take your men, Harold and Tristan, and as many mounted archers as are still here. I cannot wait for the return of Philip and Dick. We must act before more people are hurt."

Aiden nodded, "We will leave before dawn and head to the west and then north. If you follow my trail, lord, then either Edgar or Edward shall find you."

Philip of Selby and his archers arrived later that night. He looked travel-weary when he arrived and his horses were lathered. "Was there a problem, Philip?" I saw both Tristan and Harold listening.

He nodded, "We left York this morning but there was a large conroi of knights and men at arms waiting for us close

28

by Easingwold. Had my scouts not spied them, we might have walked into them. We took the road towards Arncliffe and Appleton Wiske. We discouraged their scouts and three lie dead but I did not relish a fight with so many mailed warriors."

"You did the right thing. Know you who it was?"

"From my uncle's words, I am guessing Sir Edward Fitz Mandeville."

"He is still here in the north then?"

"Aye, lord. It seems he sees the opportunity to carve out his own fiefdom. But there is more. Revolt against Stephen has sprung up in the fens. Nigel, Bishop of Ely, has risen in support of Matilda."

"That is good news indeed!"

"But Stephen has moved to nip the revolt in the bud."

"And we have Fitz Mandeville between us and the Bishop!" He nodded, "How many knights did he have?"

"I can give you detailed information on that, lord. My uncle does not like him and he told me. He has sixty knights and almost two hundred men at arms. It is why we fled. We are not cowards. He had twenty of his knights and half of his men at arms on the road."

"Do not berate yourself. Your news is vital. This Fitz Mandeville profits from the favour given to his cousin Geoffrey de Mandeville, the Earl of Essex. I have no doubt that the two of them communicate with each other frequently. Where does this Edward Fitz Mandeville make his stronghold?"

"It is Malton. The Scots burned it and, it is said, this Mandeville is rebuilding it in stone. He uses the money he extorts from the people south of the Tees."

"What of Richard of Yarm?"

"I told him of the danger when I crossed the river there. He said that his men had found evidence of this banditry!"

I was annoyed. Sir Richard should have told me! It seemed I had two campaigns that needed my attention. "And how is your uncle?"

"He is not well, my lord. His skin looked thin enough to see his bones beneath. I fear he has not long for this world."

I shook my head, "Your uncle is a true Englishman we shall miss his like. You have done well. Rest your men and tomorrow afternoon we ride to hunt Osbert Cumin and his Scottish raiders."

I turned to Sir Tristan and Sir John asked them to stay. "Sir Tristan, I will take your men tomorrow but I want you to ride to your father. Tell him about our news. I want his men to scout south of the river. He is not to act until I reach him but I must know where this Fitz Mandeville hides."

He hesitated. "Lord, I know my father. He probably thought not to bother you and that he could deal with the problem."

"I know you defend him, Tristan, as a son should. I do not condemn him. However, I would rather be bothered with a thousand questions than one of my people was hurt because of a knight riding wild in my land. Had I known of the danger that Fitz Mandeville represented then I could have done something about it. Just ask your father to keep me informed."

"I will."

When he had left me I turned to Sir John, "I need you to stay here too while we scotch this snake. We will be riding to war with this Fitz Mandeville. I want you to decide which men stay with John of Craven and which ride. I need you to decide which horses are ready for war."

"This is a great responsibility, lord. Am I ready for it?"

"You were castellan here for long enough that you know the castle as well as any. You know the men and you know John of Craven. My mind is filled with plots and plans; enemies and allies. I need someone to take some weight from my shoulders. It is what Leofric does for me in Anjou."

He stood a little straighter. "Then if you have faith in me, my lord, I will try to live up to your expectations."

He left and I went to the maps I kept in my chest. Wulfstan had been the one who had started my obsession with them. He could read and he taught me how to understand maps. Now I found them invaluable. I added to them whenever I found a new place or a new feature. I traced the route we would take. If we headed to Piercebridge and then Gainford, I could turn north and east. If Aiden was right then this Osbert would gradually pick off the outlying settlements. He would hope that I would be blind to it or perhaps he thought I would be heading south again soon. He was wrong on both counts.

With two knights, twenty-five archers, the men at arms from three conroi and my two squires, I was confident that I could deal with this Osbert if I could pin him down. His method was not new. Some of the nomadic tribes who lived on the borders of the Byzantine Empire did the same. They would hit and then run. They were past masters at it and the only defence the Empire had was a string of forts and fast-moving horsemen of their own. I would do the same. All of my men were mounted and were excellent riders. Philip of Selby had his own eighteen archers and seven from my garrison. They were excellent riders although they never used their bows from the backs of horses.

Philip protested that his men did not need the rest and were keen to ride earlier. I waved away his protestations, "I am happy at the delay for it gives my scouts the time to find them and besides it is your horses which concern me. They had a hard ride yesterday. Let us not jeopardise their health for a couple of hours."

We cut directly across the long loop in the Tees. We went due west. With two archers as scouts, I did not fear us being surprised. We were wrapped against the cold. The spring was the coldest I had ever known. Already April was almost half gone and the buds were still shy of appearing on the trees. As we neared Piercebridge, I remembered the lord who had lived there. William of Piercebridge had been a quiet knight. The Scots had not only killed him but his whole family. There was no lord there. The Roman fort on the north bank had been robbed of most of its stones and the stark, blackened shell of the wooden castle William had built lay on the southern bank overlooking the bridge and this vital crossing. It was where King David had crossed with his army two years since. I wondered if the raid on Piercebridge had been a plan to gain them access to the soft underbelly of the north.

As we crossed the bridge, I surveyed the houses. People still lived and eked out a living. With no lord of the manor, I did not tax them. What was the point? There was nothing to tax. As Richard took Rolf down to the river to water him, an old one armed man approached. He knuckled his head, "Good to see you, my lord."

I vaguely recognised him then I saw his axe held in his mighty right hand. "Why it is Tom of Ulnaby! Are you well?" He had been one of William of Piercebridge's men at arms. He had been left for dead after the raid. He had lost his left arm and all of his comrades.

He looked pleased to be recognised. "Aye, lord. I felt one of his lordship's men should farm around here but it is hard. If it is not Scots who plague us, it is raiders and bandits."

"How many men are there in the fyrd?"

"Oh, we can muster twenty but that includes four old cripples like me and five boys. The priest has gone but there is a bell in the church." He pointed to the Roman walls. "Most of the stones might be gone but they serve us yet. If a lord came..."

"I know, Tom, and you are right to reproach me. I have been remiss."

"Oh no, lord! I meant no such thing. If it were not for you then... besides, who rules the country now? If you and the Archbishop had not stopped the Scots at Northallerton, I would not be here. I am grateful." He smiled, "But I can wish and I can hope. One day there will be a lord and he will have a castle. Then I will stand on the walls once more and spit defiance at these Scottish barbarians!"

As we headed to Gainford, Philip and Harold talked of Tom. "He makes me feel humble, Harold. We have so much and he has so little yet he is grateful for the little protection we offer him. Did you see his home? It was made of wood and turf."

Harold laughed, "When I was an outlaw in the forest, a turf house would have seemed like luxury! But I know what you mean."

We had reached Gainford and night was falling. I decided to stay in the wooden walls of Hugh's castle.

We had just set off, the following morning, when Edgar found us. "Lord, Aiden sent me. We found the trail of the Scots. They attacked Walworth last night."

"Are they still there?"

"They were when we left. Edward went to Piercebridge." He hesitated. "They burned the priest alive, lord."

I nodded, grimly, "They will pay. Let us ride. "

As we headed northeast, I closed my eyes as I tried to picture the map. They would gather their ill-gotten gains and use the best road available to them That would be the old Roman Road. It went through Auckland. That belonged to the Bishop of Durham. It was a distance of about seven miles. "Sir Harold, take your men at arms and those of Sir Tristan. Ride due north towards Headlam and then find somewhere on the road to Auckland to ambush this Osbert as he returns to Durham."

"Aye, lord."

As my knight and his men left us Philip asked, "You are sure he will go that way?"

"It is the shortest way back to Durham. If he suspects we are close, he will bolt and leave his goods behind. This man has achieved what he has by avoiding being caught. He will continue to do so."

"And Sir Harold will stop him?"

"Sir Harold will indeed stop him. He knows ambush and the men at arms he leads are the equal of any. They will certainly be able to deal with these brigands no matter how well armed and armoured they are."

We had less than six miles to go and I was keen to catch them before they knew we were on to the trail. I turned to Philip. "I will charge the Scots. I want the archers to lay down a screen of arrows to the northwest. That is the route they will take. When they have fled, take your men into the village and see to any survivors."

"You will not need us more?"

"If you and your archers can thin them out then good but I want them afraid of your arrows so that they run into Sir Harold's ambush. We will catch them and have them between the hammer and the anvil. I am the hammer. Harold is the anvil. He and his men will not yield."

Edgar shouted, "It is my brother!" I looked to the right and saw the other falconer, Edward, galloping to catch us up. I now had three archers I could take with me. Unlike Philip and his archers, Aiden and his men could loose from the back of a horse. They would be my surprise.

As I had suspected, while Osbert Cumin had been disporting himself, he had had men keeping watch. As we approached the village from the south, I saw confusion. "Philip, ride! Go across country!" His men wore little or no armour and so they made good speed. Many of my men had spears and they prepared to use them. Some held them overarm to thrust while others held them underarm to punch.

I saw the enemy knights and men at arms, it was hard to tell which was which, as they fled north to the old Roman Road. Philip of Selby was riding the rougher route across fields but he would soon be in a position to send arrows after them. Had Osbert not panicked he might have seen that I came at him with just eleven men at arms and two squires.

He had a force that was fully mounted. I estimated there to be about seventy men. The thirty who galloped towards the road and led the others were the ones in armour and mail. The others, while mounted, had merely a helmet, shield and a sword. More importantly, they had poor horses. Some were sumpters. We began to gain. We rode down the road. I saw Aiden break from cover and begin to release arrows. He was less than fifty paces from them and he was deadly. Edward and Edgar began to release too. Eight men fell to twelve arrows and then we were amongst them!

One nasty looking Scot was trying to clamber aboard his horse while clutching a candlestick from the church. I lazily swung my arm as his head appeared above his saddle. I took half of his head off. Edgar and Edward were loosing arrows and targeting those who looked as though they might turn and fight. We wanted them driven into Philip's arrows. My two squires were using their spears well. It gave them an advantage over men who were fleeing. Once a crowd of men run, it quickly becomes a stampede as they try to avoid being the last man. The hedges, ditches and thin saplings channelled them in the road and they barged into each other. I saw one man thrown from his horse as another barged him out of the way. His head cracked against a tree.

I looked ahead and saw that the much wider Roman Road lay ahead. Those we pursued thought it meant they had escaped, for they would have more room and be less crowded.

I heard the wail as the arrows began to fall from Philip's ambush. Osbert and his knights, all seven of them, fared better than most. They had long shields and their armour was well made but many of the men at arms fell. Then, when the ones without armour came past my archers, more fell and the saddles were emptied. Shouting, "Leave them for the archers." I spurred Rolf. I wanted to close with the men at arms and the knights.

As we headed down the bank, I could see that we had thinned them out considerably. Osbert Cumin's banner still flew. They were beyond Philip and the archers now. I think they must have thought they had escaped us. We settled into a steady rhythm. I did not want our horses blown before we caught them. I knew that we would catch them. Sir Harold would stop them. He did not have to hold them for long because we were just three hundred paces behind them and on this old Roman Road, it would be hard for them to lose us.

I knew where Harold would spring his ambush. A wood was split by the road. When the Romans had built it, they had cut it back by twenty paces on each side. Over time saplings, scrubby growth, as well as some substantial trees, had grown. Effectively there was cover to within ten paces. I turned and shouted. "Let us put some speed on. Sir Harold will soon spring his trap."

They needed no urging and we began to steadily increase our speed. I heard the clash of arms before I spied it. Harold had led his men at arms in a broad charge two ranks deep. That was important as it stopped any man at arms from being isolated. He cut the enemy band in two. We were close enough for me to see him wheel to the left and cut off the vanguard from the road ahead. We road obliquely across the rear of their lines to stop the rearguard from escaping too.

They turned! A chase would see them all slain and it was Osbert Cumin who led the rally. He turned and with his standard-bearer rode towards us. That suited me. I wanted no man to fight my battle for me. "Gilles and Richard, stay out of the front line!

"Aye, sir."

When I saw arrows pluck three men at arms from their saddles, I knew that Aiden and his two falconers were close by. It seemed to act as a spur to our enemies who charged and roared their war cries. A knight with a black surcoat charged at me. He had a war hammer. I saw that the black surcoat had a white bird of some description upon it. It was unusual. I focussed on the war hammer. Where would he strike? His body betrayed him. I saw him beginning to stand in the stirrups. He would go for my head and use the spiked end. My secret weapon was Rolf. He could turn on a groat. At the last minute and, as the hammer came menacingly towards me, I jerked Rolf's head to the side and guided him with my knees. I flashed in front of his horse. His hammer struck air and my sword swung across his chest. He tumbled from his saddle and I heard him scream as Wilfred's horse's hoof caught and cracked his head.

Osbert Cumin took advantage of my distraction. I had turned Rolf and he rode directly at me. He still had a lance. I had no shield to bring before me. It was on the wrong side. I jerked Rolf around even as the lancehead came towards me. Wulfstan said I had the fastest hands and I swung my sword more in hope than expectation. I caught the tip of the spear and pushed it away. His face was filled with impotent rage as I galloped past him. We both turned but Rolf was quicker. I stabbed forward and Cumin tried to counter with his lance. It was the wrong weapon. He could not control it and my sword slid along his mail and into his side. He jerked his horse's head away and my sword came out bloody.

I yelled, "Yield and you shall live!" The ransom was immaterial; I wanted the leverage of a prisoner who was related to William Cumin.

"Never!" He discarded his lance and drew his sword. He charged at me.

I pulled back on Rolf's reins and he reared. His hooves flailed before him and Osbert Cumin's horse shied away. It was natural. I brought my sword down hard. He raised his shield to block it and managed to do so but my sword was well made and perfectly balanced. I had powerful arms and the shield was split in two. More than that, the sword struck his shoulder as it sliced down and I could see that he was hurt. "Yield while you can."

"My brother will avenge my death!"

He was brave and he raised his sword to bring it across my neck. I lunged forward and my sword slid above his cantle and into his stomach. He fell to the ground. He lay still. I shouted, "Osbert Cumin is dead! Yield and you shall have your lives!"

The three knights and their squires who had survived the last attack did so but the men at arms tried to flee. Wilfred led my men in a chase north. None reached Durham alive. Harold and his men at arms took the swords of those who had surrendered. Loading the arms and armour on the captured horses, I sent Sir Harold and his men back to Walworth. We would spend the night there. I stayed with Sir Tristan's men and we burned the bodies of the dead. We did not want vermin and carrion attracted by the rotting dead. I did not burn Osbert of Cumin. I had his corpse wrapped in a shroud. We would take it back with us. Our own dead we would take back home for burial. There were four. Three had died outright and one of his wounds. All were irreplaceable.

Chapter 3

Wilfred and my men returned as the first plume of black smoke rose. I looked up as Wilfred reined in. He nodded and pointed to the line of horses and mail behind him. "They are dead. I think that Alf will be using this to melt down and make ploughshares and bill hooks! They had poor protection. It is no wonder that they ran."

"It is well that some good will come from this but I fear we were too late for Walworth."

Wilfred said, "There were people still alive when we arrived. Perhaps they can rebuild."

Gilles was thoughtful. "Piercebridge is close by, lord. If there was a garrison and a knight then the people of Walworth could flee there; could they not?"

"They could, Gilles."

It was strange that the same idea could come from one so young and one so old. It was what Tom of Ulnaby had said. I could almost hear my father chastising me. He had ever been aware of the need to care for the ordinary folk. He had come from such stock. He had not been noble-born.

Philip of Selby had done a good job at Walworth. He had cleared away the enemy dead and his men had started to cook the dead horses. They were two that had belonged to men at arms and had fallen during the fight at the village. It would be hot food and welcomed by all. The smell of cooking meat seemed to make the village normal again. What he had not done was to bury the dead. I knew why he had not done so. We had no priest with us.

"Have the dead of the village taken to the church." I looked around and spied an old man who had survived the attack. "What is your name?"

He bowed and said, "John of Walworth."

I pointed to the bodies being carried by my men. "I would bury your dead for you but I know not the families. I will say words over them but I need you to make sure that families are not separated in death."

"Thank you, lord. That is thoughtful. I know them all. I will tell you. I have lived all of my life in this village. Perhaps I have lived too long. Are we destined never to have peace in our lifetime?"

I put my arm around his thin shoulders. "Peace will come one day; that I swear and I also promise you protection."

He looked sceptically at me, "Those are words I wish to hear, lord. I pray that they are meant."

Some lords would have had his nose for such an insult. But he was right. Words were cheap and mine had been glib. If I promised protection then I would have to deliver it. I cursed once more the procrastination of the Earl of Gloucester. If he had acted sooner then the civil war would be over and I would not need to leave this land so unprotected.

It was a small church. Half-timbered the only extravagance was a single bell in a wooden tower. It was not a large bell but a symbol of the hope the people had had. I spoke words as the people were buried. The body of the burned priest was a gruesome one to wrap in a shroud. Aiden and his men took that upon themselves. They had watched the cruel incineration and felt guilty. They had avenged the priest.

As we sat around the village eating in silence, I looked at the villagers. We had reached the village just in time for the enemy had not had the opportunity to slay all that they intended. There were still sixty villagers left alive. They could farm again and raise families but only if there was protection nearby. Gilles had been right, Piercebridge was the best place for a lord of a manor to use. It was better placed for a castle that could control the valley and the land around. In fact, even without the horror we had witnessed, I needed to ensure that the river crossing was protected. I needed a lord of the manor who could defend the river and watch over the land between Gainford and Yarm. I ruminated as I ate and I made my decision. That did not mean I had a lord of the manor yet, for my choice could refuse but I always slept better when I had made a decision.

We left the next morning. At first light, I sent one of the captured squires back to Durham with a demand for ransom. It was a ransom worthy of the crime. Osbert Cumin's corpse was included in the demands. I had no doubt that his uncle would wish to bury him and it served my purpose that William Cumin would have a constant reminder of the dangers of crossing me.

I looked down at the expectant villagers. "I am the Earl of Cleveland and Warlord of the North. I am sorry that you have been left unprotected and I give you my word that order will be returned. Durham is now a nest of vipers but I will rebuild the castle at Piercebridge and I will garrison it with stout and doughty warriors. If enemies threaten then flee there and send to me. I leave you four horses we took from the raiders. It is small enough recompense for your loss but you now have the means to seek help." All the men had taken a helmet and a sword from those which we had captured. "You now have weapons and you must realise that it is better to die defending your families than live and watch them abused!" The men nodded. "By midsummer, there will be a lord at Piercebridge!"

I had not spoken thus for applause and accolades but I received both and I felt ashamed. I had done little enough to deserve this. I had left them vulnerable and when I came, too late, they thanked me for that. I was angry with myself.

I waved Sir Harold and Philip of Selby next to me as we rode the short way back to Piercebridge. "What thought you of my words?"

Sir Harold knew me well. He had been my first squire all those long years ago. "You are right, lord. We need a lord of the manor here. This is as important a place as Yarm."

He stopped and I smiled, "There is a but in your unspoken words, Harold."

He smiled. "You can read minds now, lord. I see no lord you can put here. We are stretched thinly enough as it is. Do you wish Tristan or me to come?"

"Would you?"

"I would obey, my lord, for I owe all that I have to you."

"But you would not be happy."

"No, lord. I like Hartburn. It is a fine manor and I like the safety your castle affords my family but I am your oathsworn and I obey you in all things."

I nodded, "And you also know that I would not order a man to do that. I could ask but I will not ask you, Harold. You took on Wulfstan's Hartburn and have made the people love you as they did my mentor. Philip, would you be lord of the manor at Piercebridge?"

I knew I had taken him by surprise for his mouth opened and close. I smiled and said not a word. He regained some composure, "Lord, I am just an archer."

"As is Dick and yet he is now a knight."

"But he is not lord of a manor. Make him lord of the manor of Piercebridge, lord. He deserves the honour far more than I."

"Your words do you credit. Know you that I offered Sir Richard a manor and he refused. You may refuse and I will think none the worse of you. I will still knight you and I will seek another for Piercebridge." He rode in silence. "When your uncle offered me your service, he confided in me that he hoped you would fulfil his expectations. I believe you have met them. If you accept my offer and become a knight then I know you will have exceeded them."

He shook his head, "Do not misunderstand me, lord. I wish to be lord of the manor but I know you well enough to realise that you expect honesty and I am not sure that I could be as good a lord of the manor as Sir Hugh or Sir Harold."

I glanced over to Sir Harold. He nodded and smiled, "If that is your only worry, my friend, then I can tell you that all of us felt the same burden. When you ride around your manor and men knuckle their heads and say 'lord' to you then you feel a fraud. At least I did. Eventually, you will earn that respect. I warn you this though; it will change you. You will find that your feet sink into your manor and become rooted there."

"What of my archers, lord? Would you keep them with you?"

"They are your men, Philip, and they are vital to my plans. You need men at arms to guard your walls but you need men who can ride as far as Durham, Gainford and Barnard to keep watch for our enemies. Your men are fine archers. With training, they can become archers who are also men at arms."

"Is there such a thing?"

"Under your hand, I believe so!"

He smiled, "Then I accept."

"Good. I will leave you in your new manor. Before I leave for the Empress, I will ennoble you. William the Mason will come to help you build your walls. Tell the people that this year will be free from tax but this time next year they will become part of England once more. They will pay for that privilege."

Philip spent the last two miles picking Harold's brain. I had deprived myself of half of my archers and Dick would not be happy but it was the right thing to do. I knew that.

When I reached Stockton I saw that Dick had returned. He waited until we had taken off our armour and washed before he approached Harold and me. That in itself told me that the news was not urgent. Sir John and Sir Tristan joined us as we sat around the table. Gilles and Richard made to leave but I waved them back. "One day, God willing, you two shall be knights. It is right that you hear how knights plan. Stay."

Clearly awed by my knights, they made themselves as inconspicuous as they could.

"The Empress sent you her warmest greeting, lord, and this token." He handed over a seal. "It is the manor of Liedeberge, between Hereford and Gloucester." I took it and watched Dick's face. Like Harold, he was as honest as the day was long on Midsummer's day. "Aye, lord, it is close to Wales and subject to raids. A rebel-held it and I think she

42

has given it to afford her some protection there." I nodded. Did she think I could split myself in two? Dick continued, "There is a garrison there and Sir Miles has promised to watch over it until you are able to visit yourself."

I put the seal around my neck. It was a symbolic act for my knights. I now took on that office and it added to the burden of the others I carried. The Empress was protecting herself not only against the Welsh and Stephen of Blois but her half brother. The manor would warn him that Wales was not his own petty fiefdom.

"And the campaign?"

"The Empress and the Earl are busy recapturing the lands which Stephen took last year." None of my knights afforded Stephen the title he had usurped. "The Empress said she had no need of your army." He hesitated. "She spoke with me privately when her advisers were not close by. She said she needed the north strong again. She feared her uncle and his intentions."

I nodded, "King David plays a dangerous game."

"She has high hopes that the Bishop of Ely can prevail in the east and then London will be squeezed in the middle."

Sir Harold shook his head, "It is a shame that the Earl of Chester changed sides once more. Had he held Lincoln then we might have been able to take York and the war would have been virtually over."

"It is much as Philip of Selby said. There are many, his uncle included, who wish to take the side of the Empress. The Archbishop of Canterbury and the Bishop of Winchester anointed Stephen and they cannot do aught until the crown is fallen from his head."

I looked around at these. Wulfric and Edward were not there but other than that I had my most trusted of knights. I felt I could speak openly. "I intend to make Philip of Selby lord of the manor of Piercebridge. I know that deprives us of twenty archers but my visit to the lands west of here made it obvious that Sir Hugh is in great danger."

Dick nodded, "I can train more archers, lord. Already the bowyers and fletchers have made great stores of both arrows

43

and war bows. If I have this summer then I can field another thirty by autumn."

"Good, for we shall need them. This news from the Empress is as good as we could have hoped. I know that the Count of Anjou is preparing another assault in Normandy. Already our forces control much of Normandy. I see hope that the war there may be over even though the one in England is far in the future. It is to be hoped that our armies will be swollen when that side of the water is safe."

My immediate priorities were Durham to the north and, more urgently, Fitz Mandeville in the south. I decided to seek out Edward Fitz Mandeville and bring him to battle at the end of May. Sir Richard of Yarm had his scouts out and I knew that while Sir Edward was rebuilding Malton, he was content to try to extend his control of the lands to the west. He risked antagonising the Earl of Chester but I did not think that would worry him. When I told my knights, they concurred. They would prepare for the campaign. To that end, I travelled to Normanby. Wulfric and Edward were the closest of my knights to Malton. I visited Wulfric first as I was keen to see how his castle was coming along.

He had built a sturdy motte and bailey with a stone gatehouse. He had a garrison who would defend his home when he came with us. Wulfric had no wife. If he wished a woman, he took her to his bed. When he fell in battle, as I knew he would eventually, it would be the end of his line. As he took me around his castle and then to the former castle of the De Brus, I told him of Durham and my plans for Piercebridge.

He nodded his approval, "Philip is a good archer. Archers are meant to be behind walls. Me? I like to ride my destrier, Roger, and use my war axe where I can swing!"

"I know, old friend, but now that you have a manor, I would advise a little more caution. These people have just become used to a lord who will protect them. Do not abandon that."

He looked offended, "Lord, do you doubt my right arm?"

"No, but we all know that someday a young version of you will come along!"

"Perhaps." He did not sound convinced.

We had returned to his castle. "We leave in seven days. We gather at Thornaby. That way we can cross the vale to Osmotherley and miss out Helmsley. I would not waste men on a siege there."

"Good, for I hate sieges!"

"How many men will you bring?"

"Fifteen men at arms and ten archers. I have young Thomas son of Oswald as my squire. He is a handy lad."

"Then have your scouts seek this Sir Edward. Sir Richard has scouted the vale of York and we know his defences there. Malton is his stronghold. We can expect it to be firmly held."

Sir Edward was in a better position than most. Like me, the river gave him much protection and he had some stone features in his wooden castle. He also had the advantage that he could take refuge with me if things became difficult. I told him about my plans. "I will be ready, lord."

"And how many men do you bring?"

"I needs must leave a strong garrison for my family are within. There will be twenty men at arms, fifteen archers and two squires. John, my son, is under the wing of Gilles, my squire." He looked at me. "I would have Gilles knighted soon, lord."

"You can knight him yourself, Edward, you know that."

"I do but he and I would be happier if it was the Empress' Champion, Warlord of the North, the Earl of Cleveland, who dubbed him and gave him his spurs."

"Very well. Is he content to live in Thornaby yet? Does he wish his own manor?"

"Not yet, lord, but there is a manor south of here, Stainton, which someday it might suit."

"That belongs to the Archbishop of York."

He nodded, "I thought you could use your influence with him."

"Perhaps although his nephew says that he is close to death. We may lose that influence soon. I agree with you that Gilles has proved himself worthy and he is of an age. When we have finished with Fitz Mandeville, I will give him his spurs."

As we returned across the Tees on Ethelred's ferry, my squire, Gilles asked, "How long was Gilles of Thornaby a squire, lord?"

"Oh, these five years past. Why?"

"You took me from Normandy two years since. I wondered how long I would wait."

"If you were ready then I would knight you now. Do you feel ready?"

He shook his head, "I have only begun to learn how to be a knight, lord. Each time I think I am one step closer, I see you or Sir Harold do something and know I am not even close to that elevated position. I am happy to continue to learn, lord."

"Good. For you do learn. When we go to war, watch Gilles of Thornaby and see what he does. Look not at what he is ordered to do for any man can do that. It is what he is not asked to do and yet does which is important."

Sir Tristan, Sir Harold and Sir Richard of Sherwood, along with my household knight, Sir John of Stockton, would complete my conroi. I gathered them in my solar where we could discuss the campaign. John, my Steward, was there to take note of what we would need. When he knew the numbers then he would know how many sumpters and servants we needed.

"Sir Tristan and Sir Harold, I do not expect you to bring all of your men. You have manors to watch. Given that, how many men do you bring?"

Sir Harold said, "I lost one of my men at arms fighting Cumin. There will be nine men at arms and eight archers."

Sir Tristan said, "And I lost two. I will bring eight men at arms and eight archers."

"Dick?"

"I have thirty archers."

"Did you take on a squire?"

He nodded, "Aelric's son, Tom. He can use a bow but he is a fine swordsman too."

"Good, then we have our men. I will bring eleven men at arms. The Frisians can defend my castle under John of Craven. There are eighteen archers and I have my two squires. We will bring Aiden and his men with us. Dick, you will command the archers and Gilles of Thornaby the squires." Dick cocked an eyebrow, "I wish to see if he is ready to be a knight. Sir Edward thinks he is."

John, my Steward, had been adding them up. "That is a hundred and sixty of you not counting Aiden and his two falconers."

I nodded. "That should be enough. It is good to know that we leave a good half of our men here. Should an enemy come to threaten us then we would have over three hundred warriors true to fight them."

That night, when the gates were closed and the watch set, I heard a cry from my north gate. The north meant the Scots and I grabbed my sword and raced to the walls. I was relieved to see that it was not an army but a priest. It was Thomas of Leyburn and I could tell from his distressed appearance that he had bad news to impart.

"Open the gates, let him in. Send for Father Henry." I went down the steps to meet with him. "I can see your news is grave. Speak."

"Geoffrey the Bishop of Durham is dead and the Dean and many of my brothers killed."

Even I was shocked. "They killed the Bishop's Dean?"

"William Cumin's guards said he had murdered the Bishop. He had not."

"I know that. And you?"

When the guards came to find all those priests who were loyal to the Dean, I slipped out of the gate you and your men used. Some of my brothers came with me. That was two days ago. I have been hiding from his men as they hunted us."

"Us?"

"There were others. We were separated. They would have caught me too but I can swim and I jumped in the river. I am not sure how many of the others escaped."

"But you think none." He nodded. "Fear not, Father Thomas, their deaths will be avenged." Father Henry had arrived as well as Alice. "Go with Father Henry. He will take care of your hurts and Alice will bring you hot food."

She was shocked, "Of course! You poor man! Who would do such a thing to a man of God?"

Father Thomas gave her a sad look and said, "The man who now calls himself the Bishop of Durham."

Alice's hand went to her mouth and Father Henry crossed himself. "We will talk in the morning but you are safe here, Father. You have my word on that."

After they had gone I summoned Dick and Aiden. "I want you to ride tomorrow morning and look for any sign of the other priests who fled Durham."

"Aye, lord."

We found none, alive. Aiden found three dead priests. They were halfway between Durham and Stockton. They had been stripped as though bandits had done this. Bandits would never risk the wrath of God by killing priests. This had been done by someone who could offer absolution; a Bishop, albeit a false one. Father Henry and Father Thomas wrote a joint letter to the Archbishop of York and we sent it with an escort of four men at arms. He had to know what had happened and we could not risk the letter being intercepted.

While they were away *'Adela'* arrived. She was overdue and I had been worried. Fishermen brought us news that she was negotiating the bends and loops in the Tees. John and I waited for her at my quay. She was low in the water as she tacked up the river. That was a good sign. It meant her hold was laden. Her sides were also filled with new faces. They would be the men sent by Leofric. Harold Three Fingers was the first off the ship. "There are more twists in this river than a lawyer's arguments!"

"Did you have trouble, Harold?"

"Goodness no, lord. It just took more time to gather and store the trade goods and then we had unfavourable winds north. Captain William is well pleased with the voyage."

John, my Steward, asked, somewhat anxiously, "Are you whole? Can you return soon?"

He laughed, "We could go back right now but the crew would like at least one night ashore! They make fine wine in Anjou but it cannot compare with Stockton beer. I have a thirst that only Mary the Alewife can satisfy!"

I clapped him on the back. "Stay a couple of days if you wish. Ask your captain if he will dine with me this evening. I have much to ask." I pointed for I could see that he was busy on his ship. "I will not take him from his duties. John, have the new men at arms and archers sent to my Inner Bailey. John of Craven and I will speak with them."

That evening my household knights, my steward and my squires joined me as William of Kingston told us of his voyage and, more importantly, events in Normandy and Anjou.

"Your son is now a most important knight, lord. He is at the right hand of the Count and leads a large number of knights. They have almost finished quashing the rebel barons in the southern part of Normandy."

"Good, then the Empress will soon have reinforcements."

He shook his head, "I fear not, lord. The Count of Flanders has begun massing armies by the border and it is rumoured that the French are casting covetous glances at Blois. You can expect no help this year nor, in my view, next year."

That was a blow. "And Leofric, how is he?"

"His wife is with child again! He is happy, lord, and he is popular. That is rare. The people love him for he is a thoughtful leader." He suddenly looked worried. "The men he sent, they are satisfactory?"

Sir John answered for me. "They are! We can now take more men when we campaign. Are there more in training?"

"With the war in Normandy almost at an end, there are keen young men who wish to fight and it is said that the land of the Warlord of the North is the best place to become rich and successful. The ones you have are the best. The others are sent to your son's castle in Ouistreham or they stay with Sir Leofric."

John, my Steward, had listened to all of this impatiently. "And trade? Is it as good or does the end of the war mean prices have fallen?"

I shook my head. John was the son of a moneyer and it showed! William of Kingston was used to dealing with such men. "Trade is good. Alf's iron goods are in great demand and his swords are highly prized. The high quality of the wool is also much sought after."

John's face lit up into a grin. "And the leather?"

"I am afraid that the leather from Spain sells for a higher price. But look on the bright side, we sell a great deal. You were happy with your share, were you not?"

"Of course."

Harold laughed, "But although he is happy, he is never satisfied! He wants more!"

Chapter 4

We now had more men to use in our war against Sir Edward Fitz Mandeville. The last report we had was that his banner had been seen flying at his castle. That meant he was there. We had him in his lair. We gathered at Thornaby in the last week of May. It had been some time since such a mighty host had headed south. We rode down the Great North Road. We had many scouts out. Aiden, Edward and Edgar were joined by those of Sir Richard of Yarm, Sir Wulfric and Sir Edward. We were well protected. Our mounted archers guarded our flanks, our wagon with the siege machines and our sumpters. My aim was to make any spies who might see us leaving Thornaby assume we were heading for Gloucester and the Empress. We travelled slowly and stopped at the old ruined castle of Osmotherley. Alan son of Alan had been born there and all of his family had died there when I had been attacked by assassins. Arriving in the middle of the afternoon, we spent the night.

By dawn, there was no sign of us. We left in the middle of the night screened by archers. They found and killed two enemy scouts on the road across the moors. I had no doubt that they had come from Helmsley. I intended to catch Sir Edward close to Malton. His new castle was only half-built. They had used, according to our scouts, the old ditch from the castle destroyed by the Scots and they had begun to build in stone but the bulk of it was wooden still. Helmsley was stone. By using this route we cut him off from an escape to his other major castle.

We dropped down from the moors to the flatter lands around the fertile vale. This was a rich farming country. Had I wanted, I could have laid waste to it and damaged the enemies' coffers but I would not do that. They were English who farmed there. It was not the people's fault that their leaders had sided with the usurper.

I knew from my scouts that the castle was at a bend of the Derwent. They would have a fine view to the north and so we halted at the woods close to Hepton Hill. The slope and the woods gave us protection but, more importantly, we sat astride the road that the enemy would have to use if they tried to flee. Such a large host is impossible to hide and I had no doubt that rumours would have reached Sir Edward Fitz Mandeville of the threat we posed. He would, however, be in the dark for we kept our banners furled.

We left once more in the middle of the night. I wanted him to see us outside his castle when dawn broke. I sent Wulfric and Edward with half of the archers and all their men at arms across the Derwent to the south side of the river. They would appear when I had my trumpets sounded. I was trying to make Fitz Mandeville think that we had more men than we actually did. The jangling of our arms and horses would have alerted Mandeville's sentries. I did not mind now. We were in position. Even if he ran we would catch him. We unfurled our banners. We would let him know who we were. We had no need to hide.

My archers dismounted. I had fifty on my side of the castle. They moved down to within bow range of the wooden walls. Wulfric and Edward would be doing the same on their side. There had been houses below the castle but the Scots had burned them too. My archers sheltered in the charred remains and we waited. The river was not a serious obstacle. It merely slowed down an attacker. There was little point in sitting on our horses. If we fought then it would be on foot. I wondered if he would surrender. I did not know the exact numbers within the castle. I doubted that he had half as many as we did.

I made sure that my men were all ready and, as dawn broke, I had the trumpet sound. My archers let fly and the sentries on the walls fell. More men raced to the walls and were cut down too. They soon learned and we saw no more faces. We knew they were there. I turned to my knights. "Had I built this castle, I would have used stone and had a curtain wall by the river. We may not need the siege machines."

Sir Harold said, "We could attack now, lord. The archers have cleared the walls."

"There is no hurry. These are wooden walls. If they use boiling fat, it is as dangerous to them as it is to us. We have enough men to attack the wall at various places. Let us see if this Fitz Mandeville is wise enough to surrender."

Sir John laughed, "If he does then Wulfric will be like a bear with a sore head."

It took just one more flight of arrows before the standard of Fitz Mandeville was lowered and the gates opened. A pair of priests came forward. "It seems he is wiser than I thought. Come with me."

I led my knights and squires towards the gate. The priest was an old man. "Lord, the garrison surrenders."

"Where is Edward Fitz Mandeville?"

"The Baron is not within the castle, lord. He was at Helmsley the last we heard." I was not sure if I believed this priest. He held out his cross and said, "I swear, lord!"

"Then why does his banner fly from the keep?"

The priest looked down. "I fear it is a deception practised by the Baron. He likes to keep his enemies guessing, lord."

I turned to Gilles, "Ride to Wulfric and tell him that the garrison has surrendered. Sir Harold and Sir Tristan, take some men and escort the garrison out." As they waved their men forward I asked, "Who commands here now?"

"The castellan was felled by your arrows." He looked around helplessly. "I think it would be me."

The garrison soldiers, when they came out, were just twenty men. We had slain another eighteen on the walls. None of those who trudged out wore mail. Wulfric and Edward joined me. Dick shook his head, "What a waste of arrows!"

I too was disappointed. I had not been outwitted but our scouts had not done as good a job as I might have wished. I had not used Aiden and his men. I had relied on Sir Richard and Wulfric. Our clever plan had been a waste of time. The place we had avoided was the very place that Fitz Mandeville was using.

"Bind the garrison and take all that is of value then burn it!"

The castle was half-built and now it would be destroyed again. I was not being vindictive but practical. Until this civil war ended, I did not wish a castle so close to my lands be a threat. It was noon by the time we had finished. I sent the prisoners back to Thornaby with an escort of Sir Edward's men. Their fate would be decided later. The priest stayed in the stone church of St. Mary. It was the only building left standing and looked forlorn. We headed northwest. This time I sent Aiden and his scouts due north to see if there was a garrison at Pickering. A small castle, it guarded the road from Helmsley to Scarborough. As we rode, Wulfric seethed. "Next time I will scout the land myself! What did my men do? Stand atop the hill and see the banner? They did not even count the men within!"

I smiled. Wulfric was learning the problems of leadership. You chose men you could rely on. Wulfric could spot a good man at arms half a mile away but a good scout could be under his nose and he would not recognise him. I would have to loan him the services of Aiden.

"Let us concentrate on what is ahead. We worry about mistakes later. Helmsley is a stone castle and has a better aspect than Malton. This may be bloody."

"The river is not deep there and there are many fords. We can surround it easily." Edward knew the land well. Before he had entered my service, he had served as a man at arms with other lords. "And the curtain wall is a long one. Unless he has a large garrison, there may well be some point of weakness."

"Good. We will cross the river and attack from the north."

We rode down the greenways and headed north and west. It was but sixteen miles. I left a strong guard with the baggage to follow on for I was anxious to get to the castle before dark. As we approached the castle, I saw that the Mandeville banner flew. That meant nothing. There were a hundred mailed men with me and, even as we approached, I saw the gates open and twenty knights and men at arms gallop from the gate and head west. I had never seen this Fitz Mandeville but I recognised his surcoat as he fled this castle.

Wulfric smacked one hand into the other, "Will I cleave no heads again?"

"Ride!"

We rode hard towards the castle. As we did, another forty men galloped through the gates. Wulfric and his men were desperate to get to grips with an enemy, any enemy, and they pursued them. I was more concerned with capturing the castle. As Wulfric and his men at arms hastened after the last group of men to leave, we galloped over the ditch. I held my shield above my head in case there were defenders left but I entered the bailey without hurt. I was met by servants and two priests. Dismounting, I approached them. The older and rather well fed priest said, "The castle is yours, lord. The Baron has fled. I beg you to treat us mercifully."

I nodded. There was something about this I liked not. I looked around. The walls looked sound and I could see no reason why Edward Fitz Mandeville had not defended this castle. We would have bled but it would have been taken.

"Secure the castle. We will stay here this night."

The baggage had reached us and Sir Wulfric had returned by the time my sentries reported Aiden approaching. Sir Wulfric had ten horses with him. We caught some of them but they were without mail and they fled us." He patted his war axe. "At least I got to cleave some heads."

When Aiden arrived he said, "Pickering is held by twenty men. Had I had ten of our archers, we could have taken it."

I nodded. Aiden could be trusted. The reports from Philip and his uncle were that Mandeville had sixty knights and up to two hundred men at arms. We had seen nowhere near that number. I estimated that he had just six knights with him when he had fled. Where were the rest?

As my men took the weapons and supplies, I had the servants and priests gathered in the Great Hall. I sat on the lord's chair. "Bring me the two priests." The one who looked well fed also appeared more confident. The younger one looked like the other's dogsbody. "Where has the Baron gone?" Neither answered. "You know who I am?"

The older priest said, "You are the Warlord of the North."

"Then you know that I would not worry about extracting information any way I could. He left you and I want to know where he fled!"

The older priest feigned ignorance and shrugged. "York?"

I knew he would not go there and when the young priest flashed a look of incredulity, I knew that there was something amiss. "Gilles, Richard, bind this fat priest and watch him."

"I am a man of God."

"Be careful then that you do not upset me, priest or you will be seeing him even sooner than you might wish!" I put my arm around the young priest. "Come with me...?"

"Brother Alcuin. I am visiting here from Fountains Abbey."

"What is the name of the other priest?"

"He is the Baron's priest, Father Thaddeus."

"I wish no harm on any priest but I will not be lied to. If you do not wish to tell me where the Baron has gone then just say I refuse to tell you. Father Thaddeus did not do that and we both know that he is lying." He nodded. "Then I ask you, directly," I turned him so that I could see his eyes. "Do you know where the Baron has gone?"

He shook his head and said. "I do not know where he went."

I nodded, "You are telling the truth."

"But I know what are his intentions."

Hope sprang, "You do?"

"When your men were spotted he cried '*I have him now! The Warlord has fallen into my trap and is many miles from home.*'" He paused. "I did not understand that then but you are the Warlord and so..."

"Thank you, Brother, I am indebted to you."

I raced back in. "Mount. Fetch all the grain you can carry for our horses. We have to tax them this night. Sir Wulfric, leave two of your men to guard the castle, the baggage and our servants. Each man at arms, knight and squire shall bring his lance or spear!"

My knights all stared at me as though I was mad. Sir Edward said, "We have ridden far. What is the rush?"

"This is a trap. The Baron knows our plan. He has drawn us here, far from our home so that he can attack the valley. That is why he has so few knights and men at arms with him. Wulfric, make sure that the two men you leave, know how to get information. Someone here knows something. Let Brother Alcuin go but the rest are my prisoners until I return."

Wulfric's face was black with anger. It had been his scouts who had let us down, "I will leave Hrolf the Swede and Simon the Jew. They could both get blood from a stone!"

While my men mounted, I planned our action. I had no doubt that the Baron had gathered his men at Thirsk. They would have already moved towards the Great North Road and that would be their route to my castles. Yarm was a small castle and could be taken. They would give them a barrier across my river. Then they would attack Piercebridge. I had brought the bulk of my men with me. The only forces which could face Fitz Mandeville were Sir Richard at Yarm and the garrisons of Norton and Stockton. I led my men north towards Rievaulx Abbey. There was a greenway that led through the moors. It twisted and turned and eventually brought us out at Swainby. It meant we could travel parallel to the Roman Road and yet still be hidden from view. We could then send for Sir Richard and his men and meet them on the rise close to Osmotherley.

"Sir Tristan, send your squire ahead. Tell him to fetch your father and his men. Meet us south of Harlsey. Hopefully, that is where we will meet and stop this cunning Mandeville."

"Aye, lord. John, ride to my father and fetch him to the road close to the priory. Do not get caught by our enemies. The Earl is counting on you."

"I will not let you down."

"Aiden, make sure the way is clear."

It was less than eighteen miles but it took some hours to reach the track which led down from the moors to the vale below. Even in the dark, we saw the high mound of Whorlton to our right. It was the sign that we had to head west. We reached the road well before dawn and I had all the men dismount and feed and water their horses. With the grain we had brought from Helmsley, the horses were well fed. We led them down to the Wiske River and they drank too. Some of my men ate the rations they had with them but my knights and captains gathered around me.

"We will wait here for the enemy. I am guessing that they will use this Roman Road for it is both wide and well made." I pointed to the high ground to the north of us. The road rose a little and there was some dead ground behind. "The bulk of the men at arms will wait there. The knights and the squires with my oathsworn will form the front line. I wish him to see us and our banners. We will draw him on. Dick, I want you to divide the archers." I pointed to the west of the road just ahead of us. It dropped sharply down to the Wiske and there was ample cover. Put half your archers there." I pointed to the land to the east. It began to rise and led to the escarpment of the moors just half a mile away. "The rest can go on the other side of the road. There is little enough cover there but use what there is and embed some stakes."

Dick asked, "You care not if the enemy sees us?"

"He is no fool. He proved that with his cunning plan. He knows we have archers. Better that he sees you in a prepared position rather than looking for the others."

He nodded, "Then I will be with the archers to the east."

"Have as many men rest as they can."

They nodded as they headed back to their men. Aiden, Edward and Edgar waited nearby. Aiden said, "I am sorry, lord. I have let you down. I should have known."

"No, Aiden, the scouts who were sent by my other knights let us down and I have learned a lesson as have they." Out of the corner of my eye, I saw Wulfric berating his scouts. I hoped he would not inflict actual harm on them. They had made a mistake; that was all.

"We will find the enemy for you."

"Are you certain; are your horses not tired?"

"Fear not, lord. We know this land well. There is cover to the east up on the escarpment. We will not need to travel far. It will be a clear day and our vision will be unimpaired." I nodded and they rode off.

He was right. The May on the hawthorn and the cow parsley gave all the hedges a stripe of white blossom. Summer was upon us. The cold weather of a month ago had given way to what promised to be a fruitful summer. If I could not stop Fitz Mandeville then the bounty of the summer would go to our enemies.

Richard brought me a waterskin, "Do not forget to drink, lord."

"Thank you for the admonishment! You are becoming the complete squire." He smiled at the compliment. "Today, Gilles will command you. Obey him as you would me. This will be hard for our enemies may well outnumber us."

"But Sir Richard will join us."

"John of Elton has to reach him and then they have to arm and ride. It is a twenty-mile journey. I am content knowing that they will reach us sometime this morning. Now rest. Today will be a test of all of us."

I then went to speak with my other captains and knights. I needed them to know precisely what my instructions were. That done, I sat down beneath a lone apple tree. It was a gnarled crab apple. The blossom upon it promised a good harvest. How many of my men would be alive to see the fruit? I knew that the day would be bloody. It was mid-morning when my scouts rode in.

"They come, my lord!"

"Good. What could you see of our lines?"

"Had I not known that there were others on the other side of the road, I would have just seen the archers and the twenty-five of you."

"Then let us hope they think we have the death wish. You three choose your own place to fight." They nodded and I shouted, "To arms!"

I mounted Rolf but I left my shield hanging from my cantle and held my helmet in my hand. I needed to see and be seen. "Richard, unfurl the standard. Let them know who they fight." As the banner flapped in the gentle breeze, I watched the road south. There was the slightest of bends and then the road rose to a second high point to the south of us. I saw their banners appear. We were less than a mile from them. Would they turn and flee? If so then I would have to pursue them. They kept coming. They rode in a wide column that filled the road. They were not boot to boot but there were many of them.

The richly mailed knights led and were followed by the men at arms. Ahead of these were a handful of scouts. They halted half a mile from us. By the time the rear of the column had come into sight, I guessed that there were over two hundred men. There might be as many as two hundred and fifty. Only the first one hundred, however, were mailed. Their regular lines made counting easy. The rest were in a looser formation. Some had helmets and all had a shield but that was all that I could see.

Aelric commanded the archers on the right. I could barely see them but I shouted, "Aelric, wait for my command before you loose your arrows."

"I will, lord."

I wanted the focus of the attack to be on our left. They would see the stakes and the archers. They would have to turn or else their shields would be of no use.

The enemy halted beyond bow range. My archers had a well-deserved reputation for both range and accuracy. A knot of riders took off their helmets and rode to a spot halfway between us. They wished to speak. Sir Edward asked, "Do we all ride to them, lord?"

"Let us wait until they move and then we shall. I want to plant fear in their minds. I wish them to wonder why we wait." Sure enough, the five knights began to look around them. They suspected an ambush or a trap. They held a conference and then edged their horses on. "Let us speak with them now."

I ignored the conventions and took all of my knights. We halted two hundred paces from our squires. The squires and men at arms prevented our enemy from seeing the bulk of our warriors behind.

I had heard of this Edward Fitz Mandeville but never met him. He was a big man. He could wear Wulfric's armour. However, unlike Wulfric, he had some fat on his face. His jowls looked heavy. His mail was black, as was his surcoat. It reminded me of one I had seen at Durham. He was slightly younger than I was with a neatly trimmed beard. I guessed he thought himself a striking figure. I had no time for such nonsense.

I let him speak first. He had approached us. "I come to offer you the chance to surrender. Earl, you are a traitor. If you and you men lay down your arms, I promise that you will be treated fairly. We will forego execution. We will take your lands but allow you and your families to go to Normandy." He smiled as though he had made a most generous offer.

"Who are you?"

My question threw him.

"I am Baron Fitz Mandeville and my cousin is the Earl of Essex!"

"Then you should know enough to realise that you address me as, lord!" He looked stunned at my words. I continued. "We missed you at both Malton and Helmsley. I may rebuild Malton one day but Helmsley looks like a castle in which I could live. Now I will offer you terms. If you and your men surrender then I will execute you for your crimes and ransom your knights." I smiled, "That is as fair an offer as you made to me, is it not?"

Instead of being outraged, he smiled. "I am pleased that you spurned my offer. When your body lies trampled beneath the hooves of my horses, I will take your castles and the Tees will be mine. I shall be the Earl of Cleveland."

I heard Wulfric snort and I put my hand up to silence any retort. We needed none. I smiled, "Then get back to your men. We are waiting for you."

He jabbed an arm to the east. "I see your archers there but if this handful of armed men are all that you have then this will be a short day's work!"

"Do not wear my armour until you have taken it." I spurred Rolf and he leapt forward. The five were so frightened that one fell from his horse and my men all laughed.

"We came here in peace!"

"Can I help it if my horse is keen for combat? I shall look for you, Mandeville. Make sure you are in the vanguard and not hiding amongst your men." My words were deliberately insulting. I wanted his knights to hear them. He would have to lead the charge now.

I rode back to my men. I saw John of Elton galloping down the road. He reined in and I saw that his horse was lathered. "Sir Richard comes. He has forty men."

"Forty?"

"Aye, lord. He raised the fyrd. They come with their bows. They will be here within the hour. They were at Crathorne when I left them."

"Your horse is tired. Go and take shelter with Dick and the archers. Your sword and shield may prove useful there."

I turned my attention back to the enemy. As much as I would have liked to charge them, I knew that our horses, despite the water and the grain, were tired. We would charge but only at the last minute. I saw the enemy horse form into a wedge formation. The ditch which ran alongside the road would be an obstacle. It was why I had chosen this site. He had enough men who were lightly armed who could outflank us but I gambled that he would not. He had the weight of numbers and I hoped he would try to use them.

His vanguard had forty knights. They were ten abreast. Behind them came forty men at arms also ten abreast. The other twenty were a reserve. The mass of men, many of whom were on foot, were in a swirling mass with the reserve. As the column came towards us, at the trot, they walked behind. When they were four hundred paces from us I saw the black standard of Edward Fitz Mandeville rise and fall. It was a signal but what did it portend? I soon had my answer. The last twenty men at arms detached themselves and headed obliquely to their right to charge Dick and his archers. At the same time, the knights and the rest of the men at arms began to increase speed. The slope made it necessary. They were not coming at us any faster but it was taking more effort to do so.

I donned my helmet and slung my shield over my shoulder and arm. I held my spear in my right hand. I preferred a spear. It was just as long as a lance but easier to wield. "Steady and wait for my command!"

Dick and his archers were under no such order and they began to loose as soon as the twenty men at arms, who charged them, were in range. With Aiden and his men alongside them, they were a formidable force. I knew I could ignore that flank. I had to put my plan into operation. When they were a hundred paces from us and galloping, although in truth they laboured up the bank, I shouted, "Charge! For God, England and the Empress!"

My men cheered and we charged. We had a narrower front. Eight knights faced ten but my archers, under Dick's command, had struck enough of those attacking them to direct their missiles at the main column. They were loosing from the enemies' right and they had no shields to protect them.

We did not have enough time to get to full speed but the slope and the laboured gait of our enemy meant that we were travelling at the same speed and we had the slope with us. I saw Edward Fitz Mandeville before me. He was a big target. As his lance came towards me, I lifted my shield while, at the same time, I used the spear overhand to stab down at him. I hit his shoulder and he tumbled from the back of his horse. His standard-bearer, in the second rank, brought the standard down to smash into my spear before I could withdraw it. I had plunged it deep into Fitz Mandeville's shoulder. I had felt the head strike bone. My sword flashed from my scabbard. The standard-bearer was brave. He had no shield. Having used his standard as a weapon he was trying to regain control of his horse when I brought my sword diagonally across his neck. My blade clanged off his helmet and bit into his coif. It was sharp and my arm was strong. It knocked him from his saddle. My blade came away bloody.

We had forced our way into the heart of the enemy and now it was time for the second part of my plan. "Fall back!" I heard Gilles command the squires to do as I had ordered. I played my part and swayed in my saddle as though I had been struck. My men threw their spears at the enemy. We turned and galloped back up the road. We went in two lines and, as we neared the top, we dropped into the ditch. I had scouted it out before and found no obstacles.

Wilfred and Edgar led my men at arms to charge into the uncoordinated mass of the enemy and as they did so I shouted, "Aelric! Now!"

None of the enemy were looking left and the arrows, released from less than forty paces distance could not miss. Men were thrown from saddles and then my men at arms hit the survivors of the arrow attack. As we clambered from the ditch, I saw Sir Richard leading his men down the road. I waved them forward with my sword and then we followed the men at arms. The tables had turned. We now held the numeric advantage and the reserves and lightly armed horsemen who awaited us at the bottom of the slope were in for a shock.

Gilles of Thornaby was not so caught up in the moment that he forgot his orders. "Squires, follow your lords! Do your duty!"

The neat lines had gone by the time we joined the fray and it was a whirling maelstrom of swords, spears and axes. It was a cacophony of noise; horses and men screaming, the clash of steel on steel. Blood sprayed everywhere as we fought as hard as we had ever fought. Whichever side relented or backed down would lose. Richard rode close behind me and my standard drew my enemies. Gilles rode as close to me as he could get. A man at arms and a knight in a red and yellow striped surcoat charged at me. They planned on attacking on two sides. I took the blow from the axe on my shield and the blow from the sword with my blade.

Gilles hacked at the man at arms and his sword bit deeply into his leg. When the blood spurted I knew that it was mortal and the rider slipped from the saddle. The knight stood in his stirrups and tried to smash his axe into my shield. As I lifted it to block the blow, I angled it so the heavy-headed axe slid down the shield. The knight began to overbalance and I swung my sword underarm to bite deep under his arm. He kept his saddle but Richard, using my standard like a lance, punched him to the ground. As we continued down the road, he was trampled to death.

I saw that the archers had thinned the enemy considerably. "Charge those at the foot of the hill. On! On!"

With my squires and men at arms, we burst through the shocked and disorientated knights and men at arms who had found themselves surrounded by enemies. At the bottom of the slope, the reserve and the mass of horsemen suddenly realised that the Warlord of the North was descending upon them. They vacillated and that is always the wrong decision for it is no decision. Some decided to flee and some to stand. They got in each other's way and we ploughed into them. Another knight in a red and yellow surcoat tried to turn his horse to face me. He had a spear and that is not the weapon of choice in a mêlée. It banged ineffectually off my helmet and I thrust forward with my sword. It went into his side and he yelled, "I yield!"

"Richard! Take his sword."

This was no time to slow down and Gilles and I pushed on. The three warriors we chased had no armour and poor nags between their legs. I smashed my sword across the back of one, laying him open to the bone. A second threw a spear at me and it clattered off my shield. He lost his balance and fell from his mount. Gilles took his head in one blow. The third one threw down his sword. "Mercy! Lord, give me mercy!"

Those who had not managed to flee followed suit. Swords and spears were hurled to the ground. We had won!

Chapter 5

As we rode back up the bloody, body littered road, I could see that we had been lucky. I had managed to take their leader out of the battle with almost my first blow. As we neared the site of the first encounter, I saw one of his squires with him. He lay on the ground. I could see the head of the spear still embedded in his shoulder. He grimaced up at me. "End my life now! This wound means I can fight no more."

I turned to Edgar. "Bind his wound and make a litter for him. I want him alive."

"Did you not hear me? Kill me!"

"You are worth more to me alive than dead."

"You will get no ransom!"

"Who said ransom? You are the cousin of the Earl of Essex. I have no doubt he sent you up here to increase your family's domain. You sought power. Power works in two ways. I have it and I shall use it."

Sir Richard of Yarm dismounted, "I am sorry we were a little late. I wanted to raise the fyrd."

"Thank you for coming. Your arrival was timely. I would have you take the wounded back to your castle now. It will take some time to clear the field. Take and watch Mandeville. He is valuable to us."

"Aye, lord. A great victory!"

As I watched our dead being placed on the backs of their horses, I wondered. Wulfric rode across from the field where he had pursued and slain some who tried to flee. His white horse, Roger, was spattered with blood and I saw that his war axe was nicked. "Lord, you are our leader! Why do you behave so recklessly? You charged into the heart of them! You should know that a leader needs to have his eyes on the battle at all times!"

I smiled for he meant well despite the vaguely insolent and disrespectful tone. "That may be true for other leaders, Wulfric, but I trust my knights and my captains. Had there been danger then any one of them could and would have reacted. You cannot change your nature, Wulfric. The day I stop leading my men is the day I die!"

We did not manage to leave until almost dusk. The enemy dead were burned. The prisoners were tied while their horses were used to carry the armour and weapons we had taken and we headed north. I knew my men and my horses were exhausted. How could they be else? But I also knew that they had the grit and determination to keep going until we saw our home. The thirteen miles we travelled seemed to take forever. I rode with my squires for I wished to speak with them.

"You both did well. I say this because I know that sometimes deeds of squires often go overlooked. You two did your duty. You watched and protected your lord. Remember this day when you win your spurs. Gilles of Thornaby did that today. He was heroic and he was steadfast. He is the model you should follow but know that I am pleased. With you two as my chamberlains, I could sleep in a room of vipers."

Aiden and his two falconers had husbanded their mounts well or perhaps they had secrets we knew not. Whatever the reason, they left us at Yarm and galloped to Stockton to warn John and Alice of our return. The result was hot food and servants waiting to see to our needs. I was beyond sleep. I had had but two hours in the last two days and I needed to think. I went to my solar. Although it was dark and I could not see the sun, I knew where the southwest was and that was all I needed. I took a jug of wine and sat to think and ponder what I ought to do next and how best to use the prize that was Fitz Mandeville.

We had had a great victory but what would be the result of the dead on both sides? Helmsley would be a great loss to

Stephen. The land to the north and the east of York was now lost to him. Yet all would be wasted if I did not have a lord who could rule there. There was only one choice: Wulfric. I would give Gilles of Thornaby his spurs and he could go with Wulfric. Wulfric's constable would have to hold Normanby. With Malton destroyed and Helmsley in our hands, it would be easy to subjugate Pickering. One thing was clear, I needed men and many of them.

It was almost dawn before I came up with the solution. It was not a perfect solution but in these anarchic days what would be perfect? In the short term, I had ransoms to arrange and letters to write.

When Alice came up to clear my solar, she frowned as she spied me, "My lord, have you sat up all night? The Good Lord decrees that we should spend the night in sleep and not awake and worrying."

I smiled, "When a knight wins his spurs, he has to spend a night awake keeping vigil. Consider this my vigil."

Shaking her head she placed the goblet, platter and empty jug on the wooden tray." I will have a doe's liver prepared for you. That will give you strength. You are our rock, lord, and you cannot fail!"

"I pray I never do and thank you for your concern. I will be fine."

"You need a woman, lord, to keep you in check. All great men need a woman to steer their course!"

As I went to my chambers to wash and to change, I reflected that a woman did steer my course. It was Empress Matilda.

My morning was spent dictating letters. With Philip now in Piercebridge, I would have to use a written missive to inform the Archbishop of events. He was old but he had a sharp mind. He would read between the lines. The letter to the Earl of Essex was more direct. My communications with him would take some time. I had no doubt that he would spurn my initial offer. The chances that he would defect because of an errant cousin were slim but his response would tell me just how much or how little he valued his cousin. On our way north I had had Sir Edward discover the value in terms of a ransom of each knight. We had captured eight. John wrote letters to the families of the eight laying out the terms of their ransom. As all eight had rich estates to the south of us, the ransoms were proportionately higher than those we demanded from the Scots to the north of us.

Before they left, I gathered my knights and their squires in the Great Hall along with my Constable and Steward. "We had a great victory yesterday. Gilles of Thornaby, you have won your spurs. We shall knight you on midsummer day."

The decision pleased everyone. I saw Sir Edward nod his thanks. As much as he would miss his squire, he knew that it was the right decision.

"Sir Wulfric, for the time being, I would like you and your archers and men at arms to be based at Helmsley."

"And what of Normanby, lord?"

"If we hold Pickering and Helmsley then there is little threat to Normanby."

He nodded, "We will have few men to hold two such castles."

"I know. When *'Adela'* returns, whatever men are sent, you can have for the garrisons. Gilles, your first task as a knight will be to help Sir Wulfric by being constable of Pickering. It will mean that the two of you will have to reduce it by force but with Baron Fitz Mandeville in our hands that should not be a problem." I turned to Sir John of Stockton. "Sir John, I have a new role for you. I will give you a conroi of archers and men at arms. You will spend your time travelling from here to Normanby thence to Pickering, Helmsley and finally back here. You and your men will be a mobile castle. You will spend a couple of nights in each castle. It means, Sir Wulfric, that you have reinforcements within a day's ride of you at all times."

I could see that John was pleased but Dick looked worried. "We are stretching ourselves thin, lord. With Sir Philip now gone, we are short of archers. If the war was over then this would not seem so reckless an act."

"It may seem reckless, Dick, but it is necessary. Would you have me return the castles we have taken to their masters? Would you take them again? Next time it would not be as easy and we would lose more men."

"I am sorry, lord. I am still just an archer from Sherwood at heart. I cannot see the greater plan."

I smiled, "Nor can I. We seem to lurch from one crisis to the next. I would have you and John of Craven speak with the prisoners. There may be some who we can use as men at arms or garrisons for our castles."

Sir Edward said, "That is a risk, lord."

"We are knights, Sir Edward, we take risks each time we mount our warhorses. Besides, I intend to spread them out among all of our castles and only take those whom Dick and John deem fit for purpose."

Sir Harold said, "And the rest?"

"I have yet to give that thought. We will wait until Dick and John of Craven have finished their work. Sir Wulfric, Sir John and Gilles, you have tasks to complete. God speed and we will meet again here on Midsummer Day. We will dub Gilles and Philip on that day."

When they had gone and my letters despatched, I went to speak with my priest. I found him with Father Thomas. They were tending the garden which Father Henry had created. "A great victory, lord, and we have only a few men to bury. The Good Lord is truly on your side."

"I pray that he is. Father Thomas, I am pleased to see you looking better than you once did."

"Thank you, lord. You have truly saved my life. Knowing that I was the only one to survive that horror has made me more determined than ever to give my life purpose."

"And what would you?"

"I would be as Father Henry here. At Durham, we were cloistered clerks and we saw not the people. I would be like Father Henry. The people of this manor come to him as a father. That is what Christ intended for us. I would be a priest to people and tend to their needs."

"Then perhaps we can help each other. Philip of Selby is now lord of the manor of Piercebridge. There is a church in the manor but no priest. The priest at Walworth was slain. If you would accept, I would have you as priest and shepherd for those two churches."

His face brightened and then a frown came across it. "Lord, can you do that? I thought such an appointment as that was the responsibility of the church."

"It is and you are right. However, as the present incumbent of Durham is, like Stephen of Blois, a usurper these are abnormal times. I will write to the Archbishop. I am certain he will approve your appointment."

Father Henry nodded, "I concur, lord, and I think that this was meant to be. I will add my endorsement to the letter. Those poor people need you, Thomas."

"Then I accept!"

"And now, Father Henry, I need your advice and your counsel." Father Thomas made to go, "I pray you stay for your advice would help." I led them to the river where Father Henry had a log upon which he would sit and contemplate. We went there. "I intend to offer employment to some of those men we captured at the battle. My problem is the rest. I will tell you what I plan and I would appreciate it if you would give me honest counsel."

Father Thomas nodded and Father Henry said, "I will, lord, although I fear these are military matters and I am a man of the Church."

"I will give the rest their freedom, having first taken their arms from them and I will have them swear, here in this church, not to take arms against the Empress or her supporters again. What think you?"

"I think that is fair but these men are soldiers. If they cannot fight for King Stephen then you deprive them of their livelihood. They will starve."

"I am not that cruel. There are lords who fight for neither side and the Archbishop requires guards for his city. I would even give any who wished it passage to Anjou."

Father Henry nodded, "And those who will not swear?"

"They will lose their right hand. That way they cannot fight."

Father Thomas said, "That seems cruel, lord."

Father Henry said, "It is kinder than you know. After battles, most prisoners are slain. A merciful punishment is often blinding. This is more than fair for if they will not swear it means that they will bear arms again. Next time they may hurt the very people you minister to, Thomas." I could see the effect of the words on the young priest. "I will walk amongst the prisoners, lord."

"Thank you, Father Henry. We will make the offer this evening. My men are finding those who might serve us. They too will take an oath but they will make it on this sword as well as the Bible!"

We had over fifty prisoners. More than half wished to join me. John of Craven and Dick whittled that down to just eighteen that they trusted. When I offered the rest the choice of swearing not to fight against us, they all accepted the offer. Fifteen wished to travel to Anjou while the rest would travel, under escort, to York where they would offer their services to the Archbishop. I was a realist. I knew that a good third of those who had sworn an oath would find some way of breaking that vow but it would take time. I was not a naturally cruel man. Dick and Harold had shown me that men were sometimes placed in a position where they had hard choices to make. Who was I to judge? I had had a pampered upbringing. I had never known hardship. With the decision made, I felt much better.

Sir Richard of Yarm had brought the wounded who had survived to my castle a few days after the prisoners had departed for York. As the *'Adela'* had still to return, not all had yet left. Some of the wounded did not need to swear an oath. They were already maimed or lamed. The ones who would recover happily swore an oath.

Baron Fitz Mandeville had been seriously wounded by my spear thrust. Sir Richard's priest had saved his life but the Baron looked smaller somehow. He had lost weight but he had lost none of his arrogance and hatred. He glared at me when I spoke with him. I gave him a room that was constantly guarded. He was fed and he had a servant yet all I received from him were scowls and insults. I knew why. He had wanted death and I had denied him that.

"My cousin cares not for me. You will get no ransom!"

"I told you before, Baron, that money does not interest me." He looked surprised. "I know that you find that hard to understand. You robbed and stole from those with nothing. You fight for Stephen because it is your chance for riches and power. I fight for the Empress because, like you, I swore an oath to her father to ensure that came about. Unlike you and your cousin, I keep my word."

For the first time, I saw that I had said something which could not be answered by an insult. He had broken his word and he knew it. From that moment, there was a slight change in his demeanour. He was never pleasant but he became slightly less unpleasant. He was resigned to his fate.

As Midsummer Day drew close, preparations for the ceremony took over the castle and town. Midsummer Day was not a Christian festival but in ancient times the custom had been for marriage on that longest of days. It was still a time when couples married. It also meant we had many babies born in the spring, at Easter, and that too was seen as symbolic and harkened back to an earlier time.

I had had a reply from the Archbishop of York to my missive. The men who had sworn an oath were taken into his service. It suited the old Archbishop. They were warriors all and with so many wild and lordless men wandering the countryside, his city needed protection. He also thanked me for making his nephew a knight. My appointment of Father Thomas was sanctioned. In a world of chaos, it seemed somehow a normal act. When would we return to such times? Hidden within the letter was a message about the war. Stephen of Blois had taken the offensive against Bishop Nigel of Ely. He was making inroads. As the Normans had found when they tried to defeat Hereward the Wake, that was easier said than done. I wondered why the Earl of Gloucester had not taken the opportunity to launch his own attack. With Stephen in the east then London would have been vulnerable. As much as I had made the borderlands safe, I knew that I was needed at the Empress' side. He also sent me a letter for William Cumin. I kept that safe.

All of my knights attended the ceremony. It was an opportunity for the wives of my knights to show off the fine clothes they had bought with the riches their husbands had earned. It was also a chance for me to see the next generation of knights and ladies. Wulfric and Erre apart, the rest of my knights had sons and daughters.

Before the ceremony, I spoke with Philip, now of Piercebridge. "How goes the rebuilding?"

"Thank you for your mason, lord. William has many fine ideas. We have walls, albeit wooden and the gatehouse is stone. It is men I need."

"We will get them in time but use the men of your manor and that of Walworth. Train them. Father Thomas is happy?"

"He too is a good appointment. He is enthusiastic and never still. I have offered him a horse for he flies between Piercebridge and Walworth almost daily."

"Good. I will require some of your men when we go to war but, at the moment, the Empress and the Earl are consolidating. Much will depend upon Ely. I will need half of your archers and a sergeant at arms."

He nodded. "I have the men in mind for that."

My little church, where Adela my wife and my child were buried, was packed. Adela would have liked that. I found myself smiling at the memory of her. Gilles was nervous as I dubbed him and gave him his spurs. Philip was older but I could see the pride in his eyes as he was knighted. Alice had outdone herself with the feast she had provided and with wine from Anjou, it was a joyful celebration.

Before they became too inebriated, I took Sir John of Stockton and Sir Wulfric to one side. "I know that Pickering was abandoned when you closed with the castle but how goes it? Does my plan work?"

Wulfric nodded. "With the new men you sent, we have the garrison we need and Sir John here has proved most adept at capturing and hanging the brigands who preyed in the remote villages. Gilles will be a good knight. If you so wished, you could make him lord of the manor. He is young but he has learned well from Sir Edward."

"Perhaps. Pickering and Helmsley are temporary. I hope that when the war is over then the Empress will appoint her own lords there. I would have you and Gilles closer to home." I pointed to Erre. "He has no children. When he dies I will need a lord at Norton and that manor is special for it was my father's."

"Aye, lord. We forget the past at our peril."

Chapter 6

I had had to house and home knights held for ransom before. Normally I came to like the knights even the ones who later turned against me. Edward Fitz Mandeville was the most unpleasant guest I ever housed. Perhaps it was his wound or maybe it was his nature but he was offensive to all. It was when he insulted Alice that I finally took action. He was able to move around and I allowed him the freedoms of my Great Hall. It was a mistake. He took to wander as though he owned it. That I might have pardoned but he insulted the women. He seemed to take great delight in demeaning them. When Alice fled in tears after one of his outbursts, I confronted him.

"While you are in my home then you will treat all within with respect."

Laughing, he had said, "Servants are like dogs and should be treated as such. And as for women..." The leer left me in no doubt about his attitude towards women.

"As for women, I command that you treat them with respect; all of them!"

"You do not command me! I did not surrender my sword. I will speak as I choose and no man tells me other."

"Then as you do not think yourself to be my guest then you are my prisoner and you shall be treated accordingly." I had him put into my dungeon. It was well kept and had a bed but it had a locked door and a guard. He also had the indignity of using a bowl for his toilet. That shamed him. His vile insults towards the women of my home made me glad that I had rid myself of his unpleasantness.

The letter I had sent to the Earl of Essex through the Archbishop of York took some time to reach Edward's cousin. The reply to my offer reached me at the end of June. As I had expected, the offer to release his cousin if Geoffrey de Mandeville ceased hostilities against the Empress was rejected. He made a counteroffer which was a large ransom. I reluctantly sent a letter rejecting the amount and demanding a higher figure. I say reluctantly for I wished to be rid of my prisoner. The ransoms for the other knights were paid promptly and we were all the richer for it. The captured armour and horses were also invaluable and I felt more confident.

My dilemma was the lack of communication from both the Empress and the Earl. I felt cut off. I had no idea how the campaign in the west fared and my only news of Ely's campaign was second hand. When *'Adela'* docked just two weeks after Midsummer's Day, I had more second-hand information. The Bishop of Ely was now deep within the Fens and Stephen of Blois was closing with him. The putative rebellion in the east had apparently failed. Once again the procrastination of the Empress and the Earl had cost us the opportunity to inflict another defeat on Stephen. I was frustrated. Had I not had to watch my prisoner and await his cousin's next offer, then I would have visited the Empress. I also learned that King David had met with the Empress and told her that he would appoint William Cumin as Bishop of Durham. The meeting had ended acrimoniously and the Empress had refused. My letters to her and the news they contained had not been wasted.

My ship brought more men for us and our garrison was swollen by another twenty men. I hated the inactivity of just waiting and so, leaving my new men in my castle, I took Dick's archers and eleven men at arms to patrol to the north and see what Cumin had been up to. I left after sending my ship back to Anjou. My townspeople had much to trade with Anjou. William of Kingston promised me a fast voyage.

I did not take Rolf with me as I headed north. He had picked up a wound in the battle and it had not healed. It was not a serious wound but I did not want to risk him. I took a new horse we had captured at the battle. He was not a true warhorse but Lion was a horse with a heart. A golden copper colour, he reminded me of Scout. I did not know him well and a journey north would enable me to get to know him.

We halted at Thorpe. William of Wulfestun had been a captured prisoner forced to be a bandit. He had helped the survivors of an attack on Thorpe and they had taken to him. He was now married to Hilda, one of the women, and acted as a headman. He was a good man. We halted there so that I could speak with him.

"Have you seen aught of men from the north?"

Thorpe was on the Durham Road and none passed north or south without that William knew who they were.

"No, lord. Since you passed south and warned me, I have kept a wary eye open. I thought that the lack of a lord might mean more bandits but there has been none."

"You do well to be vigilant. We intend to travel north and see how the land lies."

"Fear not, lord. I will watch this road and send word if I see any danger."

As we headed north Dick said, "A castle there would give us more protection, lord."

I smiled, "A man born and bred in the forests advises me to build walls?"

He laughed, "Let us just say, lord, that I have seen the advantage of loosing arrows from the walls of a castle."

"Perhaps you are right but if Durham belongs to the Empress then we have no need to protect our northern road. Cumin is a distraction that is all."

"You do not think he will attack us?"

"Cumin? No. However, he has allegiances to Scotland and King David. It may be that he encourages the Scots to come south. That is what I fear. And if it was Scotland then a castle at Thorpe would not aid us except to dilute the number of men we would have to defend Stockton. If the Scots come again, they either attack us or Piercebridge and now we have a garrison there. I think Sir Philip could hold out until a message was sent to us. He has stone walls and a river."

78

Gilles had been listening. Since the dubbing of the two knights, he had become increasingly interested in such matters. "Your purpose in this ride, lord, is it to warn Bishop Cumin?"

"He is not anointed Bishop, Gilles, but you have it aright. I do not want him to think that we have forgotten him and his treacherous act. He knows not that Father Thomas escaped. He thinks all the priests who fled are dead. I also have a letter to give to him from the Archbishop.

"Why is he not Bishop of Durham, lord?"

"The Prince Bishop of the Palatinate is appointed by the ruler of England. Cumin is King David's man. Stephen will not appoint him. Pope Innocent will not sanction the appointment of a bishop where there is such conflict." I patted my saddlebag. "This letter I have from the Archbishop will confirm, I have no doubt, that Cumin has no right to be in Durham. Of course, the letter alone cannot shift him and I am loath to lose men in an attack on the walls of Durham but the delivery of the letter will weaken his position."

Gilles nodded and Dick said, "What you wish, lord, is for Cumin to be foolish enough to try to take on our men."

I nodded, "It will not happen for he is no leader. However, the prisoners we spoke with told us that Osbert Cumin has a brother, William, and that he serves Prince Henry. He may be more of a threat than his uncle. We shall see."

We saw no sign of armed men as we headed north. When the travellers we met spied my banner, they approached us. They told us of depredations continuing in the Palatinate. One older woman pleaded, "Lord, end this tyranny! This new Bishop is a cruel man! His riders still prey upon us."

I nodded, "I can only offer hope for the future and not for the present. Until the Empress' son is crowned king then I fear I cannot do as much as I might wish."

I waved a hand south. "There is land by the river and I can promise you that you and your families will be safe there."

The old woman looked at her family. "That seems an honest answer."

The father who was also a grey beard said, "But my family have farmed the land since the time of the Conqueror. Can you offer us land which is as good?"

Dick shrugged, "A dead family cannot farm at all. That is your fate if you remain here. The Earl has not yet enough men to face King David and it is his men who rule this land. I would take the Earl up on his offer."

"I go now to Durham and I will speak with this Cumin on your behalf. My offer stands. If you present yourself at my castle then you will find land."

It was not an idle offer. Hartburn, Elton and Norton all had good land for farming. Stockton had slightly less for we were more popular. We reached Durham in the early afternoon. We halted out of bow range with our helmets removed. Dick had two of his archers with arrows at the ready. We waited to be addressed. Four men appeared. I recognised one as William Cumin and the other two, from their looks, appeared to be of his family. The fourth was a Sergeant.

"What is it you want, wolf and murderer?"

I did not wish to engage in a useless exchange of insults. I was no murderer and he knew it. Instead, I held up my hand with the letter from the Archbishop. "I have a letter here from the Archbishop of York!" I handed it to Richard.

William Cumin shouted, "He has no authority here! This is now part of Scotland and King David has appointed me!"

"And the Empress has refused to confirm it. I come not to bandy words with a usurper. I come to deliver a message."

I nodded to Richard who trotted forward. I saw one of the young men who flanked Cumin turn and speak to someone. A crossbow appeared. Before it could be used, Henry Warbow's arrow had plucked the would be assassin from the battlements.

"Any more treachery, Cumin, and I will have my archers slay you and your kin!"

They ducked behind the battlements and Henry Warbow snorted. "If you wish them dead, lord, then it matters not where they hide."

He was right for my archers knew how to loose an arrow vertically. At this range, my archers could clear the gatehouse with just ten arrows. Richard threw the letter to one of the guards and then backed his horse all the way back. It was intended to insult those within by telling them he did not trust them to send a bolt to his back.

When he reached me I said, "Bravely done, Richard." Then I shouted, "And I have a message for you. If you send your barbarians to rampage through this land, they risk my wrath. I give you fair warning that I will hang any I find whether they be lord or commoner. I will not seek a ransom."

One of the young men who flanked Cumin shouted down, "And here is a message from me! I am William Cumin and you slew my brother, Osbert! I will have my revenge upon you!"

I laughed, "Then have it now. Come down and try your lance against me!"

The silence was deafening. I saw the guards along the wall look to him. He should have accepted my challenge but, instead, he said, "I will bide my time!"

My men all laughed. The guards on the walls hung their heads. How could they follow a man who refused a challenge? My visit had been worthwhile. I turned my horse and we headed east.

"Where do we go, lord?"

"We will head to Bishop's Auckland. I know there is a hall there. I would keep watch on the castle. Have two of your archers wait close by. If armed men leave the castle then I would know."

Dick nodded, "Aye lord." He turned to two of his most experienced archers. "Rafe and Long Tom. Hide in the woods yonder. We ride to the Bishop's hall at Auckland. Fetch us if men leave."

"Aye, lord."

In the days of Geoffrey Rufus, the hall at Auckland had been popular. There was good hunting nearby. King Henry had even visited and hunted there. As we rode in to the small village, it seemed almost deserted. There were just two priests at the wooden church and a handful of mean huts. We reined in and I dismounted. The leader of the two priests came over to speak with me. "Earl, we are honoured by your presence. I am Father James. We have not seen you since..." His voice trailed off.

"Since Bishop Geoffrey ruled the Palatinate. I know." I waved a hand around the village. "It seems the estate has fallen on hard times. How do you manage?"

He shrugged, "We eke out a living."

"Do the men hunt?" The priest hesitated. Hunting on the Bishop's lands was punishable by death. "The man who calls himself Bishop has not been appointed by either the Church or the throne. There is no Prince Bishop at the moment."

"Even so, lord, none of the men would risk it and we dare not condone the act."

I nodded. "And you would starve. I am not bound by such conventions and rules. Dick, send your archers to hunt in the forests. It is richly filled with game."

He grinned. At heart, he was still the young man who had lived off his wits in the forests of the Sherwood. "Aye, lord! I will not have eaten sweeter meat since I lived as an outlaw!"

As they rode off I said, "We will not take food from your mouths but we will use the Bishop's lodge this night and we will share whatever my men hunt with you and your people." He still looked uncertain. "We are here for a while. I intend to stop the raids on the homes of the poor of Durham. When I am satisfied that there is no danger then I will leave."

"Thank you, lord. I meant no offence."

"And I took none, Father James."

I handed my reins to Richard and went to the lodge. The door groaned as I opened it and inside it smelled damp and musty. Edgar said, "We will clean it up, lord, and make it fit for us to use."

I nodded and, after taking off my cloak and laying my helmet and shield upon it, walked around the village. I saw that only half of the huts were occupied. Pale faces peered fearfully at me as I passed. I smiled, "Fear not. We are not here to harm any of you." I knew my words would not

reassure them. If I meant them harm, I might say the same
thing. By the time I had walked the village, my spirits were
low. It had taken a short time for this prosperous estate to
fall into ruin. It was a reflection of the whole country too. I
knew now that the valley I ruled was an oasis in a wasteland.
The Scots had tried twice to do us harm and we had not
suffered. It made me more determined than ever to continue
to resist them with every ounce of my being.

"It is ready, my lord!"

When I approached the hall I saw that my cloak, helmet
and shield had been taken within, The horses were stabled
and, as I entered, Gilles and Richard were attempting to
make a bed. "Do not worry about comfort. We are on
campaign now. I need no goose down. I will make do with
straw."

Edgar shook his head, "There is precious little of that
either, lord!"

My archers had done well and the animals they brought
back were gutted and skinned in next to no time. Dick tried
to give the skins and the bones to the villagers but they
shook their heads fearfully. Father James explained, "If they
are found in their homes, they will think they hunted them.
They will eat your food but all traces of the animals must be
removed, lord. I am sorry."

"I understand."

The villagers ate well. I guessed that none of them had
had meat in some time. Leopold of Durstein took it upon
himself to cook all the bones. It made a fine stock which
would give more taste to the vegetables and greens they
normally ate. "When all the meat has been taken from the
bones, we will make a bone fire. They can spread that on
their fields."

My men were rough, hard men but they hated to see any
people mistreated.

I decided that we would stay in the village until Rafe and
Long Tom contacted us. It allowed my men to help the
villagers spread the burned bone on the fields as well as the
horse manure which our mounts provided. It would not help
them in the near future but, eventually, it would. No matter

what man did to the world, nature kept life going. It was a reassuring thought.

Rafe and Long Tom arrived on the third morning of our time in the village. "Lord, a large number of knights and soldiers have left Durham."

"How many and whither went they?"

"There were four knights and ten men at arms. I would guess there were thirty soldiers. They were poorly armed. They took the road south."

"What lies in that direction?"

Rafe said, "The only large place is Stockton but there are villages, lord."

Dick said, "If we head due east, lord, we can be at the Roman Road in six or seven miles."

"Then let us do so. Mount!"

It was a greenway that led east but we were all good riders. Rafe and Long Tom rode ahead. I kept my banner furled. I could not believe that Cumin would risk my wrath by sending men to raid my lands. However, he might be scouting out my borders to see how well they were guarded. That would make more sense. I knew that the village of Fissebourne had been prosperous once. It lay on the road to Hartness. Could that be a target? I was speculating and I had to find them. When we struck the Roman Road, we saw their sign upon it. Rafe waved to us. He was north of where we had joined the road. Horses had travelled upon it and they had left marks showing that they were heading east.

"What lies east of here?"

"Middleham, lord."

In the distance, I could just make out smoke rising from the settlement. Long Tom said, after leaping down to examine some horse droppings, "This is fresh, lord. They passed here not long ago."

I spurred my horse, Lion, and led my men on the turf road east. I hefted my shield. If they were just ahead then we needed to be ready. We spied them within a mile of leaving the road. They were ahead of us and making their way to the small village. Larger than Auckland it had a palisade running around it. I think it was to keep animals out, for a horse could mount it easily. I did not need to give orders. As I drew my sword, I heard the rest of my men at arms and squires doing the same.

The raiders were racing towards the village in a mass. There was no order save that the knights and men at arms were at the fore. I heard the screams as the villagers realised they were being attacked. The thunder of our hooves made those at the rear look over their shoulders. When they saw us, I heard a wail and shouts of alarm. As I brought my sword across the back of one of the men on foot, I knew that the shout had been too late. We were among them. My sword laid open the leather jerkin and his back to the bone. He fell silently to the ground.

Those nearest me tried to flee out of the way. When I saw arrows pluck some from their saddles then I knew that Dick had dismounted his archers. I could leave the ruffians to him. It was Sir William Cumin who turned first and tried to form a line to face us. It was too little and too late. They were stationary and we were galloping. I had no need to make for William Cumin. He wanted revenge but he did not come alone. I saw that the knight next to him had the same livery and had been stood on the gatehouse with him. He was another cousin.

They came at me on either side. I had to focus on William for he came at my sword side. I would rely on my shield to protect me from his cousin. We met sword to sword and they rang like church bells as they clashed. My shield arm took a heavy blow from the sword of the younger Cumin. I pulled my reins to my right as I heard Gilles shout to Richard to attack the knight. Cumin's squire jabbed a spear at my shield as I passed behind Cumin's horse. I kept my saddle but only just. Out of the corner of my eye, I saw Gilles swing his own sword at Cumin's squire. I found myself behind an unsighted William Cumin and he was desperately trying to see where I was. My men at arms were amongst his and mine were the superior of any. I brought my sword over my head and struck him on his left shoulder. He shouted out in pain. Something had broken. His reins were in his left hand and his horse just kept going. The Scottish knight tried to turn to face me but he could not. I spurred Lion and he leapt forward. I brought my own sword before my body and, as I passed him, I swung it across his body. It hit his chest and he tumbled over the back.

As I turned my horse around, I saw Richard struck from his horse by the last Cumin. He cruelly tried to make his horse trample the helpless squire who lay winded on the ground. An arrow came from nowhere and struck the knight's shield. He turned and fled with his squire.

Gilles reined in next to me as did Edgar. They protected my sides.

"See to Richard!" I turned my head as Gilles leapt from his horse. Richard Cumin and his squire were galloping north. I could see their shields were stuck with arrows. Dick had done his best. The rabble, the ones who remained, had also fled and all that were left were two men at arms and William Cumin who groggily stood.

I remembered the villagers in Auckland. I rode up to William Cumin. "You have no honour, Cumin. You and your uncle are bandits both!"

His helmet had fallen to the ground and I saw the sneer on his face. "The treasury in Durham is full. Ask for your ransom!"

"I told you before I wanted no ransom."

He looked at me with surprise, "You will let me go?"

"I will release you, yes! Hang them!"

He tried to move towards me, "I am a knight!"

"You are a bandit and a villain. Hanging is your punishment. Wilfred, Edgar, strip him of his armour. Let him die naked. That is my order!"

The two men at arms were resigned to their fate. From their scarred faces and arms they were veterans. They knew what to expect. William Cumin was stunned. He dropped to his knees before he was unceremoniously hauled up again and his mail lifted from him. With ropes around their necks, the three of them were dragged to the nearest tree and the ropes were thrown over. My men at arms looked at me and I nodded. They began to haul on their ropes. The men at arms went limp until they were halfway up and then they violently threw their legs to one side. Their necks broken, they died relatively quickly. They had seen men hanged before. They did not want to choke to death. Better a broken neck than that death. Cumin, however, did not and he wriggled like a fish on a hook. I saw his cheeks and face grow purple. He gasped for breath. It was not a quick death. Without his armour he was light and it took some time for him to die. Eventually, his body went limp and began to sway gently from side to side.

"Leave their bodies there. Collect the horses, armour and weapons."

I rode back to Richard. He was standing when I reached him. "I am sorry, my lord. He defeated me."

"He was a knight and you are a squire. There is no shame." I saw that Gilles had slain the squire who had tried to kill me. "And thank you, Gilles."

He grinned as he held up the dead squire's broken sword. "Alf's sword proved stronger, lord. The squire had fine armour but his sword was cheaply made."

I nodded, "Your sword should be the best that it can be. Ride to the villagers, yonder. Tell them they can have the dead horses but they should leave the bodies there until they are collected." Two of the enemy horses had been killed. Their flesh would not go to waste.

Richard asked as he mounted, "Who will collect the bodies, lord?"

"Cumin will know of our attack and he will send men to recover his nephew."

"And us, lord?"

"We will head back to Stockton. The danger here is passed. I have no doubt that more men will raid but not for some time. I have other plans to make."

We captured two of the stragglers as we headed back to our castle. I thought to hang them but then realised that they were just ordinary warriors. Both had the accents of the Scots who came from north of Bamburgh. We took them back to our castle and put them in the dungeon with Edward Fitz Mandeville. I tired of using my own men to wait on him hand and foot. It amused me to use the Scots to do so. The

87

fact that they were meanly dressed displeased him. It was a petty victory for me but one I enjoyed, nonetheless.

Chapter 7

We now had so many horses that I was forced to send some to my other knights. They would not go to waste. The mail and armour went to Alf. He reused the ones which were poorly made and repaired the rest. I saw that we had had an influx of refugees from the north. The privations of Durham had driven them to shelter. There was now a wasteland to the north of us. It was as though a plague had descended and wiped out life there. I resolved to visit with the Empress when my ship next returned. I would take a small number of men at arms. I could make the journey in ten days. I would wait for my ship in case she brought any news.

In the meantime, I held sessions. The crimes were petty but my people needed to see that justice was done. It was a necessary part of my task as lord of the manor. As William the Mason had returned, I sat and planned more improvements for my castle. Now that the leat had been cut for the waterwheel which would grind the grain, I needed some protection for it. He and his sons built a small extension to our curtain wall and improved the tower which overlooked it. If the Scots came again, they would be in for a shock.

As August approached, I prepared to leave. We expected *'Adela'* daily. My oathsworn were all ready to ride at a moment's notice. I was, therefore, surprised when a rider from Sir Hugh Manningham arrived one evening. It was Oswald. He was a scout often used by Sir Hugh. I knew him well. When he began to speak, I understood why he had been chosen.

"My lord, Sir Hugh sent me with dire tidings."

I nodded. The outer bailey was no place for such discussions. "Come to my Great Hall. Gilles, find my knights and captains. I would speak with them."

When they were gathered I said, "Speak. What is the message from your lord?"

He looked around at my knights. He knew them and seemed satisfied that he could speak, "My lord warns you that you have upset Prince Henry, the Earl of Northumberland. William Cumin and Osbert Cumin were both his knights."

"How does he know this?"

Oswald seemed a little uneasy. He was not noble-born but he was trusted by Sir Hugh. "Sir Hugh has had to come to an understanding with Prince Henry, lord. We were alone and..."

"I understand. Neither you nor your lord needs to apologise. We have left him isolated far from any help. So, Prince Henry told your master that he was angry with me?"

"More than that, my lord. He said he would send men to teach you a lesson! My lord sent me to warn you that he would come south and punish you. He is gathering an army north of the Tyne."

I looked over to Dick who shook his head. He said nothing but Dick had a wise old head on his shoulders.

"And did your lord know where the attack would come?"

"He said that Balliol was in the Earl's company and he believed that he would attack Barnard Castle and recover his lost land."

I nodded. "I thank you, Oswald. You have risked much." I gave him a gold piece. "Richard, take him to Alice and have him fed. He can sleep in the warrior hall this night."

When he had gone I said, "Well?"

Dick shook his head, "Prince Henry is no fool. Remember the battle at Northallerton, lord? He nearly wrested victory from us. He intended Sir Hugh to believe that Barnard Castle was the intended target."

I saw Gilles and Richard look at each other. It was obvious that they had not thought of that as a ploy.

Sir Harold said, "Last time they attacked Barnard Castle, we met them there. Stockton was left with a tiny garrison."

I nodded, "I gambled and won. Perhaps this time it is Prince Henry who gambles. He knows I am spread thin but he does not know of the reinforcements we have received from Anjou."

Sir John asked, "Would we stand behind Stockton's walls, lord?"

I shook my head. "That would allow him free rein. If we were trapped here, he could pick off Piercebridge and Gainford. He could destroy Norton, Hartburn and Elton. We would give him the Tees valley if we did so. No, we meet him on the field of battle."

"Where, lord?"

"We force him to attack Norton and we fight him there on that boggy ground."

"And how do we do that, lord?"

"The same way Prince Henry did with us. We tell him." I saw the confusion on their faces. "I will devise a way. Tomorrow, Dick, I want you to ride to Barnard Castle and warn Sir Hugh. I may be wrong. If so, he must hold out alone. Then ride to Sir Philip and ask him to keep watch to the southwest of Durham. Sir Tristan, your father needs warning and I need him and his men at arms. Sir John, I need Wulfric and his men at arms and archers."

"If Prince Henry brings a mighty army then we will be outnumbered."

"Perhaps, but we have a good defensive position. If things go awry, we can fall back to Norton and thence to Stockton. I will go to Sir Edward myself and give him the information."

After they had gone I sent for Aiden and his men. I gave them precise instructions. Oswald left before dawn with a letter to his master from me. I took Richard and Gilles and went with Wilfred and Edgar to the dungeon. "Come to mock me again? Were these two savages not enough punishment?" I saw the look of hatred they gave him.

I shook my head. "Your cousin has still to accede to my demands but that will have to wait. I fear I must move you. I have just had intelligence that the Scots under Prince Henry intend to attack us here in the valley. I need to move my forces to protect my castles. I must take you to safety for you are valuable."

He frowned as though he suspected something. "Where will you move me?"

"Just across the river. Your servants can go with you."

"I beg of you, Earl, do not leave me with these savages! They stink and I cannot understand their gibbering!"

I nodded, "They can help you across the river and then they will be returned to the dungeon." They both glared at me. "You insolent pair! Think yourselves lucky that you were not hanged like your masters!"

"Sorry, lord."

"Now pack the lord's belongings and do not try anything. My two men at arms will cut your throats as soon as look at you."

My gesture seemed to placate Fitz Mandeville. He became almost civilised. "If the Scots come here, will you wait behind your walls?"

"I dare not. It is likely they will attack either Barnard Castle or come down the road from Durham. I will wait to the north and west. Hopefully, I will find out which way they come and then meet them."

He shook his head. "You gamble!"

"When you have as few men as I do then you have to. If lords like yourself fought the Scots instead of me, this would not be happening." The two prisoners had gathered Mandeville's things and they now stood. "Come, we will walk to my ferry."

Ethelred had been warned of our arrival and he had the ferry already there. It was a high tide which was on the turn. The water was flowing quickly towards the sea. He had to stand at the steering oar holding it against the powerful current. "Wilfred, Edgar, watch Baron Mandeville. You two, load the ferry." The two of them carried the Baron's belongings to the front of the ferry. They had no sooner dropped them than they hurled themselves in to the river and were soon swept towards the sea.

Wilfred shouted to the two archers who stood guard there, "Loose your arrows."

Although they released three arrows each, they failed to hit anything. I shook my head and grinned at Wilfred, "Take the Baron back to the dungeon."

Baron Mandeville stared at me and then his face became redder. "You used me! You never intended to move me at all. This was a ploy to deceive the enemy!"

"It is time you paid for your keep. Take him away. I must see Sir Edward."

As Ethelred took us across the river Gilles said, "How do you know they will survive?"

"I don't. The Baron was correct. I am gambling but I think it is likely that they will. If they run all day and night then they can reach Durham and I have no doubt that the Cumin family will ingratiate themselves with Prince Henry and tell him all."

Sir Edward found my trick highly amusing but he became more serious when I explained my whole strategy. "What would you have from me, my lord?

"As many men as you can spare. We will tie the ferry to the south bank. If this all goes wrong then there will be survivors and they can flee to my castle. Your family could join them."

"But you do not believe that you will fail."

"No. We will use Dick's archers to have a screen reaching from Hartness to west of Thorpe. Sir Philip's archers will cover the western flank. We are all mounted and I cannot believe that Prince Henry will be. He will be slower than we are. I will adjust my plan if I am wrong."

My men began to trickle in to my castle. I met with Alf and the men of Stockton. I told them what I needed from them. They were happy to defend my walls along with John of Craven and my Frisians. I waited for news from Aiden and his men but none came. *'Adela'* docked two days after Oswald had left. This time she only brought ten more men but they were welcome. They would have a baptism of fire. I wrote a letter to the Empress telling her of the possible attack. I had planned on visiting with her. I would have to defer that now until the autumn. He also brought the unwelcome news that the Bishop of Ely had had to flee to Gloucester. His attack had failed. I was now the only island of hope for the Empress.

We had some good news the following day. Sir Hugh and Sir Philip had ambushed and destroyed a column of forty men marching from Carlisle to aid Prince Henry. It was doubly welcome news for it also meant that the attack would be in the east rather than the west. I sent my men at arms to begin to prepare the defences on the ridge close to Wulfestun. I had stakes prepared. I intended to funnel my enemies to where my archers could make a killing. The stakes would be kept until we knew the ultimate destination of our enemy.

It was Edgar who brought the news. The Scots were heading south from Durham. It was a smaller army than I had expected. They numbered less than four hundred. It was just the Prince's men who were coming south. I knew that most of his better knights had fallen at the Battle of the Standards two years earlier. It gave me hope. I sent Sir Harold with fifty mounted men at arms and my standard. He went to block the Durham road at Thorpe. The rest were with me north of Norton and we waited. I watched the sun set in the west. The sky looked threatening and I wondered what the new day would bring. Aiden and his two scouts had arrived. They looked weary.

"The Scots are camped north-west of here by Fissebourne. There are three hundred and fifty of them."

"Has he lost some?"

"He sent scouts out and not all returned." He grinned, "Ten of them fell to us but I will not take credit for the rest."

"Good. Eat and then make sure they are heading this way."

"Aye, lord." He nodded to Edgar and Edward. "They both did well. They can scout without me if you wish."

"I will always need you, Aiden, you know that!"

The Scots liked to use lightly armed warriors on small ponies. They could cover great distances. They were, however, vulnerable to my archers. I had no doubt that

Dick's archers had slain those that Aiden had not. After dark, we heard the sound of movement to our left. I had the men stand to. It was with some relief that we saw it was Sir Harold. He dismounted and his squire handed my standard to Gilles.

"It went as you expected, lord. His scouts saw us at noon. We chased them and my men slew four but we managed to miss the other three. I had Will Red Legs follow them. They met with the Prince on the Fissebourne Road and headed thence. When they camped we came here to join you."

That was good news. They were seven miles away. "You have done well. Get some food and rest. Sir Edward and Sir Wulfric are preparing the defences for tomorrow." The high ground on which we stood had a swampy area behind us and to the east. There was a road that led to Hartness but the main road headed directly for Norton and then turned to Stockton. We had made the lower ground by the road as difficult to travel as possible. We had stakes on the side of the road and a barrier across it. Dick and his archers guarded that. I had every horseman with me on the high ground. If the Prince tried to attack us, he would have to charge uphill. If he tried to winkle out my archers then we would sweep down upon him from the high ground. I had given him a dilemma. They had seven miles to march and the day promised rain. Dick and his archers would keep their bowstrings dry until the last moment.

It was just before noon when the first of the Scottish scouts appeared. We were not trying to hide my whole force. My knights and their men at arms were spread out across the top of the high ground. I did have some men waiting behind the trees but that was because we could not all fit on the ridge. We watched as the Scottish army formed up on the high ground half a mile away. It was lower than we were and it descended into a swampy narrow valley. The stream which ran through it would not stop a man let alone a horse but the ground was boggy. The rain which had begun at dawn only stopped shortly before the Scots arrived.

I wondered if they would talk first. The Scottish Prince formed his men up in three battles. The centre one was made

The Fallen Crown

up of his wild foot warriors; they were the Galwegians. They were half-naked with spiked and limed hair. They had a small shield and a curved sword. They had been used to try to break us at the Battle of the Standards. They were ferocious fighters who had to be struck many times before they died. His horsemen formed the two flanks. I could see that he intended to knock us off our ridge. As his three battles marched down the slope, I saw that he had kept one-third of his men as a reserve. He remembered the last time he had fought us. He stood on the ridge. I saw that the army which descended was led by Gospatric's son. He rode a large black horse and had five knights with him. He led the left-hand column and would be the closest to Dick and my one hundred archers.

They came down steadily at first and then some of the wild warriors began to run as they neared the stream. When the first ones had leapt over, the others began to run and soon it was a wild mob which ran up the hill towards us. Dick and his archers sent four flights of arrows over and they thinned them out. Amazingly some ran with three or four arrows sticking into them. There had been a hundred of them and now there were less than seventy. I waved my sword and led my front rank of horsemen towards them. I left Sir Edward with the second line of forty-five horsemen. We had spears and there were fifty of us. Gospatric's son saw what we intended and he hurried his battle towards the stream. Instead of crossing and then forming lines, they jumped over and tried to join the fray. Some sank up to their knees in the boggy ground. I had to concentrate upon the men on foot first. Dick would have to deal with the horsemen. I led the line. Rolf was eager to go to war and his powerful hooves ate up the ground. I pulled back my spear and, as a limed warrior tried to throw himself and his sword at my horse's head, I punched my spear. It tore into his chest. I must have hit his heart for blood spurted. I pulled out the spear and stabbed a second time at the warrior behind him. This time I hit him in the stomach. Even though he was dying, he managed to wrench the spear from my hand and I drew my sword. The stream was just two hundred paces from me and

96

I knew we would have to retreat soon. As I leaned forward to hack into the neck of a wild Scot I yelled, "Wheel left!" As we turned, we charged across the front of the horsemen lumbering up the hill. Dick and his archers rained death from one side. We charged into the other.

It was their shields that faced us and not their spears. Some of my knights and men at arms still had spears and they did the greatest damage. They knocked knights from their mounts. Wulfric had his war axe and when that struck, it knocked man and shield from the back of the horse. I saw Sir Harold, Sir Tristan and their squires charge Gospatric's son and the last three of his oathsworn. Sir Harold and Sir Tristan were both powerful knights. It was an uneven contest and the four Northumbrians were hacked to death. The whole of the rest of the Scottish right flank turned and fled.

"Fall back!"

As we headed up the hill, I saw that the last battle had seen their opportunity and they charged obliquely up the hill towards us. Sir Edward and the last of my men charge down the hill to meet them. As our horses struggled to make the top, I heard a clash of metal on wood as my knights and men at arms struck the shields of the Scots. Dick had taken it upon himself to send half of his archers closer and they began to pick off horsemen and horses. By the time we had reached the ridge and turned, the Scots had been broken and the survivors of the three battles limped and trudged back to their Prince.

We reformed and I saw empty saddles. We had not emerged unharmed. The enemy still outnumbered us but it was not by much. More importantly, they had seen us break three of their attacks. As the afternoon drifted towards dusk, I saw them pack up and turn around. They began to head back the way they had come. Sir Richard of Yarm and Sir Edward had slight wounds and I left them with the wounded and Sir Richard's men at arms. They would collect the horses and clear the battlefield. The rest of us followed the Scots. I did not want them to rest. I wanted them far from my land. Dick and his archers led the pursuit. They had not used their horses which were fresher. We saw evidence of their harassment of the enemy as we passed bodies with arrows in them. We were weary but I rode Lion. Rolf had done his work and pursuit was better suited to my new horse. As darkness fell, we closed ranks but our archers ahead of us protected us still. We passed the old Scottish camp at Fissebourne. We could smell the fires they had used to cook their meals and still we followed. As I had expected, our pursuit ended at Durham. When we saw the huge fortress above the Wear ahead, we halted and I ordered my men to make camp.

We had last eaten at dawn but no one was ready for food. I had one man in two sleep while I sat with my knights and watched the castle as the moon came out. As dawn broke behind us, I saw that the standard of the Bishop of Durham had been replaced by the standard of Prince Henry of Scotland. My men had procured some food and we ate a cold breakfast washed down with water from the Wear. I saw the battlements lined with the enemy. Taking off my helmet and with open palms, I rode towards the gates. Dick and his archers had their bows ready. Sir Harold and my two squires accompanied me. I had thought to take Sir Wulfric but I knew his temper.

We stopped a hundred paces from the walls. I shouted, "I have come to talk."

Prince Henry appeared and William Cumin was next to him, "Talk, but we hold this castle!"

I nodded, "Aye. This is the second time you have escaped me and taken refuge in a castle although I must confess you have brought more men back with you this time."

"Do you have something to say or are you just here to insult me?"

"I am here to tell you that this man whom you have tried to appoint Bishop is a murderer and he will pay for his crimes. This is not Scotland. Each time you come down to my land to try to take it, you lose more men. I am becoming tired of this. Know you this; if you or any other Scottish rabble come to the Tees then I shall come north and make such a wasteland of your country that it will be worse than when William the Conqueror did so."

I let my words hang in the air. All remembered the slaughter perpetrated in the land by William the Conqueror.

The Prince pointed at me. "You hanged one of my knights!"

"I hanged a murderer and a thief. I will do the same again so be warned." I pointed at the third Cumin knight, Richard. "If you wish to live, young Cumin, then stay away from my sword!" He shrank back in fear.

The Prince said, "We will not come south again. Not until my father decides that we will take back what is ours."

I nodded and said, "Then if you do, make sure that I am dead else I will hunt you and your father down and you will die. You have the word of the Warlord of the North and I am never foresworn."

I turned my horse around and headed back to my men. It was over.

Chapter 8

Of course, such things are never over. There are twists and turns a leader does not have time to consider. I had done what I set out to do. I had stopped the Scots from raiding my lands. I had damaged their ability to do so again in the near future and, as August drifted into September, I planned my visit to the Empress.

We had been back a week and I was immersed in the many problems my leaving would create. Just after dawn, I was summoned to the town gate. Alf stood there with two of the town watch. They had two bound baskets before them and their faces were drawn. "What is it, Alf? Is something amiss?"

"Lord, these two baskets were placed before the gate sometime in the night." He glared at the two sentries. "The men know not when."

I smiled, "The walls still stand and we are safe. I think the two baskets hardly constitute a threat to us."

Alf nodded to the two men. They opened the baskets. I peered in at the dead eyes of Sir Hugh Manningham and his son in one basket and Oswald the scout and Ralph, his squire in the other. Alf said, "I did not recognise them, lord, but I can see that you do."

I nodded, "He was an ally and more than that, a friend. We had the victory but he paid the price. Fetch them to the church. I will have Father Henry inter them."

Alf said, "The Scots, lord?"

"Aye, the Scots. You were right to be concerned. If they could get as close to our walls as this then there is the danger that we could be surprised. Have the undergrowth cut back from the walls and have oyster shells laid before the gate. They will give a warning. Is the ditch in a good state of repair?"

"It is, lord, but there are no longer any stakes within. We worried about children falling in."

"Tell the children to be careful and plant the stakes." I turned and looked back at the town. "The town watch should have dogs. See Aiden. If they have dogs, they will give a warning. They will bark at danger."

"Aye, lord." We had reached the church and the two men laid down the baskets and hurried away. They were eager to be away from Alf's tongue. I had no doubt that any admonition they had received before would now be doubled.

I summoned my household knights and told them of Alf's discovery. All were shocked for we had fought alongside Sir Hugh many times. "How did they manage to do this, lord? Sir Hugh was a canny fighter."

"He was but he was taken in by Prince Henry and deceived. I am guessing that there was a spy in his household. As I discovered this morning, our watches are not as rigorous as they should be. This is a warning to us; especially as I leave within the week."

"We will be vigilant, lord. We will examine and interrogate all who wish to make their home here. Our enemies will not find it so easy the next time." Sir Harold's family lived in my castle. He would ensure they were safe. He had more skills in that area than any other knight. "Whom do you take?"

"I will just take my men at arms, Dick and Sir John. I go not to war but to speak with the Empress. The hope that we had in the spring has withered. However, whilst I am gone I wish you all to be aggressive. Mounted patrols should ride in all but the worst weather. I want the road to Durham, Piercebridge and Barnard Castle patrolling as though they were my castle walls."

Sir Harold nodded, "And who commands in your stead, lord?"

"You command the castle and Sir Edward the valley. I will speak with him before I leave. I will inform John what is required too."

"How long will you be away, lord?"

"It could be a month and it could be half a year. I told William of Kingston that I wish him to use Bristol on his way back from Anjou. That way I can send secure messages. Do not use the land to send messages. It is too dangerous."

I visited with Sir Edward and told him the same. He agreed with my strategy. "We have more men now and more horses than we know what to do with. I will have our men hunt the forests and scour them of enemies."

I had thought I was ready to leave when a rider arrived from York. It was one of the Archbishop's most trusted clerks and I knew him well. I admitted him straightaway and saw him in private. "Lord, I bring a written missive from the Empress. The Archbishop spoke with her at the peace conference the Bishop of Winchester arranged at Bath." He handed over the letter.

"Do you know what it contains?"

"No, lord, but the Empress asked that her messenger should wait until you had read it and be available to take a reply back to her."

I nodded and I read.

My Lord Cleveland,

I thank you for all your efforts on my behalf in the north. You have excelled yourself and once more my son and I are indebted to you.

This peace conference has not gone as well as it might and this insidious war goes on. I beg a boon of you. The Earl of Essex has a cousin whom you hold. I would have you release him and send him under escort to York. I know that you could have great ransom for him but this act may do more for our cause than you know.

I need to see you. I would have you join me in Gloucester at your earliest convenience. I know that the journey will be difficult and I would not ask you unless I needed you. I do need you. If this war is to be brought to a speedy conclusion then I have to have you by my side.

Your Empress and friend,
Maud

I looked up at the messenger. "Let us go down to my hall. You will be returning later. I will have some of my men escort you."

As I went to fetch Baron Fitz Mandeville, I wondered how this could aid us. I would obey but I was not happy about it. I also knew that I had to change the plans for my journey. I might be away for longer than I had expected. When we reached my Great Hall, Alice was waiting with refreshments. "See to our guest, Alice." Sir Tristan and Sir Harold approached. They had heard of our visitor. "Sir Tristan, I wish you to escort the Archbishop's clerk and Baron Fitz Mandeville back to York."

"Aye, lord, has the ransom been paid then?"

Shaking my head I said, "He is to be treated now as a guest. Go fetch him and find him a horse. On your way back, call in at Helmsley and tell Sir Wulfric my plans. He will need to be alert to danger too."

As he left Sir Harold said, "You like this not, lord."

"No, Harold, I do not but it is the Empress' command and I obey. I will need to take more men with me. I intend to take seven of the new men at arms too." I held up the Empress' letter. "The Empress has need of me. I may be away longer than expected. I will never write to you, Sir Harold. If I need anything then I will send someone you know and trust. These are dangerous times. The people I trust are in this valley and nowhere else. We need to walk and speak carefully. Keep a good watch."

"I will, lord. I have a son now and my wife is with child again. I have more to defend than my life now."

"And I will write a letter to my son and to Sir Leofric. Have them sent on the *'Adela'* next time she docks."

The Baron looked confused as he was led into my hall. "What is this, lord? Another trick to fool the Scots? Do you torment me again?"

I pointed to the clerk. "Sir Tristan will escort you and the Archbishop's clerk to York. You are free. I have no doubt that the Archbishop will explain all."

The clerk came over and said quietly, "The Archbishop is not well, my lord. The journey to Bath proved to be a trial. When I left he was confined to his bed. The Earl of York rules in his stead." I had fought alongside William of Aumale at Northallerton. He was a good warrior but a little like a straw; he bent with the political wind. I had no doubt that he would agree to support the Earl of Essex.

I turned to the Baron. "Your cousin, it seems, has asked the Empress for your freedom. I have granted it."

He smirked, "And my arms and armour?"

"He asked for you. He will get you and nothing more. We will loan you a horse to carry you to York and that will be the end of our association. Do not be under any illusions, Mandeville. You and your cousin are still my enemies and I do not forgive easily. The privations you inflicted upon the people of the north are too close to be forgotten!" Sir Tristan and the clerk nodded. They were ready. "Leave now!"

The air felt cleaner somehow when he had gone. I did not mind losing the ransom; it was merely gold but I hated dealing with dishonourable men.

I left the first week of September when the nights were drawing shorter. The land was still fresh and filled with nature's bounty. My land would have a good harvest and my people would be fed over the winter. I was leaving it in good hands. With a ring of knights and castles surrounding the river, I felt secure. I had frightened both Cumin and the Scots. They would not bother us; at least not for a while. The day I left, as I headed west, I met a rider bringing news. Archbishop Thurstan had died. He was an old man but he was the most honourable churchman I had ever met. It had been he who had masterminded the defence of the north against the Scots and I would be forever in his debt. The thought that he had passed on was doubly saddening. He had been an ally in York. I did not doubt that there were others there who would think favourably of me but I was their enemy. My circle of allies was shrinking. Sir Hugh had been murdered and the Archbishop had died. I was more alone than I had been for some years.

After we had collected my squires' new swords, I also picked up the short sword I had made for Henry Fitz Empress. I had ordered it when I had returned from Gloucester and been waiting for the leather scabbard which I had also had made by the skilled leather workers of my town. It was beautifully decorated and I was pleased with the gift. I could not give my son much but I could give him this.

It would be a gift from a knight and as such, he could accept it.

We were a powerful conroi. Although I had but two other knights, we had over twenty men at arms as well as four squires and twenty archers. The six servants we had brought with us were all capable of handling weapons. They led our spare horses. I brought Rolf but rode Lion. The others I had left in my stable. Aiden would care for them and, if they needed it, ride them. If they needed schooling then Harold would do that. We rode to Piercebridge first where I gave Sir Philip the news about his uncle. Like me, he was sad. He owed as much to his uncle as I did. He took me around his castle while we spoke. His defences had improved. He was an archer first and foremost. He had looked at his walls and made them so that they favoured the bow. The land was cleared further than was normal and he had all manner of devices to deter horsemen. He had ten men at arms to garrison his fort and when he was able to collect taxes from his people, he would hire more. I told him what we were about and left him confident that the river crossing of the Tees would be contested if an enemy came close. He and Sir Hugh had developed an understanding and riders passed between them on a daily basis. I did not ride to Barnard Castle. I crossed the river at Piercebridge. Once I did so then I knew I was in enemy territory. More likely than not, anyone we met would not be our friend or ally!

Instead of heading west, I took my men south. Dick asked, "Why this way, lord?"

"I would gauge the mood of our enemy and besides, this way takes us close to Lincoln. There the treacherous Earl of Chester lives. I wish to know how he is received by his new subjects." I smiled, "Besides, it is an easier road than travelling over the windswept top of England, is it not? You should be happy; we will pass close to your home!"

He nodded, "Aye. I am not unhappy with the route; we have danger whichever direction we take but it would be a foolish knight who tried to stop the Warlord of the North. I fear, however, that we will have little comfort on our journey south."

In that he was right. That first night we stayed in the ruins of Osmotherley Castle. Alan son of Alan, my man at arms had lived there. We always felt safe there. We could have ridden further but I wished to make a longer ride and evade scrutiny from York. With the Archbishop gone, I knew not whom I could trust there. I decided instead to ride the one hundred miles to Lincoln. It was a good road and by leaving early we could make it in one day. As we ate in silence, I noticed that one of the new men at arms had a familiar look to him. I had not met them all yet. Edgar had chosen them. I called him over.

"What is your name and where do you hail from?"

"I am Günter from Swabia."

"I thought I recognised the armour and the weapons. I am pleased that you serve me. I was a brother of four fine Swabians who served the Empress."

He nodded, "I know, lord. I sought your service for I am Rolf's nephew. He often spoke of you and in our village, we all respect King Henry's Champion."

"And I am glad to have someone who knows how to wield the two handed sword. You are welcome."

I slept easy that night for it was as though we were a family. So long as my men surrounded me then I was safe.

As we neared Doncaster, in the late afternoon, we could see the forest stretching out to the south and west of us. If we had trouble at Lincoln, we could flee there. Dick and many of his archers knew the forest as well as they knew my castle. I sent Walter of Crewe and Richard of Middleham ahead of us. They went in disguise. If there was danger then they would return to us.

It was getting on for dusk as we saw the walls of the city in the distance. This had been one of Rome's first fortresses and that Empire's mark was still on both the city and the landscape. My two archers rode out to meet us. I think we can stay there, lord. The Earl is not in the city. He is in Derby but his wife is in the castle."

I looked at Dick. He smiled. Lady Maud was the daughter of Robert of Gloucester and she was a friend. If I could not trust the Earl of Chester, I could trust the Countess with my

life. The castle lay at the western edge of the city and was
north of the river. "Sir John, take command of the conroi.
Camp by the river and stay out of sight of the castle. Take
care of my standard. Dick, bring two archers. Edgar, come
with me. We will come to you on the morrow."

"And if there is a problem, lord?"

I shrugged, "Then we fight our way out."

I was not worried. We had managed to gain entrance to
the castle when it had been held for Stephen. I was confident
that Lady Maud would, once more, come to our aid. As we
approached the gate my surcoat was recognised. I heard a
shout go up inside, "The Earl of Cleveland! The Wolf is
here!"

The sergeant at arms approached me apprehensively, "My
lord?"

"I am here to see the Countess of Chester." I smiled, "We
are old friends." I saw him hesitate and I nudged Lion
forward. "Come, you cannot fear seven men. I swear we will
not take the castle."

I almost burst out laughing when I saw the relief on his
face, "Your word is good enough for me, lord. Enter." As we
did so, I saw him peering out to see where the rest of my
men were.

We clattered into the inner bailey of the castle. "Richard,
stay here with the horses. Gilles and Dick, come with me.
We will see how the land lies."

I left my helmet and cloak with my horse and strode
towards the Great Hall. The Countess came to greet me as I
entered the keep. She threw her arms around me. She never
bothered much with ceremony. She was a clever woman who
had a mind of her own. She exuded power. "Alfraed! What
brings you here?" As she took my arm to lead me into the
Hall she said quietly, "You love taking risks do you not? Or
did you know that my husband was absent?"

I smiled, "I knew, but I also knew that you would bid me
welcome." I stopped and pointed behind me. "Four more of
my men wait with our horses."

Without turning, she said, "Ailred, go and see to the Earl's
men. Have their horses stabled and find chambers for them.

We will have a feast tonight. It is good to have some real warriors in the building once more!"

She was an excellent hostess and wine, bread, ham and cheese were fetched to offset our appetite until the main meal was ready. We spoke of neutral events such as the deaths of the Bishop of Durham and the Archbishop of York. She did not know of the involvement of the Scots in the death of the Bishop but she was not surprised.

Ailred approached, "My lady, the rooms are ready for our guests."

I nodded to Dick and Gilles, "Go and see to our rooms. Clean up and prepare for the feast."

"Aye, lord."

After they had gone she said, "You have true warriors about you. These two seem as though they would be ill at ease at court."

I laughed, "That would be true of all but a handful of my men. Sir Tristan and Sir Hugh apart, they are all warriors first and courtiers second."

Nodding she said, "And now that they are gone we can speak, can we not? You can tell me the real reason you are here. Do you wish my husband to change sides again?"

"I believe that you would like nothing better yourself, would you not?"

"And you have not answered my question. Come, my lord, you can be honest with me. You know that."

"No one has asked me to do so. I called here if you want the real reason because I am heading to Gloucester and this seemed a good opportunity to test the water, so to speak, before I meet with your aunt."

"And my father." She saw me look away. "You need not be coy around me, Alfraed. Like you, I know my father's faults. I see his attributes too but I would that he was more like my grandfather."

"We could have had the war won but we lacked unity. If I am to be truthful that began with your husband's defection. When we took this castle, I thought that the war was won and then it was handed to Stephen."

"His half brother has a desire for power. He is now Earl of Lincoln. It pleases his wife who is also greedy for power. They seek fine thrones on which to sit." I liked Maud. She spoke plainer than any woman barring my deceased wife. If she had been a man then the war would be over. She would have prosecuted it until the end.

"Is there any likelihood of his changing sides?"

For the first time, she appeared nervous. "I fear he may."

"Why should you fear that which you wish?"

"Because the change may not be my husband's decision. The people of Lincoln like not having an Earl. Lincoln was a royal manor until my grandfather died. They would wish it so again. The taxes were not as high as they are now. My spies tell me that they are making representations to King Stephen to have the status of my husband and his half brother revoked."

"In which case, he would be likely to turn to your father once more."

She leaned forward and touched my hand, "But that would mean we would lose this castle. This castle may be the key to the Kingdom. London is full of fickle folk. They are a law unto themselves and the King allows it. There is little point in taking London but Lincoln controls the road to the north. If my father held this then York would soon fall for you are a real threat in the north."

I sipped my wine. "And you would like me to tell your father this."

She laughed. It was as though the room was lit up. "I had not thought of it until you came but now it seems a good idea for of all the knights in this land, I know I can trust you, the English knight, the Warlord of the North, the Wolf who terrifies my aunt's enemies." She looked around, although there was no one else in the hall. "I held this once, for my husband and you. I could do so again. If my husband falls foul of King Stephen then tell my father that I will wait here for him. I can hold it."

"I believe you can. I will tell him and I will go further. How would it be if I left four of my men at arms and six of

110

my archers here? Could you disguise their presence? I guarantee that they would be of great help to you."

She nodded, "I think so. I have been asking for a bodyguard for some time. The people in the streets are most unpleasant sometimes. I have tunics for them. Yes, that would work."

"I will send for them now." I ran to the stairs and found the steward. "Take me to my chambers."

"Aye, lord."

Once in my room, I quickly explained to Dick what I wanted. Gilles fetched Edgar. Between us, we selected the men and Dick went for them. It was dark by the time they entered the castle and Ailred brought them in through a side door so that no one saw them. I gathered them around me. "I am asking you to stay here at Lincoln and serve Countess Maud. A time will come when she may have to hold the castle against our enemies. I know you are my oathsworn but I will not order any of you to do this. It is your choice."

Cedric laughed, "It will be a pleasure, lord. We dine well out of the stories of our adventures. This will just be another. We will guard the Countess as though it was the Lady Adela."

"Then I can ask no more!"

I had to smile when I saw them in the livery of the Earl of Chester. They looked markedly different from the others. Maud assured me that they would not be noticed and would soon blend in. I think she was looking forward to the deceit.

I left as soon as the gates were opened and rejoined my men. I now had positive news to take to the Empress and, for the first time, felt that something was going our way. We had an even harder ride ahead of us for I was heading for Sir Brian Fitz Count and his fortress at Wallingford. It was over a hundred and thirty miles but we would be safe there and could rest up for a couple of days. We had left some archers and men at arms at Lincoln but we were still a powerful force. As we headed south, we saw hunting parties and groups of knights but none approached close enough to us for there to be any danger. The danger lay in their anticipating where we were going. My archers scouted ahead of us so that we did not ride into unforeseen dangers. I kept up a hard pace. If any were to get ahead of us then they would need the wings of a Pegasus to do so.

When we were ten miles away from the mighty castle of Wallingford, I sent four archers to warn Fitz Count of our arrival. He rode out and greeted us three miles from his gates.

He gave us an effusive and warm welcome. "Good! Your arrival means that this damned war will actually start again! I am heartily fed up with sitting on my arse behind my walls! The war is always more interesting when the Wolf of the North leaves his lair and comes south! I will give thanks to God tonight in my chapel!"

I laughed, "And it is good to be in your company again, Sir Brian!"

Chapter 9

It was good to be in the company of such a plain-speaking knight. He held the forces of Stephen at bay with a garrison less than I had at Stockton. His one advantage was that the Earl of Gloucester and the Empress were less than forty miles away. If a large force threatened then they could relieve the siege as we had done earlier in the war. I did not mention the Countess' plan. It was not that I did not trust him but the message was intended for her father and the Empress. If they chose to spread it then that was their decision. Instead, we spoke of the Bishop of Ely's attempt to rebel in the east and Fitz Count asked me about my battles in the north.

"I envy you. You get to fight as a knight should, from the back of a horse using lance and shield."

"We are normally outnumbered."

"Aye, but when you win, you get all of those ransoms. When we win, all we are left with are the bodies of the bastards who fall inside our walls!"

"It will change. I hear that the Count of Anjou is mopping up the last of the Norman rebels."

He nodded, "That is not all. The King of France is threatening Theobald. Stephen does not have as much support from his brother as he once did have and the peace conference held by his other brother Henry was a disaster for him. I am not certain that they are on speaking terms."

I shook my head, "All the more reason to strike now. When the Bishop of Ely rebelled was the time."

"To be fair to the Earl, he regained all of the lands lost when Stephen attacked last year."

"So we are back to where we were?"

He laughed, "Do not be so despondent. Now that you are back, the Empress will smile once more and the ordinary knights will be uplifted. They will be fighting alongside the Empress' Knight and King Henry's Champion. I can tell you now that they all relish the opportunity. You have a well-deserved reputation."

I told him about Sir Hugh Manningham and his face darkened. "I will have prayers said for their souls. Those Scots are barbarians! They are one short step away from being savages with painted faces fighting naked!" Despite being a great warrior, there was something of the priest about Sir Brian. I often wondered why he did not become a Templar or a Hospitaller.

I found myself laughing at his description. The Galwegians were, indeed, quite close to that description. "And they can fight whilst studded with arrows! They are almost not men!"

When I left two days later with rested men and horses, I felt better. Both Fitz Count and his men were just like my own and it gave me hope that there were enough men of a similar mind to make a difference to our cause. The weather turned as we headed north and west. The first rains of September hurtled in from the seas to the west. We rode into a gale and arrived at Gloucester cold, wet and miserable. The weather had undone all the good work of Fitz Count. We were despondent. As we dismounted, Sir Geoffrey Talbot greeted me and told me that the Earl was away hunting but his army was with the Empress. That was a little better than it had been. Geoffrey apologised for the Earl. "I am certain that had he known you would be here, he would have stayed, my lord."

"Do not apologise. I came because the Empress summoned me. It is why I brought only my household men at arms and knights."

"Many hoped that you would bring all of your knights and their men."

"And leave the north unguarded?" I shook my head. "I am like the guard dog who sleeps behind the sheep pen guarding the animals. If I left then the wolves would fall upon them. They only survive because we are vigilant. I am afraid that this small conroi will have to do."

"And it is more than enough, my lord!" Those eight words were enough to tell me that my beloved Matilda was behind me. I turned and dropped to my knee. She put her hand under my chin and raised me up. "You kneel to no one, my lord, least of all me. Without you, I would be as nothing."

Behind her, I saw Henry, our son. He had grown. He was dressed in a small hauberk and he had a dagger strapped to his baldric. "And is this fine warrior Prince Henry? If so, he has grown since last I cast eyes on him."

He grinned, "It is, my lord! Have you been battling mother's enemies again?"

"Always, and I look forward to the time when you can fight alongside me as your grandfather did."

"Have you beaten the Scots again?" I nodded. "I met their King. He is my mother's uncle you know. I did not like him. He smelled funny!"

I laughed, "I am not over-fond of him myself." I turned to Gilles. He handed me the sheepskin. "Here, you are almost a warrior. My smith has made this for you. It is slightly longer than your dagger and no one makes a better sword than Alf of Stockton."

He unwrapped it and his eyes widened as he drew the shining blade from the richly decorated scabbard, "It is beautiful, my lord! Look, mother! Is it not the most beautiful thing you have ever seen?"

Her eyes were on me as she said, "It is. Now go and show it to your brother. I daresay he will be jealous!"

He ran off and I turned to my squires. "See to the horses. Sir Richard, arrange quarters for our men."

Geoffrey Talbot said, "If you will follow me, we have a hall for you. The owner had a disagreement with the Earl and fled. You can use that while you are here. There are stables." Dick nodded and followed.

Matilda said, "Your arm, my lord. You can walk me back to the hall. I would have a conference with you."

Her two ladies, Judith and Margaret, were waiting for us in her antechamber. They both had huge smiles on their faces. Margaret said, "You get more handsome each time I see you, my lord!"

Matilda said, "Margaret!"

"Well he does and God likes us to speak the truth; it shames the devil!"

"Leave us!" I could tell that she was smiling beneath her words.

When they had left us, she threw her arms around me and kissed me. I kissed her back and then held her. I said, quietly, "You must like the smell of horse!"

"I just want my arms around you for however brief a moment. This will be our only time together, my love. My brother is ever suspicious and once he knows you have returned, he will cease hunting."

I did not want to let her go. I nuzzled her hair. It smelled of rosemary and thyme. For something to say, more than anything, I said, "Our son grows."

"And each day looks more like you."

I stepped back, "He does?" She nodded, "Then I shall grow a beard. We cannot have any suspicions."

She kissed me one more time. "Now you should go to your chambers and change. Tonight we shall talk of the campaign."

Before we do, I have news for you from the Earl's daughter. Your niece. I have been to Lincoln and spoken with the Countess of Chester. I was going to speak of it in the presence of you both but he is not here and I am anxious to unburden myself. She believes that her husband will split with Stephen soon and that means he will return to our side. I know he is untrustworthy and I would disregard his defection save that Maud says if he does, she will hold Lincoln until her father can get there."

"Truly?"

"She is a strong woman. She reminds me of her aunt."

116

She smiled and suddenly looked much younger. "Has she the men that she can trust?"

I nodded. "I left her some of mine to augment those that she could trust but it is important that we are ready to act as soon as Stephen breaks with the Earl and he will. He is going to take back Lincoln. We both know that the Earl likes his manors and his power."

"Then that is good news and you are wise to speak of it privately. When my brother returns, we will talk more. Thank you, my lord."

"It was Maud and not me."

"I know that you make these things happen. You are too modest!"

I was about to leave and I hesitated, "My lady, Mandeville. It did not sit well with me surrendering him. He is a bad man. I did not mind losing the gold but he is not a noble man and there is little about him which is knightly."

"Sometimes, my lord, we must choose strange bedfellows. The Earl of Essex is contemplating defecting to our side. He controls London. We could take that city without a fight if he were on our side. It seemed worth the gamble."

I nodded, "I can see now why you did so but London is not England, my lady. It has always looked after itself. I think it is because there is no lord to whom they owe allegiance. Be wary of London."

"Thank you, Alfraed. As ever, your words are both wise and welcome. I am glad that you are by my side again. I believe our cause will be furthered now that you have joined our ranks once more."

Gilles had laid my clothes out for me and had managed to get a bath for me. I suspected that Margaret and Judith had thought of that. It was such a pleasant experience that I confess I fell asleep and Gilles had to wake me. I saw him take out the knife he used to shave me. "I think I shall grow a beard, Gilles."

"A beard, lord!"

"I have whimsy to grow one. When I was younger, I could never manage one. I think I shall try."

"Very well, lord."

"But you can cut my hair. That is getting too long."

"You always wear it long, lord. You said Wulfstan wore his long."

"Aye, but he wore his in pigtails. It is not the fashion now. I will try it shorter." I shrugged. "I can always grow it long again."

"As you wish, lord." I could see that I had mystified my squire.

The Empress nodded approvingly as she saw me enter her Great Hall. It was filled with knights. It was lucky that there were just the seven of us. We would have struggled to find a seat had it been all of my knights. Sir Pain and Sir Miles Fitz Walter sought me out as soon as I entered. We had fought together at Worcester. They were both reliable knights. Sir Pain was a huge man. He reminded me of Wulfric in many ways. "It is good to see you, Earl. While we have sat over the summer, you have been fighting I hear."

"There is always fighting in the North. If it is not the Scots then it is Stephen's men and if not them then robber barons who seek a throne for themselves."

Sir Miles said, "We should have gone to the aid of the Bishop of Ely." He pointed to the prelate who sat by the Empress' right hand. "He is a good man. He has not complained that he was abandoned but I have spoken with him and it would not have taken much to go to his aid. Now the east is lost and many good men too."

The feast went well. Everyone seemed in good humour. The Empress glanced over to me many times during the feast and smiled. They were small gestures but I read much into them.

After the food had finished, the Empress stood and silence descended upon the room. "My lords, your Grace, today we have been joined by our Champion." There was a cheer and goblets were banged on the table. Matilda waited until the room was quiet once more, "He has come fresh from more victories against those who would harm us and he brings tidings for my brother and me. I give you a toast, the Earl of Cleveland, the Champion of England!"

The room roared, "Champion of England!"

Sir Miles said, as the room subsided and more wine was fetched, "She thinks highly of you, lord." I nodded. "There are just two left now of the knights of the Empress."

"Two? What of Sir Guy?"

"Did you not hear? He was killed when French forces attacked his lands and those of his brothers. France is flexing its muscles. I fear that Count Geoffrey may need aid there soon. He may be winning the war in Normandy but this new French king is anxious to make a name for himself."

Sir Pain said, "Aye, but the young wolf, Sir William of Ouistreham is now as powerful in Normandy as his father is here. You have a son in whom you can be proud, my lord."

"I am proud." As I drank, I reflected that it was sad I had to hear that from someone other than my son. He had never been a great writer and I suspected that he was busy. I yearned for news of him and my grandson. Yet I knew I could not leave England. Our paths seemed fated to diverge.

I listened more than I spoke as Sir Miles and Sir Pain told me of events beyond my valley. I had had little news over the last year. That was understandable. The Archbishop had not been well and letters could be intercepted. The result was that I had much to think about as I headed back to my chambers. I discovered that I had a good manor in Liedeberge although it was, occasionally, subject to Welsh raids. Both Sir Miles Fitz Walter and Sir Pain knew it well. I decided that when I had spoken with the Earl, I would visit it. I would also have to speak with the Bishop of Hereford for he was also my liege lord.

The Earl did not arrive for two days. I suspected the delay was deliberate. It would be seen as an insult. It did not upset me for it gave our animals time to recover and I was able to spend time with young Henry. It afforded me even more opportunities to be close to the Empress without any suspicion falling upon us. Henry Fitz Empress was a clever boy and I saw quickness in his thinking. He understood things beyond his years. When we spoke of my new manor, he asked if I would subjugate the Welsh.

"These are not my lands, lord. They belong to your uncle. It is for him to take that on."

119

"But if he will not, do you not have a duty as my mother's Champion to do so? England's destiny is to rule the Welsh. My grandfather began that rule." I nodded, amazed at his understanding of such matters. "When I am king, I shall conquer it and you will lead my armies."

"And I will gladly be there with you!"

The Earl of Gloucester made a loud and noisy entrance when he did return. He came accompanied not only by his own knights but also by Welsh allies including the Lord of Powys, Madog ap Maredudd. He was the brother of the Welsh king. It was a statement of his power and I wondered if he had delayed his arrival so that he could come by so many men. Perhaps I was becoming cynical.

When he leapt from his horse, he greeted me warmly. The Empress had warned me to curb my tongue and think of the greater good. She knew how I felt about her brother. I smiled as he greeted me. "It is the Wolf of the North! We are all grateful that you keep us safe from the privations of the Scots."

"And it is good to see you too, lord. I have much to tell you."

He waved an airy hand, "Good, good. This is my good friend the Lord of Powys."

The Welsh lord looked just like any other Norman save that he was Welsh. He dressed the same as any Norman knight. However, when he spoke his accent made it difficult to understand all that he said, "I have heard much about you, Earl Alfraed, Warlord of the North. It is good to finally meet you. I look forward to the day we fight alongside each other. I have heard that you, alone amongst the English, have archers who are the equal of the Welsh."

"We find that they are useful when fighting the Scots, lord, and I have good ones." I gestured for Dick, "This is Sir Richard, he leads my archers and is the finest bowman I know."

Dick bowed and the Welshman said, "A knight who is an archer; interesting."

Dick smiled, "I was an archer long before my lord knighted me. I use a sword but I prefer the bow."

Madog laughed, "Spoken like a true archer. We must talk."

I think that the Earl was irritated by the lack of attention on him. "You say you have news, my lord?"

"It would be better spoken of in private. Perhaps in the Empress' antechamber."

"These are all friends."

Matilda said, "And it is too public, brother. The Earl is right."

"Very well." He turned to his knights. "We will enjoy the fruits of our hunt this night!"

Once in the antechamber, he said, "Well, what is so precious that it has to be heard in secret as though we are conspirators?"

I took a deep breath as I saw the warning in the Empress' eyes. I spoke calmly, "I visited Lincoln, lord, and spoke with your daughter." I could see that I had taken him by surprise. "She believes that her husband will be stripped of his new titles by the King and that Stephen will invest Lincoln with a royal garrison once more."

"And how does this help us?"

"She will hold Lincoln for us but we need to go to her aid."

"Not her husband?"

Matilda said, "Ranulf is like a straw, brother. Your daughter is made of sterner stuff it seems."

"Aye, it looks like my fate is to be surrounded by strong women."

Matilda gave me the slightest shake of her head. Her brother had insulted her but she wished me to ignore it.

"Lincoln is far from here."

"It is and winter approaches."

He gave me a shrewd look, "Can my daughter hold?"

"She did before, and I left her some of my men. I believe she can."

The Empress leaned forward. "We cannot act yet. We must wait until Stephen has broken with the Earl."

"From what Maud told me, lord, that will not be long. The people of Lincoln grow tired of your son in law."

"Then we need to gather our army. Lincoln is in the heart of the enemy's lands. It would take many days to reach there."

"Perhaps we could gather at Wallingford, lord."

He looked at me, "Wallingford?"

"Fitz Count holds it still and our enemies might think that we are preparing for an attack on London down the Thames Valley. It would be more logical than a strike a hundred miles north, to Lincoln."

He laughed, "You are a true Greek! Your mind could unravel the Gordian knot. It is a good plan but we must do this slowly. Fitz Count will need time to prepare quarters for us and we will need supplies."

The Empress shook her head, "We cannot take them from our people."

"Then we take them from Stephen's. The harvest will soon be in. We raid along the borderlands. It will weaken the resolve of our enemy and empty the lands through which we must travel." This was the old Earl.

"Let us keep this plan to ourselves, brother. We can tell our knights that we raid but not the grand strategy. We must give Maud every chance!"

He nodded and we were all in agreement. "Aye, she is the fruit of my loins and no mistake!"

That seemed to set the mood for the next few days. The Earl seemed both enthusiastic and confident in our enterprise. He took it upon himself to visit Wallingford and prepare the camp there. We wanted all of our men in place before we began the raids. The Empress also sent spies to London so that she could assess the likelihood of Lincoln reverting to the crown. I took the opportunity of visiting Liedeberge. Sir Miles came with me. He knew the area well. I just took Sir John, my squires and my men at arms. Dick and his archers were scouting the sites we might raid.

Liedeberge was a quiet manor. It looked to me as though it had been largely a hunting lodge that had expanded into a small manor and village. There was no castle but the hall had a wall around it. I realised it would never bring in a huge income but it was a gift from the Empress and, as such, should be held in high regard by me. The reeve was an old man, Ralph of Liedeberge. He appeared to be related to everyone in the manor. He was pleased to have a lord and took us around everyone who lived within a mile of the hall to introduce us. My title impressed him. He seemed a good sort. His three sons had the three best farms and his four daughters had all brought other farmers to the others.

"What sort of income can I expect, Ralph?"

I do not know if he expected me to be a typical knight who used the manor for hunting but he was in for a surprise. "Income, my lord?"

"Yes, Ralph. This war against Stephen the Usurper costs money. I have knights and men at arms to support. You do want Empress Matilda to win, do you not?"

"Of course, lord." He rubbed his grey beard. "This year has not been as good a year as we might have expected."

"Why? Did you have storms when you were gathering in the harvest? Your barns look full. Perhaps you were raided?"

Sir Miles said, "Stephen got no closer than Wallingford, lord."

I went close to the old man. "I am a good lord. Ask my people in Stockton but I expect the truth. Do not try to deceive me. I will expect you to bring an account of the manor to Gloucester in two days' time." I swept a hand around the village. "It would not please your family if I brought in another reeve would it, Ralph?"

His shoulders sagged, "I am sorry, my lord. No, my family would not like me to be replaced. I swear that I will answer all of your questions honestly."

"Good. My men will use the manor while we are in the area. Sir John here will act as my constable." I nodded to Sir John. He knew what to do. "Come, Sir Miles, we have pressing matters in Gloucester."

As we rode back Sir Miles laughed, "Ralph was just seeing what he could get away with, lord, you know that?"

"Of course, and that is why I left Sir John there. Sir John was castellan at Stockton. He worked closely with my Steward. He will give me an accurate assessment of the worth of Liedeberge. Let us see how truthful the old man is."

"I can see why you have gained so much power at such a young age. Nothing gets by you."

"When you live surrounded by enemies, it is what you have to do. One mistake can prove disastrous as my friend Sir Hugh Manningham discovered."

"And yet you did not avenge him. I was surprised by that."

He said it mildly but I whirled to face him, "When I have time I will avenge him. Had I gone charging up to the New Castle, it would have availed me naught save the loss of irreplaceable men. I will bide my time and Prince Henry will feel my wrath."

"I am sorry, lord, I did not mean to offend you."

"You did not. The memory is too raw and I berated myself on the journey south. I am the one who knows when I have done wrong or made a mistake. The death of Sir Hugh haunts my dreams and I will have vengeance but on my terms and in my time!"

As we neared Gloucester he asked, "You are in the Earl and Empress' confidence; tell me what this massing of men and supplies at Wallingford means. Do we attack London or Oxford perhaps?"

"I cannot divulge the Earl's plans but suffice it to say that we will see action soon. It is why I wanted affairs at Liedeberge putting in order."

As we approached Gloucester, I could see more knights and their men heading for Wallingford. Soon Gloucester would be emptied and the citizens could get their lives back to normal. The Empress' household knights and the garrison of the town walls would be all that remained.

Chapter 10

Sir Brian Fitz Count was happy that his castle would be used as our home for a month or two. He confided in me that it would give him the chance to ride his horse to war and see how his knights fared beyond the safety of his walls. Dick had suggested Banbury for our raid. It belonged to Alexander, Bishop of Lincoln, but he had fallen out with Stephen and had had his castles confiscated and was imprisoned. I concurred with my knight's decision.

The night before our raid I gathered my men. "Our aim is not to hurt the people. We will be taking their livestock and their grain but they should not be harmed." They nodded. My men did not like making war on those who could not defend themselves. "My plan is quite simple. "Dick and the archers will conceal themselves close to Banbury Castle. I have no intention of taking the castle. It will be a waste of men. I will lead the knights and men at arms to frighten the farmers from their farms and flee to Banbury. Hopefully, they will leave their animals and grain. After all, the Wolf and his pack will be abroad!" My men laughed. "If any try to take animals then Dick and his archers will be able to capture them. When we approach Banbury, I suspect that they will risk trying to capture me. After all, we have few enough men. Dick, you will spring our trap then."

"And after, lord?"

"Then, Sir John, we drive the animals back to our camp and scout out another target."

"I meant after the raid, lord. We are collecting animals and grain for a purpose. What is that purpose?"

"That is out of our hands. Suffice it to say it is a great prize. This winter we seek a crown!"

Dick and his archers left before dawn. They had scouted out the town walls and knew where to hide. Their hiding place was well within bow range. We had the luxury of just approaching any farm. We did not need to be silent nor did we need to be cautious. We just rode. The first farm we spied had just a wooden palisade. It was to keep wild animals out and not men. We were spied when we were a mile away by a cowherd. We saw him run and I guessed that he was shouting. They had two horses and the family crowded on the backs of the two beasts. The farmer led them as they fled towards Banbury. We slowed as we approached for I wanted panic. While John of Norton and Peter Strong Arm began to herd the animals together, Richard and Gilles went to find the grain. We knew that the farmers in this county had gathered their grain in already and it was conveniently stacked in sacks in their barn. Leaving the two squires and men at arms to secure our booty, we hurried after the farmer and his family. When we spied Banbury's walls, just half a mile ahead, we stopped as though we had been deterred by the walls and I led them along the greenway to the next farm we had selected.

This was a more substantial farm. The house was partly made of stone. They must have spied the other family fleeing for, as we neared them, I saw that they were already heading across the fields to Banbury. They had a cart pulled by two horses and it was laden. There were others driving their animals before them. We began to catch them and the men driving the animals abandoned them and took to their heels. They fled towards the town and stone keep. The cart kept ahead of us for some time and when they saw the castle just half a mile away, they must have thought they were safe.

Sir John and his men spurred on their horses and began to catch the cart. The farmer and his family had lost the race. As we closed with them, I saw that the women and children were running for the town and the six men had drawn their weapons. Two had swords while the rest had daggers and farm implements. When they saw the rest of us galloping up with drawn weapons, they turned and fled. They were safe. I had no intention of chasing them. Even as I reined Lion in, Sir John's squire, Robert, had taken the reins of the cart and was heading back to Wallingford. It would be a long ride. We had over forty miles to cover before dark and we had to avoid Oxford.

I was about to signal Dick when a column of mounted men left the town and galloped towards us. There were twenty of them and they outnumbered us. "Edgar, take Henry of Langdale and escort the cart back to Wallingford. We will catch you up."

"Aye, lord!"

I now had two knights and ten men at arms. I felt confident. "Form line!" We had no spears but we were all mailed. I did not wait for them to come to us, we charged. They did not expect that. The knight at their fore tried to form a line. Sir John and I headed for the knight and sergeant at arms. I left the others for my men at arms. They could deal with them easily. The knight tried to approach shield to shield. At the last moment, I jerked Lion's head around and jinked to the left. It took him by surprise. I swung my sword just above his horse's head. He tried to block it with his own and failed. My sword bent his and, more importantly, cracked into his chest. He almost threw himself from his saddle. I reined Lion around and saw that John had slain the sergeant at arms.

The knight's squire halted before us and drew his sword. "Sheath your weapon, boy, and see to your master. Tell him the Warlord of the North has spared his life!" There were just ten of his men still mounted and the squire looked at them. They began to back their horses away from us and the squire sheathed his sword and dismounted.

Sir John said, "A wise decision. One day you will make a good knight!"

We wheeled our horses around. I looked to my left and saw my archers galloping towards us. I turned and saw the relief on the faces of those who had survived our encounter. They were wise enough to know what the outcome would have been had they fought.

We caught up with the others by the village of Bloxham. I saw that my squires had loaded the grain we had found on the cart. It made for a better journey. We now had more men to help drive the animals and we made better time. Aetheling and Grant rode ahead of us as scouts. We were deep within enemy territory. I had chosen Banbury for that reason. It was so far behind the enemy's line that they would think themselves safe. I had also chosen it because it was on the road to Lincoln and when we did travel thence, I wanted to know the lie of the land.

We were close to Cumnor, a small inconsequential village not far from Oxford, when danger arrived. Grant rode in. "Lord, riders approach from Oxford. Aetheling has stayed to slow them down."

Dick nodded, "Archers, follow me!"

The narrow greenways and sunken roads which were bordered by hedges suited my archers. Dick would slow them down from ambush. "Keep moving and keep the animals close to the cart. We have come this far. Let us not lose them. Squires, your job is to protect the cart and the animals. The cart is the priority."

"Aye, lord."

We hurried down the lane. Dick and his archers appeared. "There are thirty of them, lord. Four knights, five squires and the rest men at arms. There were some light horsemen but they fell to our arrows. We kept ambushing them. They will be cautious for they think we wait for them again. They are persistent. Would you have us delay them longer?"

"No, Dick, we keep driving the animals. If they catch us then we will fight." I pointed to the standard held by Gilles. "I hope that discourages them."

A small village lay ahead. I heard the hooves as our pursuers hurried after us. "Stop the cart in the village and put the animals on the other side. It is time we faced them. Besides, the horses need a rest."

The cart stopped and I shouted, "Dismount! Dick, archers behind the cart. Today we fight on foot."

I stood before the cart as the horsemen appeared. I glanced to my right and saw Günter the Swabian. He held his sword in two hands with his shield around his back. He was grinning. "Now you will see if I am like my uncle!"

The horsemen charged us. They had lances. The knight who led them had a blue and yellow surcoat and a full-face helmet. He was not a clever leader. He had his men in a column of twos. The lane would have allowed him four men abreast. Had I been the one chasing, I would have sent half of my men around the village. They came on. I knew that their horses could not jump over us and they would baulk at riding over us. That meant the only thing they could do was to pull back on their reins and make their horses rear.

I prepared my sword and, like Günter, held it in two hands. Wulfric would have had his mighty war axe but our swords would have to do. As I expected, the two knights made their horses rear as they stabbed down with the lances. Their blows were weak for their horses were rising and they had not practised this move. We swung our swords across the animals. Günter's long sword hacked through the legs of one horse while Sir John and I hacked our swords into the neck of the second horse. Dick and his archers rose and loosed arrows. It proved too much for the men at arms who fled along with one of the knights. The two whose horses we had killed lay stunned while the third knight lay dead.

"Alain, grab that horse." I stepped closer to the knights and placed my sword at the neck of the leader. "Yield or die!"

He took off his helmet, "We yield." As he tried to pull his leg from under his dead horse he said, "I think my leg is broken."

I nodded, "Alain, put this knight on the back of the horse." I pointed to the other. "You can lead his horse."

"But I am a knight!"

I laughed, "Until you get another horse you are not. The walk will do you good!"

It was dark by the time we entered the camp. The Earl had ensured that we were well protected with ditches and stakes. It took some time to negotiate them safely. The grain was sent into the castle. Half of the animals would be slaughtered immediately while the others kept for winter which would be upon us soon enough.

The next morning my men rested while I went to see the Earl. He looked pleased, "That was a good haul and you captured Ralph D'Aubigny and his brother. They will fetch a tidy ransom. The other conroi did not fare as well but it is a start."

We walked the camp acknowledging the compliments from the men. "My lord, you know this land better than I do. What are the winters like? Are they as bad as in the north?"

"Occasionally, they are worse but normally any snow which falls lasts but a few days. Why do you ask?"

"It is at least a two-day ride to Lincoln. If it is in winter and there is snow then it will be hard going."

"Then let us pray for a mild winter. When we do leave, I want you and your men in the vanguard. Your warriors have a nose for trouble."

"How many men do you think we shall take?"

"Madog will be bringing many Welsh knights, archers and men at arms. If we leave a garrison here and at Gloucester then we should have over a thousand men."

"I pray that will be enough."

"If my daughter can hold the castle then it will be."

"And Ranulf, what of him?"

"He is not the son in law I would have chosen, Alfraed, that is for sure. Had you not been married at the time, I would have suggested she marry you!"

"I am flattered, sir, but I will not marry again. I had but one love and she is dead."

He looked at me curiously, "Just the one love, eh? Then you are unusual, Alfraed. My father had women all over this land and I have had my fair share."

"Stockton is remote, my lord."

"Aye, it is that!"

We did not raid again for the Earl was anxious that we be fresh to lead the attack on Lincoln. Others foraged far and wide. That autumn was a hard time in Oxfordshire. When November arrived, it came in like a lion with icy blasts of wind which chilled to the bone. Winter had arrived and we still waited.

Every couple of days I met with the Earl, Madog and the other leaders. There was increasing dissension in our camp. The early success of the raids seemed a distant memory, The Earl was now older and liked his comforts. He yearned for a castle's walls. After one such meeting, I headed back to my camp with Sir Miles and Sir Pain.

"It is a pity that Sir Robert D'Oyly did not side with the Empress. I know he favours her."

Sir Miles shook his head, "But, Sir Pain, he sided with Stephen instead and that is why he is within Oxford."

"I know but I believe he would change sides; for the Empress."

Their words set my mind to speculating. I often did this. Usually, it was in my solar in Stockton. Here the process took a little longer.

Our raids continued into Oxfordshire. I led my men north towards Oxford and its castle. I did so not because we needed food but because I did not want my men to become stale. The camp was becoming a little quarrelsome. The Earl's Welsh allies frequently clashed with the Earl's Englishmen and dice and gambling were rife. Both resulted in violence. Our raids had meant that there was little left to be taken in the countryside close by our castle. What little we had left had been taken within Oxford and its secure walls. I also had another reason. I had come up with a plan to gain us another castle.

Sir John asked as we headed north, "Where do we go, lord?"

"Oxford."

Sir Dick said, "Surely you do not intend to attack that mighty city, lord!"

I smiled, "There are many ways of attacking without scaling walls. We will go and speak with those within Oxford. Perhaps our privations have persuaded them that it may be in their interest to change sides."

I had found out as much as I could about Sir Robert. He was the son of Sir Nigel D'Oyly and had married one of

King Henry's mistresses. That gave me an insight into his mind. He would be closer to Matilda than to Stephen. It was the position of his castle that dictated his allegiances. Until we had begun raiding, Oxfordshire had been secure and close to London. Now it was isolated. I gambled. I did not risk much. I doubted that they would make a foray to try to take me and all I risked was the humiliation of being rejected and sent hence. It was why I just took my men.

The days in December were short and it took us some time to reach the castle. The ground was frozen hard and our breath formed a fog as we spoke.

When we reached the castle, we headed for the west gate. I said, "I will go forth and speak with those within. Dick, take charge."

"Be careful, lord."

"I will, Dick. I have no death wish upon me. I serve the Empress and I see a way of doing so here."

I took off my helmet and rode with Gilles and my standard towards the castle gates. I reined in close enough to shout, "I would speak with Sir Robert D'Oyly. Tell him that the Earl of Cleveland wishes conference with him."

A grizzled man at arms shouted, "Try no tricks, my lord. I have six crossbows aimed at you and the boy!"

I nodded and turned to Gilles, "Are you afraid, Gilles?"

He smiled, "No, lord. You would not have brought us here if you thought that this would end in bloodshed."

"How do you know?"

"I have served but a short time yet Sir Richard and Sir John have told me how you always weigh up battle with talk and always choose wisely. I am content. Besides, my shield is close and my mail is strong."

A short while later a knight somewhat younger than I appeared, "I am Sir Robert D'Oyly. What is it you wish?"

"To speak."

The man next to him pointed a finger at me and shouted, "That is the Wolf! He is not to be trusted."

"Peace, D'Elbeuf." I had met a knight with such a name before, Sir Hugo, and he had been a black-hearted villain. I wondered if my suit might be a waste of time. Sir Robert turned to me again. "He is right, my lord, you do have a reputation for cunning. Why should I speak with you?"

"Because there are just two of us. You have counted my men behind me and seen that there are not enough to worry you. It will not cost you much to listen."

I saw him nod, "They say you are cunning but they also say that you are a man of your word." He shouted down, "Open the gates and admit the Earl and his squire but no one else!"

The gates were opened and we rode through. I saw that the guards were wary and it made me smile. They feared the two of us. We passed over the River Isis and through the barbican. We crossed another bridge over the Isis again and then we were in the bailey. This was a well-made castle. I admired the design. This would take a long siege to reduce it. I dismounted and handed my reins to Gilles once we were in the bailey. I also gave him my helmet. "This will not take long."

Sir Robert and the knight called D'Elbeuf headed towards me along with two other older knights. Sir Robert said, "I have heard of your deeds against the Scots. It affords you a conversation, no more. Come, we will go inside. It is too cold to stand out here."

I could feel the hostility from D'Elbeuf but I ignored it. I had many enemies. They did not worry me. It was those who feigned friendship that I feared. We did not go into the hall but a guard room in the west tower.

"Well, Earl, you have your audience, speak."

"My lord, I will speak plainly, you are fighting for a usurper. I know not if you were in Westminster when we swore the oath to King Henry to support the claim of his daughter for the crown but I know that your father was." I waited.

"I was not there but you are right. My father swore an oath to King Henry. What of it."

"I ask you this; would King Henry wish Stephen of Blois upon the throne? Would he want this chaotic civil war?"

"King Stephen was anointed." I sensed that he was spouting what he had been told and that his heart was not behind his words.

"His brother, Henry, managed to manipulate that event while the Empress and the Earl of Gloucester buried their father, the King. It was not England who crowned Stephen it was London."

D'Elbeuf snorted, "He is trying to trick you, my lord!"

"Sir Roger, keep silent or leave. It is I who speaks with the Earl and this is still my castle."

In answer, he said, "I cannot stay here in the presence of this traitor. I will leave!" He stormed out.

Sir Robert gave an apologetic shrug, "He likes you not, my lord."

"He has reasons and it offends me not. I serve Empress Matilda."

"I know. You were her champion and the King's Champion. It granted you admittance to my castle. Now tell me, plainly, what do you want?"

"I will speak as one knight to another for I believe you to be a man of honour. I wish you to support the claim of Empress Matilda and her son Henry Fitz Empress." I expected rejection but there was none. The other knights looked at Sir Robert. I sensed that he was vacillating. "You know that the Earl of Gloucester has an army not far away at Wallingford." I saw his eyes flash and I held up my hand. "I threaten not. You know I speak the truth and I tell you that there are no plans to take this castle." I smiled, "To speak clearly, this is such a well-made castle that we would lose too many good men if we tried to do so. If you reject my offer of peace and friendship then I will return to Wallingford. This is not a threat. There is no sword hanging over you."

"I like your honesty, lord, and I can see from your eyes that you speak the truth. My people are hungry." He smiled, "That is the result of you and your army but I take comfort that you hurt none of my people in your raids. Was that deliberate?"

"When this war is over, and it will be one day, we will all have to live here. I would not wish to be remembered as an English knight who slew ordinary English folk. My fight is with the enemies of England both within and without. I fight for the Empress and England for they are the only things worth fighting for."

"I would not have my people suffer more."

"I give you my word that they will not."

"I need to speak with my counsellors." He waved a servant over, "Fetch the Earl some mulled ale."

I nodded, "And some for my squire too."

Sir Robert looked surprised. "It is what I have heard of you. Despite your elevated position, you care for all who serve you."

I shrugged, "The day I do not is the day I have lost the right to rule. The title has a responsibility as well as rights. I am well aware of both."

It took until afternoon for him to reach a decision. "I have decided I will join the Empress' cause but I would speak with her personally. I trust your word but I would look into her eyes as I have looked into yours."

I nodded, "As would I. My men and I will escort you to Gloucester if you will allow us."

"If we leave now we could reach there by tonight."

"Aye, Sir Robert. The roads are clear and my men are well mounted. I will send my squire to fetch my men to the gate."

Sir Robert showed his confidence in me by only bringing two knights, their squires and six men at arms. I sent Alain of Auxerre back to Wallingford to tell the Earl of Gloucester that I would be returning to the hall. He would wonder the reason but I could not worry about hurt feelings. If we could regain Oxford then it was a blow as great as the capture of Lincoln. I sent Gurth and Alan son of Alan ahead to warn the Empress of our arrival. I did not need to send an elaborate message; the Empress was one of the cleverest women I had ever met. She would be ready to entertain Sir Robert.

We rode swiftly and spoke as we rode. After I had been closely questioned about my campaigns and victories, I asked about Lincoln.

"Lincoln, my lord? What brings that to mind?"

"I was there with the Earl's daughter and helped to capture it. It has a place in my heart."

"Then I fear you may not like my news. The citizens of that city have appealed to King Stephen to return it to royal rule. The Earl of Chester and his brother are unpopular rulers."

"Where is the King now then?"

"I have heard that he is gathering forces with which to invest Lincoln. I was asked to be ready to defend the borders should the Earl of Gloucester attempt to intervene."

I realised that the usurper was as sharp as ever. He had almost anticipated our plans. Did we have a spy, I wondered? Then I put the thought from my head. Of course, we had a spy. There were probably many of them. When knights like the Earl of Chester and Geoffrey of Mandeville were willing to swap sides more frequently than they changed their breeches, it was highly likely that lesser knights would be in the pay of another. The only ones I could truly trust were my own men.

We reached Gloucester after dark. We were cold and we were hungry but the warmth of the Empress' smile and the welcome more than made up for it. Sir Robert needed no persuasion. He was smitten as soon as he laid eyes on the Empress. He dropped to one knee, "I swear to be your knight unto death! Oxford Castle is yours, your majesty!"

She raised him up and kissed him lightly on the cheek. "And I am doubly pleased that you are now on the side of right and of England. Come, let us warm you." Unusually for one in her position, she took Sir Robert and me by our arms and walked us into the fire lit hall. "I am blessed to have two such fine knights on my arms. How all the ladies will envy me."

In that moment she sealed the compact she had made with Sir Robert. He was hers. He proved to be faithful, as he said, unto death.

After we had retired, Margaret came to my chambers, "The Empress would have a word with you, lord."

"Is it safe?"

She nodded, "It is safe. I have Edgar and Wilfred watching the corridors. You will not be observed."

My men at arms would not question any of my actions and the secret of our meeting would go with them to their graves. I knew my men. There were none more loyal or trustworthy.

They nodded as I passed. Margaret waited by the door after I had entered. We were not alone but the Empress could speak. "How did you persuade him, my lord?"

"I suspected that he was a supporter of your father and it proved so. Our raids into his lands had weakened him anyway. Although Oxford is a strong castle; one of the strongest I have ever seen, I am sure we could have taken it. He knew not that we plan to take Lincoln back."

"Then our plans move on apace."

"They do, but when I return I will urge your brother to move to Oxford Castle. From what Sir Robert told me, I fear that Stephen may be ready to take Lincoln back from the Earl of Chester. If he invests the castle, we will never take it without great loss of men. The Countess can only hold it for a short time."

"Then you must urge him." She put her arms around me and kissed me. "You are ever my rock. I know not what I would do without you."

"That is a worry you need not have. So long as I have breath in my body, I will serve my Empress and our son."

Chapter 11

I knew that there would be ramifications from my visit to Oxford Castle. The Earl liked to be in control of events. I rode directly into the keep of Wallingford Castle where the Earl and his closest advisers resided. I knew that he was more than a little intrigued when he leapt up as I entered the Great Hall where the lords were all gathered. "What took you to Gloucester, Alfraed?"

There was little point in small talk and I would not lie. I spoke the truth. I came directly out with it. "I negotiated the surrender of Oxford Castle, my lord, but Sir Robert D'Oyly wished to surrender to the Empress in person."

While the rest of the room seemed delighted, the Earl frowned. "Come with me. We must talk!"

Sir John and Dick looked surprised at the Earl's brusque manner but I was not.

He led me to a small antechamber. He snapped at the sentry, "Let no one enter!"

Once inside he said, "Do you try to usurp me? Would you lead this army?"

"No, my lord."

"Then why went you behind my back?"

"The idea came to me as I rode. I did not expect the result which ensued, my lord. What difference does it make? The castle surrendered to the Empress and not to me. We now have a base from which we can advance to Lincoln."

"So you do wish to control the army. You try to tell me what we should do."

"I will speak plainly for that is my way as you know. It seems to me that you would argue that black was white. It appears I have offended you yet I know not how. I thought our plan was to go to the aid of your daughter when she summoned us. This makes it easier. Oxford is closer to Lincoln, is it not?"

"Do not try my patience, Alfraed, Earl of Cleveland. You are what you are because I made you."

"No, my lord. There you are wrong. I am what I am because of my deeds. It was your father who made me Earl and not you."

He drew himself close to me. "I could have you...."

"Have me what? Thrown in the Tower? You forget, my lord, that we control a tiny part of this land. If we fight amongst ourselves then we do Stephen's work."

"I do not need you. Take your men and go hence!"

I could see that he was white with anger. It took all of my self-control to keep my sword sheathed. I had to think of the greater good and the Empress.

"Very well, I will quit the camp in the morning."

His eyes narrowed, "Where will you go?"

"I am leaving this camp to keep the peace but do not think for one moment that I am afraid of you. I think of the Empress and her son. I will not tell you where I go for it is none of your business."

His hand went to his sword.

"If I were you, Earl, I would move your hand for if you draw that sword then you will die and all that we have worked for will be wasted."

"You would fight the King's son?"

"No, I would fight the King's bastard!"

He pushed me aside and barged from the chamber. As I passed through the hall, Sir Miles and Brian Fitz Count accosted me. "My lord, have you upset the Earl? He stormed out of here like an enraged bull."

"It seems I should have asked his permission before I sought the surrender of Oxford. I am no longer needed here and I will quit the camp on the morrow."

They both looked shocked, "My lord, we need you! You have helped us to be in this position. Come the Spring we could attack Stephen and win!"

"Fear not, Sir Brian. I ride to Gloucester to be with the Empress. If I am needed then send a rider. I will come even if it means coming to blows with the Earl."

"We will speak with him."

"I fear it will do little good. It seems he has his Welsh allies now and I am no longer needed."

Sir Miles said, "My lord, you are worth a whole Welsh army. Stay close I beg of you."

"It will take death to stop my support of the Empress. I will fight alongside you once more. Fear not."

And so I spent Christmas at Gloucester with the Empress and my son. It was unexpected and I enjoyed it but, at the same time, I knew that it brought disharmony to our ranks. The Empress was sympathetic for she knew her brother and his ways. Since his father's death, he had changed. Those traits which had been submerged when King Henry ruled, now rose to the surface as the prospect of power grew.

"I think that my brother sees himself as the King of Wales and the west. He and Madog spent hours together before you came. I think Madog has aspirations to be King of Powys in his brother's stead."

"Then our hope lies in a brave maid. Maud is our only chance. Your brother will go to her aid of that I am sure. The only problem is the time it will take. Were I in command, we would be there in less than three days. I fear that the Earl will take longer."

As December drew to a close, we had two messengers. One was the spy the Empress had sent and the other was a messenger from Geoffrey Mandeville. They both said the same thing. King Stephen was marching north and that could only mean one thing, he was heading for Lincoln. I was keen to ride back to Oxford and urge the Earl to act but Matilda shook her head, "No, Alfraed. I will write to him and give him the information. He will not leave his daughter in the clutches of Stephen. Even though my cousin would treat her well, my brother's honour would be impugned. He will act."

January came and still the Earl sat in Oxford. Finally, on January the eighth came the dire news we had been expecting. Ranulf, Earl of Chester, and his half brother had fled Lincoln when Stephen had captured that city, seventeen knights and besieged the castle. But Maud had done as she had said. She had held the castle; however, the army which had been intended to rescue her was a hundred and fifty miles away.

As soon as I heard the news, I roused my riders. I was angry and my anger showed in my last words to the Empress. "I foretold this! And yet I sat here doing nothing! I am just as bad as your half brother! Does no one wish to win this war?"

I saw young Henry clutch his mother's arm. His face was fearful.

Matilda nodded, "You are right to chastise us so. I pray that you will reach my niece in time. If any can save this situation it is you, my lord, my champion."

"I hope that I can live up to your expectations."

"Do you ride to Oxford, my lord?"

"No, my prince, I ride to Lincoln. I made the Countess of Chester a promise and I will not let her down. If I have to fight Stephen's army alone, I will go to her side!"

As we headed north, I knew that we had a slightly shorter journey and we would travel much faster than if we first went to Oxford. I hoped to reach Derby by the end of the first day. I prayed that the Earl of Chester was there. If I could put some marrow into his backbone, we might be able to threaten Stephen and make him face us rather than the Countess. I needed time for the tardy Earl Robert to reach his daughter. It was just over ninety miles to Derby and despite the short days and cold weather, we had grain for our horses and remounts. We rode hard.

Dick and Sir John flanked me as we headed north. "Do we know how many men the enemy have, lord?"

"No, Sir John, but it matters not. He began the siege two days since. The Countess hoped to hold out for three, perhaps four days. If we reach Lincoln by the morrow then that will be the fourth day. We face whoever we find. I left warriors with the Countess and I will not abandon them."

Dick said, "They knew the risks, lord, when they volunteered."

"That matters not. It is what I said that matters. I promised that I would return and return I will!"

We skirted every castle we saw. I knew that some would be supporters of the Empress but I could neither take the chance nor spare the time. I had scouts out and we rode hard stopping only to feed our horses grain and changing any who showed signs of fatigue.

We were close to Burton when my scouts returned, "Lord, armed knights are heading down the road towards us."

"Dick, ambush!"

My archers split into two groups and disappeared. We formed a solid column of knights, squires and men at arms. It was with some relief that I recognised the Earl of Chester and his banner. He reined in, "Alfraed! What are you doing here?"

"I am heading to Lincoln. Your wife is still there. I go to her aid. What are you doing here?"

He rode close to me and dropped his voice, "I begged her to leave when Stephen began to attack but she said she would stay and that her father would come."

"She was right. Her father is bringing an army now, even as we speak. So tell me, Ranulf, why it is that she wears the shift and you the armour. It seems to me that she has more right to be a knight than ever you have."

We were so close that only our squires heard the interchange. "You insult me!" His hand went to his sword.

"Be careful, Earl. You have changed so many sides that if I slew you here and now many would say I was doing the Empress and England a service by ending your miserable and pathetic life."

He subsided for he was afraid of me and quite rightly so. I was angry. He shook his head and held his hand out for me to clasp, "You are right, Earl, I have behaved badly but I see the error of my ways. Come, let us return to the Earl and we will retake my castle."

I knocked away his hand, "Get out of my sight. I will ride to Lincoln! I will do what needs to be done!"

I spurred Lion. His scouts had to jerk their reins around to avoid us knocking them from their saddles. We had just passed Burton Abbey when I heard a cry from behind. "Lord, we are being followed."

I wheeled my mount around and waited with sword drawn. It was Sir William Montague, one of the Earl's knights. He had twenty men at arms with him. "Lord, let me follow your banner."

"Why?"

"I was ordered to leave Lincoln by the Earl. I did not like leaving the Countess alone. I will ride with you for honour demands it."

"Then you obey my commands and unlike your lord, I mean what I say!" As we rode I questioned him to gain as much intelligence as I could. "Who remains at Derby?"

"It is a small garrison only."

"Who commands?"

"Old Ralph of Derby. He served the previous lord of the manor."

"Then we spend the night there. Where does Stephen have his siege engines?"

"From what I heard, he has some in the town but most of them are close to the Fosse Dyke and the river."

I remained silent for the last few miles to Derby. I was thinking and I was planning. Stephen could take the castle in five days but not without siege engines. I decided that we would disrupt his attack. If he chased us off then so much the better. He could not besiege the castle and chase us. The sight of my banner and my voice opened the gates of Derby to us. We had shelter and food. While the food was prepared, I studied the maps which were in the castle. An approach from the side we were approaching from would mean we would have to cross the dyke and the river. That meant we would have to approach from the north. That suited my purpose. Stephen's spies would have reported that I had left the Earl's army. Perhaps my approach from the north might make him think I had brought my valley army south. That would frighten him. He would take that threat very seriously. Small in number but not stature, we were a force to be reckoned with.

When I had made my plans, I summoned Sir William. We four knights sat apart. "You were in Lincoln recently. Tell me how it stands."

"It is in the hand of the Countess, her garrison and the men you left. All seventeen knights were captured when King Stephen captured the town." He shook his head. "It seems that the Countess kept the men at arms and her garrison confined within the castle, as though she expected some disaster."

"How did you know this? Presumably, you were with the Earl."

"We were, my lord. A clerk escaped. He rode to us with the news that the castle had fallen."

"When was this?"

"On the sixth of January, lord."

"And what did the Earl do then?"

"He sent a message to the Empress and prepared to head back to Gloucester, lord." I glared at the knight. "I know, lord, there was no honour in this but the Earl is my liege lord. I have to obey."

I relented. He was correct. "You are right but I hope you fight well for we will be outnumbered."

"You intend to take King Stephen's forces? There are almost fifteen hundred of them."

"Have you never read of the Spartans?" He shook his head. "In ancient times, three hundred of these Greek warriors held off an army of ten thousand for over a week. I have seen where they died. It is not numbers that are important, it is the heart that wields the sword. We will prevail."

He looked at Sir John and Dick who were both grinning. He shrugged, "It seems I am with madmen!"

Dick laughed and clapped him about the shoulders. "Now you begin to understand us. When you fight for the Earl, you do not ask how many, you ask, how?"

Sir John added, "And then you do it! It is simple."

144

We left before dawn. Dick sent Ralph of Thirsk and Aelric
to scout the road ahead. Until now we had been relatively
safe but we were getting closer to the enemy. I wanted to get
as close as I could before we were sighted. They rode back
when we were just a few miles northwest of Lincoln. We
were close to the village of Brandsby. It helped that we had
Sir William and his men with us. They knew the area and
identified some of the places we passed through.

Aelric said, "Lord, they have a line of scouts north of
Lincoln. There is no village nearby and they watch the road.
There are ten of them."

I trusted Aelric. Along with Dick, he was one of the
longest-serving archers I had. He had good judgement.
"Could our archers take them?"

He laughed, "Ralph of Thirsk and I could have taken
them, lord."

I smiled, "Let us take no chances. Take the archers, all of
them, and eliminate these men. I want their horses. Leave no
trace of them." I turned to Sir William. "Is there a village
north of here?"

"Not on the road, lord. It is Roman and travels straight and
true towards York." He pointed to our left and, in the
distance, I could see smoke rising from a collection of huts.
"There is one there. It is called Scampton. There are few
people who dwell within."

"Aelric, do as I commanded and then bring their horses
back to the village."

As we headed for the crude huts centred around a tiny
wooden chapel, I explained my plan to the others. "I want to
draw Stephen north. The Earl is approaching from the west
and I want the Usurper looking to us. Dick, I intend to take
the men at arms and progress down the Roman Road. I have
no doubt that these sentries will be relieved or someone, at
least, will check up on them. Your task is to wait until we
approach and then ambush whoever comes. We will wait
until the archers return before we begin."

I turned to the servants. "This will be our camp. If the
villagers stay, do not harm them but warn them that they
cannot travel south. They must head north or west."

While my men went about their business, I dismounted. I would ride Rolf for Lion had done his fair share for the day. I had my knights and men at arms arm themselves with spears. "When we ride put more space between you than is normal. I wish them to see more men than there are. Sir John, make sure you have a banner. I want them to see knights and, Richard, make sure you hold my wolf banner high. Gilles, today you carry a lance with a gonfanon."

He said, "But I have not got one!"

Sir John laughed, "Then make one! Use a spare surcoat."

Aelric and Ralph returned leading a string of horses. "They are dead, lord. We hid their bodies in the ditch. They will find them only when they begin to smell."

"Good, Dick, you know what to do. Send me a message when they approach."

There was no road for us to the Roman Road and so we crossed the frost hardened fields. The dips and the folds hid us but there were no enemies to spy on us, yet. When we reached the road, I had the men dismount. The squires either had their lord's standard or a gonfanon. We all looked to be knights. It was getting on to late afternoon and that suited us. I wanted dark behind us. Men are more likely to see threatening and sinister shadows in the dark. Men multiply enemies when the night is upon them. I spent the time explaining to my men exactly what they would do.

I wondered if anyone would come at all as I saw the glow that had been the thin January sun sink in the west. Will Red Legs rode up, "Lord, a large patrol has ridden from Lincoln. There are forty riders. They are a Roman mile away."

"Mount!"

Our horses were rested and we cantered down the road. I did not want to hide. I wished them to know that we were coming. The horses' hooves drummed on the Roman stones. It made us sound more than we were. We covered the first half mile quickly and then we saw them. As they saw us, they reined in and I shouted, "Charge! For the Empress! The Warlord of the North rides!"

As we galloped, faster and looser than we normally did, Dick and his archers began to rain arrows into them. Panic

146

ensued. These were men at arms and they ran. No knight led them. Some were plucked from their saddles and some horses were struck. The rest headed back down the road.

We halted at the site of the ambush. In the time it had taken to charge, night had fallen. One horse lay dead. Already three of my archers were butchering it. The rest were taking all of any value from the twelve who had fallen. Others would arrive back with wounds and some of those would die but it was the message they would deliver that was most important. They would report that the Warlord of the North, with many knights and men at arms, had ridden south. I relied on my reputation and the fact that Stephen knew me well. He knew of my tricks and my nighttime attacks. He would halt his attack on the walls and prepare for my men striking that night. I did not intend to do so. Instead, we would eat horsemeat, sleep well and be ready to harass them on the morrow.

As we ate, Sir William said, "That was a clever ruse, lord. I thought that you were just a good tourney knight who led men."

Dick laughed, "The Earl would have made a good outlaw. He knows how to use the land and the enemy's fears to win. I could not believe the panic when they saw your banners, my lord. We were close enough to hear their shouts. They believed that all of our men had come south with you!"

Sir John asked, "And tomorrow; what then, lord?"

"Tomorrow we move and we strike. Our men at arms hold them while Dick and his archers thin their numbers. The Usurper will know by evening how few men we have. He will have patrols seeking us out. Until they report back, he will believe that I am up to some trick. And then I pray that the Earl of Gloucester will have arrived for if not, then the siege will begin again on the next day and I am not certain how long the Countess can hold out."

We slept as well as men can in the middle of winter out in the open but we were warriors all. The addition of Sir William's men had aided me for it gave me a larger number of mounted men to use. The key would still be Dick and his archers. I was just grateful that we had brought so many arrows. It looked like we would need them.

I led my men east, across the Roman Road. I wanted to draw Stephen's eye away from the west. Using Dick's archers as a screen, we headed for the east gate of the town. I knew that it would be guarded. I also knew that there would be men watching for us. Had it not been for Dick then we would have stumbled upon them but, as it was, we had a warning.

Rafe galloped up, "Lord, Sir Richard sent me. There are fifty men ahead. Four knights and the rest are mounted men at arms. Our men are falling back along the road."

"Sir William, take your men into the fields on the left. When we have their attention, attack them in the flank!"

"Aye, lord."

"Tell Dick to pull back; we are coming!"

I held my lance across my cantle. If these men had been sent to look for us, they would have neither lances nor spears. Ours might make the difference. As I looked ahead I saw my archers galloping towards us. They were safe from the enemy for they wore no mail and their horses were light. They could outrun them. The men at arms and knights wasted energy spurring their horses after my archers. The ditches which lined the roads were no obstacle to horsemen and my archers leapt across them when they spied us. The result was that the enemy suddenly saw my column of men bearing down upon them.

Their leader tried to form a line. It was a good move and would be effective for the land around us was flat. What they did not know was that Sir William was bringing a line of men at arms to strike at his right flank and my archers were preparing to dismount and loose arrows. I concentrated on the leading knight in the line. He was their leader. I could see him gesticulating with his arm. I had Gilles on one side of me and Sir John on the other. Gilles was having to play the part of a knight thanks to the prevarication of the Earl of Gloucester. If anything happened to my brave young squire then the earl would pay!

The enemy line began to labour towards us. We had speed. I pulled back my arm and as our two lines approached each other, I pulled my shield tighter and punched hard with my spear across the cantle of the leader of the knights. He was slow to bring his shield across and his cantle deflected the head of my spear up. It tore through his surcoat and mail and ripped into his organs. I felt the tip strike the wood of the cantle behind him and he was thrown from the saddle. His fall took my spear with it and I let it go. As I drew my sword, I saw Sir William and his men hitting the right flank of the enemy line. I shouted, "Wheel right!"

A man at arms swung his sword at me. I blocked it and then he was passed. I heard a shout as Jean of Angers hacked him in two. Our dual lines were effective. As we swept right, I saw men at arms being plucked from their saddles by the arrows from Dick and his archers. As we hit the shocked and leaderless remnants, they broke and fled.

"Halt!"

I did not want us to pursue the enemy. They might count our numbers. This way the survivors would report greater numbers than we actually had. They would tell Stephen that there was a large number of men attacking the east gate as well as the north. It would make their flight understandable.

"Gather the weapons and horses. Back to the village. Fetch our dead and wounded."

Chapter 12

As we ate the last of the horsemeat, I reflected on the situation. I had besieged castles before. Indeed, I had done so with Stephen when fighting for King Henry. I had set him a new puzzle. He now knew that I was to the north and the east of him. He would have no idea of the actual numbers of men. His scouts had just seen a screen of my scouts while those who had returned from the encounters would give an exaggerated picture to him. He was a clever commander. I would never underestimate him. He would be devising a plan to continue the siege while finding me and my men. I could expect him to hunt me the next day. So long as he hunted me then he could not attack the castle with all of his forces. I felt certain that the Earl would be close by the end of the day. To that end, I sent one of Sir William's men at arms to look for him on the road.

Before we retired for the night, I warned my men what we could expect. "Günter and Alain, I want you to guard the servants and spare horses. If we are found then take them and head north and west. Dick, your archers will give us protection while we head north and east towards the road. We will make our enemy think we are protecting our way home."

Sir William nodded, "In reality, you are keeping the King's eyes away from the Earl of Gloucester."

"That is all we can do. We have hurt him. He has lost knights and men at arms to us. We need to do more. I want him afoot. If we can weaken his ability to use horses then we help our cause. We hit and we run." I laid out my plans for

150

the next day. My own men knew what to expect but Sir
William and his men at arms struggled to understand how we
could make such fluid plans and expect to succeed. They had
proved an asset up to now but I wished they were my men
from the north.

I was awoken while it was still dark by Walter of Crewe,
one of my archers, "Lord, I have heard horses. There are
men on the road."

That could mean only one thing; they were hunting us.
"Rouse the men but do so silently. Let us slip into the night."

Gilles and Richard had already been roused when Walter
had woken me. They had Lion saddled and ready for me by
the time I had made water. They helped me into my mail and
I mounted. I rode east towards the road and Dick ghosted
next to me. Even on a horse, he could move silently. His
bow was already strung and hung from his cantle. We did
not speak. Noise carried long distances at night; especially in
winter when there was little animal noise. He pointed south
and east towards the road. I nodded. Unsheathing my sword I
followed him. I soon heard the sound of hooves on the road.
They had put sacking around them but in the silence of the
night, they could still be heard. This was open country but it
was dark. Both Dick and I were cloaked and our horses were
dark in colour. We were as invisible as it was possible to be.
I glanced behind me and saw another eight of Dick's archers.
The rest of my men would be following and Alain and
Günter would be leading the servants and spare horses to
safety.

It was Dick who spied the first enemy scout. His horse
had blotches of white which showed up in the night. Dick
had an arrow ready and he loosed it from the back of his
horse. The scout fell from the back of his mount. He grunted
as the arrow hit him in the chest. Startled, his horse galloped
north towards us. The sound of the galloping hooves alerted
the other scouts. They shouted to each other and we knew
where they were. Dick waved his archers to flank us and we
moved in a long line across the open country. Soon we
would be seen, despite our black apparel, but it mattered not.
No matter how many men sought us, we would have the

advantage of numbers over the scouts. We stopped in an oblique line across the road. Loosing from the back of a horse was neither easy nor accurate, even for my skilled archers, but the scouts approached so close to us that even I could have hit my target.

The arrows flew and the scouts died but some died noisily and I heard the cries of alarm further down the road. I pointed to the east and Dick, nodding, led his archers thence. My squires, Sir John and my men at arms formed up behind me. I could hear, coming a little more slowly than my men, Sir William and his men. We formed a line ten men wide across the road. The scouts who had not been slain had galloped south down the road to rejoin their comrades and we waited. Movement could be seen. I could hear that they were cantering up the road and that suited me.

I caught sight of a white horse amongst the mailed men who rode towards us. As soon as I detected where they were, I spurred Lion and he strode forward eagerly. It made us into a mobile wedge as we trotted down the road. The sound of our hooves told them that we were coming. I wanted my men as close to me as possible. I did not know the numbers we would meet and I wanted us to strike the head of their column as hard as we could. When they came into view, I saw that they were four abreast and less than thirty paces from us.

I shouted, "Charge!" As I dug in my heels, my horse leapt towards them. He was a powerful beast and was eager for battle. I had my sword behind me, ready to strike. Lion galloped between the two leading knights. A night battle is always hard for you can misjudge where to strike. I just aimed my sword at neck level. The knight to my right failed to raise his shield and my sword slashed across his ventail and throat. My blade came away bloody.

To my left, I felt the knight who was there stab at me. It was the wrong stroke for it merely hit my shield and then Sir John showed him the correct blow by striking diagonally across his chest. My wedge was forcing the column of men apart and that would give us an advantage, but only for a short time. Eventually, if the column was big enough, we would be surrounded. I stood in my stirrups as I swung my sword overhand. I brought it down on the head of the man at arms who tried to slash at my side. My sword struck first and it smashed through his poorly made helmet. As I stood I could see that the column was a long one. It was time to break.

"Wheel left!"

Wilfred and Edgar were at the extreme right of my short line and they were both experienced warriors. They would have the task of protecting our right flank as we turned to the left. We took the men before us by surprise as we punched a hole in their ranks. Then we were on the hard, frozen fields which bordered the road. I led my men, now a ragged formation, north and east. I knew not where Dick and his archers were but they would be ready to ambush the column as it blindly pursued us. A lightening of the sky ahead told me that dawn was not very far away. It meant another day bought for the tardy Earl of Gloucester.

I saw two horses without riders galloping next to me and I recognised them as belonging to our men. We had not escaped unscathed. Ahead I saw a low hedgerow. We could have jumped it but I suspected that Dick and his archers waited there. "Through the gate!" I led my men through the open gate I had spied. I glanced over my shoulder and saw that the enemy were just fifty paces from us. This time they were using a long line to try to sweep around us. They had the advantage of numbers. I knew that they would think to leap the low hedge. As we passed through the gate, I saw my line of archers, all twelve of them with bows arched. As soon as the last of my men at arms was through the gate, they released.

"Turn and face!"

My men at arms turned and formed a line some twenty paces behind my archers. Dick's men were pulling and releasing as quickly as they could. A skilled archer is beautiful to behold. Unless you have tried it yourself, you cannot know how hard it is to pull back the yew bow and launch the ash arrow as accurately as they did. They made it seem so effortless and yet I knew it was not. Sixty arrows were released in the time it takes to mount a horse in full mail. Not all found flesh. Some found mail and some horses but enough of the sixty struck home.

Six knights and men at arms burst through the gate. We charged them. Sir John and Sir William reached them first along with Edgar and Wilfred. There was a flurry of blows and three saddles were emptied. Three knights headed back through the gate and from the way one hung on to his reins, I knew that one was wounded. I saw the enemy reforming in the gloom of winter dawn.

"Dick, mount your men. We head north. Let them think we retire to our home."

We rode quickly north and west across the field back towards the road. As daylight filtered slowly from the east, they would see our paltry numbers. They would now know how few men we had brought. Stephen would realise he had been duped. Our threat was that of an insect. It would do them little harm. We did not stop until dawn had fully broken and the thin late January sun shone across the frost filled fields. They stopped pursuing us shortly after we reached the road.

It was two of Sir William's men who had fallen. I was just congratulating myself on a relatively easy victory when Richard slumped from his saddle. Gilles and I quickly dismounted. His surcoat was bloody. "Henry!"

Henry of Langdale had some skills as a healer. He jumped down from his horse and came over as Gilles and I took off Richard's surcoat and then his mail. A spear had penetrated his mail. There were torn rings and it had pierced his side. Henry took the skin which held watered-down vinegar and washed my squire's side. He was, thankfully, unconscious. Henry peered into the gaping wound.

"His organs look intact, my lord, but this will need either stitching or burning."

Dick said, "It will take too long to get a fire going, Henry. Stitch."

I nodded. "Gilles, Robert, hold his arms lest he flails around."

As Henry set to work, I saw others seeing to the wounds some of my men had received. Compared with Richard's they were minor but my men knew that wounds left untended could go bad.

"Alan, son of Alan, go and find the rest of our men. Fetch them hither. We will seek a new camp and hope that the Earl reaches us soon." It took until mid-morning before our servants and horses arrived and Richard was ready to ride. We had to ride slowly for fear of undoing Henry's work. We needed somewhere to rest up.

By noon, we had found shelter in a village whose inhabitants fled at our approach. We stayed there for the day while we licked our wounds. I sent James son of Robert in a wide loop to spy out the siege and to let me know how it was going. We had still to have word from the Earl. He seemed to be dragging his heels in his march to rescue his daughter. If it had been my child then I would have moved heaven and earth to reach her!

We kept two archers at the Roman Road as sentries. A messenger sent from the Earl would head for our last position. We used one of the deserted huts for Richard. "How are you?"

"I am sorry I was injured, lord."

"It is my fault. I have used you as a knight and yet you have barely begun your training as a squire. You did well and you bore the pain well."

"Henry was gentle, lord. I am grateful."

"You will stay with the servants until you are healed."

He shook his head defiantly, "I know I cannot fight, lord, for that would jeopardise another but Gilles is repairing my mail. I can hold your standard. You have perilously few enough men as it is."

"And you have shown great courage. Very well, you may carry the standard but I want you to retire if danger threatens. I am pleased that you took my offer of service."

"I could not imagine serving another, lord, and I will learn from this wound."

"How so?"

155

"When Henry was stitching me, he said that had I worn a thicker and wider leather belt around my waist, it would have stopped the spear thrust. When we return to Stockton, I shall use some of the money I have gathered and have the women make me a better belt."

I nodded, "Henry is wise. You might also buy a padded gambeson. It too will prevent hurts."

"I am learning, lord. Each time I fight for you I learn something new."

James returned in the mid-afternoon. My knights and I sat with him while he outlined what he had seen. "They have a ram trying to attack the western gate. I think there is one in the city too but I could not be certain. They are building towers and they have the parts for a stone thrower. It is not made yet."

"Where are these?"

"They are to the west of the castle lord; they are close to the Fosse Dyke."

Sir John asked, "Do they have horse lines?"

"Aye, lord. They are north of the town walls. They are guarded."

"What is in your mind, John?"

"When the Earl comes we will bring them to battle. If they have fewer horses then they will have to fight on foot. It might help. We could drive off their horses or even capture them. It would also prevent them from scouting in force."

"That is good. Then tonight, Dick, take your archers and try to capture the horses. It matters not if we do not get them all. Any would be to our advantage."

"Aye, lord."

"Sir John, we will take our men and infiltrate their lines in the dead of night. Let us see if we can set fire to their machines of war." He nodded.

Sir William said, "And what of me, my lord?"

"You will wait with your men and guard our horses. We will be going in on foot. When we flee we will be pursued. You and your men at arms will have to charge those who pursue us and allow us to get to our horses."

"Aye, lord."

After dark Sir William's weary man at arms found us.
"Pray tell me that the Earl is close to hand."

He shook his head, "I am sorry, my lord. It is the reason I
have taken so long. He and the army are at Derby. It is,
however, a mighty host with many Welsh men as well as the
men of the Earl of Chester."

I bit my tongue for this was just the messenger. He did not
deserve my wrath. "Go find food."

I put the Earl from my mind. I would still do what was
needed. We took off our mail. It would encumber us and we
needed to be swift and silent. We left our helms and shields
at the camp. Each of us took extra weapons. I took a mace
we had taken from one of Stephen's dead knights. Edgar took
a flint and Wilfred organised the kindling. Before we left our
camp Dick said, "Lord, smear some of the charcoal from the
fire on your hands and faces. You will stand out less in the
dark."

It was wise advice from someone who had evaded capture
in the woods of Sherwood for many years. We parted at the
Roman Road. Dick headed east and we went south. We went
cautiously and when we saw the fires of their sentries on the
road, we left our horses with Sir William and slipped down
to the watery dyke. My plan was simple. We would wade
down the shallow side of the dyke. If we spied sentries, we
would duck below the water. It would mean the kindling
would be useless but we could improvise. The water was icy
as we slipped into its black waters but the bank hid us from
view. We made our way along it. We could hear the noise
and the conversations from those in the camp but we saw
nothing.

Alan son of Alan was leading and I was close behind him.
He held up his hand and we halted. I saw a shadow appear
some ten paces from us. The overhanging grasses and reeds
hid us but when I heard the hiss and the splash in the dyke, I
knew that he was making water. Alan waited until he had
gone before he waved us forward. We went another thirty
paces. James had told us that the war machines were
between the camp and the castle walls. They were guarded.
When we heard the murmur of the camp fade, we halted. I

slowly raised my head, acutely aware that the charcoal on the back of my hands had been washed off by the water. I saw that we would not need the flint for there were three fires. They were there to keep the guards warm. I counted eight men who were guarding the war machines. Turning, I waved the others to the bank and I started to pull myself out. After the icy waters, the night air actually felt warm! I knew that it was an illusion. We were hidden in the dark and the eight men around the fires had no night vision for they were staring at the fires.

I waved my arms left and right. My men began to crawl along the ground. I wondered how we were going to creep up and slay them silently when I heard an alarm. It was far away from us and I realised what it was, it was Dick and his archers stealing the horses. The eight men stood and looked in the direction of the horse lines. To our left, some way off, I heard someone shout, "To arms! They are stealing the horses!"

The commotion was too great an opportunity to miss and I rose, mace in hand and ran towards the eight men. My men joined me. The mace is a powerful weapon, especially when used against unprotected heads. I caved in the back of one skull as Gilles stabbed the second man in the back. As another turned, I swung my mace and demolished his face. All eight were dead and no one looked in our direction.

We ran to the machines and Wilfred spread the kindling amongst them. I helped my men to gather the spare firewood for the fires and used that too. When all was in place, we each grabbed a burning brand and threw them under the machines. I did not wait to see if the kindling caught; instead, I led my men back through the camp. It was a risk but there was so much movement that I doubted any would notice another group of men running. I took my sword in my right hand and held my mace in my left. We ran.

We were halfway through the camp and approaching the sparsely populated northern end when someone took an interest. A sergeant at arms shouted, "Where the hell are you lot going?"

Edgar rammed his sword into his middle and hurled his body to the side. His companions looked around and we hacked and stabbed at them. The damage had been done and all eyes, in that part of the camp, turned to us. "Run! Sir William!"

I swept my sword in an arc and managed to rip it across the arm of a man at arms. As I ran I sensed someone on my left. I stopped and held up my mace. It blocked the blow from the sword and I stabbed the man at arms in the thigh.

"Hurry, my lord!"

Gilles' voice spurred me and then I heard the sound of hooves on the road ahead. I ran even faster. When my feet touched the Roman, Road I risked a glance behind. The enemy horsemen were in hot pursuit but behind them, I saw the war machines blazing away. We had succeeded; now could we escape?

Sir William's voice shouted, "To the side, lord!"

We needed no urging and we threw ourselves into the ditch. Sir William and his men at arms were all mailed and they hit the lightly armed and sleepy soldiers like an avalanche hitting a stand of young trees. They swept them before them. We regained the road and ran to our horses. Sir William had left horse holders. As we mounted I shouted, "Fall back!"

We held our swords and waited. Sir William and his men galloped up but one horse was riderless. These were true warriors and I was grateful that they fought at my side!

When we reached our camp Dick apologised. "I am sorry, my lord. We were seen as we got into position and the alarm was given."

I shook my head, "It was meant to be, Dick, and besides, it aided our escape. When the alarm was given, we were able to break through their lines. We captured their horses. Some are war horses."

"I think that the usurper will regret his decision not to keep his war horses secure. They will be a grievous loss."

Sir John asked, "And now, what, my lord?"

"We have done all that we can do. His war machines are damaged and he will have to begin building them again. His ability to range far and wide with his horses has been diminished. We will wait here and prevent any reinforcements from the north arriving and await the Earl."

"Derby is not far away, my lord."

"Sir William, it is a lifetime away for some of our men. I pray that the Earl hurries and applies some of the determination I have seen from our heroes."

Chapter 13

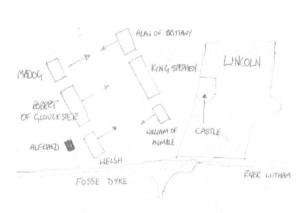

    The Earl did not reach us until February. However, the valiant efforts of my men had delayed the real assault on the castle. Stephen had to make new siege engines and that took time. The Earl was wise enough to realise that our position was the best one from which to assault the castle. If we attacked from the other side then we would have the town to negotiate first. This way Maud, the Countess of Chester, could use her archers to harass the rear of the enemy. Of course, it might be that Stephen would decide to abandon the siege and withdraw. If he did so then it would be a victory for us; we would have Lincoln. From what I knew of him, I did not think he would. Even though we had not attacked since destroying his siege engines, we had scouted. I had gone with Dick and his archers to spy out the enemy. I knew who some of his commanders were. We had spied their banners.

William of Ypres was from Flanders and was a favourite of Queen Matilda, Stephen's wife. He had been involved in every battle they had fought and was not to be underestimated. Alan of Brittany I had met whilst campaigning in Normandy and William of Aumale was another close confidante of Stephen. I had fought alongside him at Northallerton. He was solid but cautious. I did not see the banner of de Mandeville. Perhaps the Empress' strategy had worked and by giving up his cousin, she had bought his friendship or his neutrality at least.

It took some time for the bulk of the army to reach us. They were stretched out for many miles along the road. The majority of the Welsh were foot soldiers and they made up almost two-thirds of the army. I wondered at Prince Madog's motives. I did not know him but neither did I trust him. What was a Welsh prince doing in England fighting for the Earl who controlled the richest part of Wales? Could we rely on the soldiers who made up almost two-thirds of our force?

I was greeted warmly enough by Robert of Gloucester although Ranulf, Earl of Chester, and his half brother were lukewarm in their praise of our actions. "Thank you, Alfraed. Once again you have valiantly held the line until we could reach you. The roads were treacherous and the weather vile. I am disappointed it took so long for us to reach you but we are here now. I take it you have their dispositions?"

"We have scouted them, lord," I told him whom I had seen. "He has almost fifteen hundred men although we captured or drove off a large number of his horses. His siege machines are destroyed."

The Earl nodded, "We have, with your men, a thousand. We will be outnumbered but that should not bother you, my lord. You seem to do even better when the odds are against you."

I said nothing but one day it might be interesting to fight when we outnumbered the enemy.

The Fallen Crown

Prince Madog, who was a squat, powerful-looking warrior said, "Fear not, Earl. My Welshmen are as solid as the mountains of our homeland. We will not falter and we will hew these enemies of yours."

I noted his use of *'enemies of yours'*. What did that imply? It confirmed my suspicions. This prince had ulterior motives.

I was anxious to begin the battle. The army was here and we could begin to prepare. "How will we fight on the morrow, lord?"

"We will fight on the day after. Tomorrow we will frighten my cousin. We will array our men so that he may see the full force we can bring to bear."

I heard his words but I knew the true meaning. His men were too tired to fight the next day. They needed time to recover.

"My lord, that is a good plan but should we not just show him our strength but also meet with him tomorrow and try to put fear in his heart."

"How mean you, Earl?"

I spoke slowly for I wanted no misunderstanding. "My lord, they see an army which is largely Welsh. If we hint that we have more men coming from the north and the west it may change the way he deploys his army."

I saw the Earl as he took in my words. It made sense. Everyone knew that the best warriors were from the Tees. The small contingent I had brought would suggest that the bulk were still waiting to attack or to join us.

"The idea has merit. The three of us will speak with Stephen on the morrow. Perhaps you are right and we can frighten him into surrender."

I did not think for one moment that would happen but it suited my plans to go along with his.

The next day, the three of us, with squires and banners, rode in peace towards Lincoln Castle. I had a different motive. I wanted Countess Matilda to see that we had come. Stephen was too wily an enemy to believe that I had more men heading south. He knew I would not leave my land undefended. I wanted to look him in the eyes so that he knew my purpose. We headed towards the castle and I saw that

163

Stephen had already arrayed his men in case we made a surprise attack.

He approached and was flanked by William of Ypres and Alan of Brittany. Although he spoke to Robert, Earl of Gloucester, he looked at me all the time he spoke.

"Robert. I see you have brought Welsh mercenaries to terrify us!"

"I bring allies, Stephen. Will you surrender now or when we have slaughtered your men?"

He ignored the Earl and I could tell that Robert of Gloucester was not pleased. He huffed and snorted as Stephen said, "I see, Alfraed, that you are up to your usual tricks." He waved a hand at the charred remains of his war machines standing like the skeletons of some blackened primaeval beast.

I nodded, "Until the rest of my men arrive that is all that I could do. It stopped them from being bored. To be truthful, it was all that I could do to stop them from attacking you. Soon you will feel the full weight of the men of the Tees. Then you will know fear!"

He laughed, "God but I wished you had chosen my cause. This land would be at peace now!"

"But I chose the honourable course. I remained true to the oath I took. You did not!"

I knew that would anger him because it was true. He had sworn at Westminster with the rest of us.

He turned to the Earl of Gloucester. "Do what you will, Gloucester, but by the end of the week, Lincoln will be mine! I have more men than you do. The fact that you had to bring these Welshmen shows me that you lack numbers."

The Earl had regained his composure for we had made the threat of reinforcements. "That, cousin, is in the hands of God and the men I lead. You can surrender now or when we have defeated you."

"We will fight you!"

"And you will lose. We will see on the field of battle. We will decide there who rules England and Normandy; you or my sister."

We rode back to our lines and the Earl said, "You frighten him, Alfraed. More than any of us he fears you. We will use that threat on the morrow."

"How mean you, lord?"

"You and your men will be the reserve. I want Stephen to see you and wonder when you will attack. I want him to fear the men you might bring. He will have his own reserves and he will not commit them until you have joined the battle. He will be distracted and my Welsh allies will use the distraction to break his lines."

I was not sure about the strategy but I was happy to go along with it for it meant I could choose when I attacked Stephen. This battle would be decided by combat between the two of us. He knew that, as did I. I was fighting for a promise given to King Henry; more than that, I was fighting for the Empress and my son. If I let them down then I did not deserve to live.

The Earl of Gloucester knew how to prepare for a battle. The leaders were gathered together and he explained his plan. "We fight in three formations tomorrow. The largest will be led by me in the centre. Our Welsh allies will form two further battles on our flanks. The Earl of Cleveland will have his men and those of Sir William as a reserve. He will draw Stephen on and, should we suffer a reverse on the field, then he will attend to that."

As a plan it had simplicity. Our weak flank was the Welsh infantry who were close to the Fosse. The left flank had the Welsh cavalry with the infantry and they were led by their prince. The centre was a solid phalanx of knights, squires and men at arms. They were all mounted.

The Earl of Chester flashed me a triumphant look, "I shall be in the fore with you, my lord! I will have a place of honour! Tomorrow will be a great and glorious day!" I ignored the glare. The battle would not be decided in the first attacks. We were not fighting half-naked Scotsmen but an army almost identical to ours. It would be a bloody slog.

Sir William followed me to my men so that we could prepare. "This is a great honour, my lord. I shall be with you on this most momentous of days."

I had seen the glares from the Earl of Chester and his brother, "I fear you have incurred the wrath of your liege lord. Perhaps the Earl sees this as a punishment for having followed my banner."

"That may be so, lord, but if a knight has no honour then what is he? He is little better than a hired sword or a brigand with a title. I am content that tomorrow we ride with you."

Richard was still too weak to ride to war. That upset him. "But I can still wait with the reserve, my lord. I can keep your spare horse there."

I smiled, "That you can, squire." I would be riding Rolf but if it was a long battle then I would need Lion too. Gilles and Richard put edges on my weapons. I chose my own spear rather than a lance. I would have my newly acquired mace too. When you fought another man in mail and your weapon was blunted then a mace or a club could smash bones protected by mail. With my hauberk cleaned and oiled then I was ready. Each man is alone with himself before a battle. A formal battle meant that you knew what you would be doing. There would be few surprises. This field had nowhere for one of us to outflank the other. We would have to destroy one flank first. Men would have to die to do that. You contemplated death and your own mortality. I prayed alone and silently by the Fosse. I knew that I might die but I asked God to make my death worthwhile. I asked him to ensure that my son would be king. Then I rose and returned to my tent. Passing the tents of the Earl of Chester, I heard them carousing and boasting of the men they would kill.

As I approached my quieter and more contemplative camp Sir William asked, "Lord, I have not fought in a battle such as this. How will it go?"

I waved a hand at the darkness lit by so many flickering fires that the frost seemed to sparkle. "The site means that there is little opportunity for a flanking move. The dyke protects one flank and we know that Stephen now has fewer horses than he did. We will advance upon each other and slog it out. When they fight, it will be knight against knight and they will be pressed close. There will be little opportunity for skill. It will be the strength of your arm, your

weapon and your armour which decides the day. Our task is
to watch in case the enemy breaks through or to see a
weakness in their lines. If they do then we attack."

"We have less than forty horsemen, lord. What difference
can we make?"

"You forget Dick and his archers. When we advance then
they will too and when we charge, their arrows will range
ahead of us and make our attack more effective. Dick and his
men double our strength. Besides, we do not attack a whole
line; we either plug a dyke or exploit a hole. We will be
enough."

He nodded, "I hope that I may prove to be worthy."

"You have proved it already, Sir William. My men and I
would now lie dead had you and your men not held the road
for us as you did."

After he had retired I went to the horse lines. Lion looked
content. I had not owned him long but already I felt the
connection that would make us a single fighting machine. He
understood my slightest move. He would respond to a nudge
of my knee or the flick of a spur, in a battle that could make
all the difference. I stroked his mane and whispered,
"Tomorrow we shall see your true heart. Tomorrow we go to
war." He nodded his head as though in agreement. I patted
his neck and I retired. I had done all that I could. It was now
in the hands of God.

We woke and prepared for the battle in darkness. Edgar
made sure that all my men ate. Wulfric had drilled that into
him. Who knew how long the battle would be? The horses
were fed with grain and watered. We walked them to our
position. Dawn brought a cold and grey day. I hung the mace
I had captured from my cantle. I had my sword, a dagger and
a short sword. Along with my spear, I was as well armed as I
could be. I allowed Rolf to nuzzle me as I gave him the
gnarled apple I had found in one of the deserted huts. He
swallowed it in one. Then he raised his head up and down.
"Today, we must be as one!"

We watched as the three battles formed up before us. The
Earl's looked the most colourful as the front rank was filled
with the banners of the great lords who supported the

Empress. The dour Welsh infantry to the right looked plain by comparison. My eyes were drawn to the enemy. I saw that Stephen had dismounted most of his knights. They would fight on foot. The two flanks were a mix of horsemen and infantry. The left of the enemy line was commanded by William of Aumale while their right by Alan of Brittany. As with all such battles, it took some time to get into position. We did not mount while they moved into place. The weakness of both armies was the lack of archers. Had I been the Earl then a third of my men would have been archers but there looked to be perilously few. It was too late to worry about that for we could do nothing about it.

We were close to the rear ranks of the army. Dick and his men planted stakes in the ground for protection as the two behemoths closed with each other. Then they remounted.

As the army advanced to meet the enemy, who stood and waited, we advanced too. I wanted to be as close to the fighting as I could in case we were needed. Then Earl Robert made his first mistake. He did not use his archers to weaken the enemy. He should have halted and loosed his arrows but he did not. I saw then Stephen's plan. He was emulating Hannibal. His strong centre would not move but his mobile flanks would. William of Aumale and Alan of Brittany charged the Welsh!

I felt as though I had the power to see into the future for I could see what would happen. I turned, "Dick, dismount and prepare to loose your arrows."

He knew me well. He might not know what was going to ensue but he trusted me. "Aye, lord!" He and his men had already planted more stakes in the ground behind them in anticipation of having to dismount and they tied their horses to them and then strung their bows.

"Richard, stand behind the archers and let my banner fly!"

We were closer to the right flank for that was where I had feared the enemy would break through. I saw the horsemen of William of Aumale strike the Welsh infantry. He was an experienced knight and his men were well trained. Their lances were held by knights who were knee to knee. Archers sent arrows from behind the knights and they struck the

Welsh line. Men fell and it was no longer a solid wall of shields and spears. There were gaps. When the line of horsemen hit it, there was a sound like a blacksmith striking iron. Then I heard the cries of death. The frozen ground meant that the horses were travelling quickly. I saw the banners of Aumale and his men as they bowed and bent the Welsh line and drove deeply into it. It was like a branch of a tree. It bent until it could bend no more and then it snapped. The Welsh broke as the knights broke through the front ranks and into the heart of it.

"Ready, Dick!"

He had seen what I had seen and he nodded. "Aye, lord."

"Mount!" My men, already in our lines, mounted our horses.

The Welsh ran not along the dyke for they feared the icy waters but flowed between the earl's undamaged battle and my men. William of Aumale and his men pursued them. The stakes which my archers had planted afforded some protection. They channelled the fleeing Welsh and meant any horsemen could not attack my archers. As soon as the enemy horse were in range Dick shouted, "Release!" Their arrows fell amongst the knights. They were no longer a solid line and both horses and knights fell. It was only one or two who fell but it slowed the advance. To the left of us, I saw that the other two battles had joined with their enemy and the lines there ebbed and flowed. The dismounted battle of Stephen held the knights of the Earl. It was this right flank that would decide the outcome.

"Prepare!" We had to stop the horsemen or else they would turn and attack the flank of the Earl's men. If they broke then it would be the end of the battle. As Dick's archers got into their stride and released more arrows, so more of the horsemen fell. I heard the Welsh knights trying to rally the fleeing Welsh foot. We had to strike at that moment. A charge from us might rally the Welsh.

"For God, England and the Empress! Charge!"

We were not a long line but we rode together, knee to knee. We struck William of Aumale's men on their shield side so that they could not strike a blow in return and we hit

them when they were already blown and spread out. I pulled
back my spear and punched as hard as I could at the white
shield with the red boar upon it. The knight's cantle only
held his front and rear. He tumbled from his horse and as
Rolf galloped over him, I heard the sickening crunch as his
skull was caved in. I pulled back my spear and looked for
my next target. A knight with a blue and yellow quartered
shield tried to turn his horse. He had shattered his spear
already and he faced me with a sword. In trying to turn he
stopped his horse. I was galloping and had a slight slope with
me. I punched forward and this time the spear caught the
edge of his shield and was then driven deep into his chest.
As he fell, the head of the spear was broken and I threw
away the broken end.

I heard a trumpet sound the recall and William of
Aumale's men began to withdraw. I knew it was his style. He
had been cautious at Northallerton. His men turned and
began to move back towards the city walls. I know not why
but many of the magnates and powerful men in Stephen's
army thought that signalled defeat and, incredulously, began
to flee. Some of Aumale's men joined them. Behind me, I
heard the Welsh cheer and they began to rally.

I halted to allow Rolf to rest and to assess the situation.
The magnates who had fled had allowed Prince Madog to
push back Alan of Brittany's men. But in the centre, the
dismounted men of Stephen still held the line. They were
solid and the horses of the Earl could not penetrate the steel
and wooden wall. Horses fell and formed a barrier
preventing more horses from approaching. Had I been Earl
Robert, I would have dismounted my men.

I saw Stephen himself as he wielded his axe. Horses and
knights fell before the Usurper. I had fought alongside him
and knew that he was neither a coward nor a poor warrior.
Even as I watched, I saw him take first one and then a
second knight with two mighty blows. Men fell back
reluctant to face certain death. It needed a champion to fight
him. I saw none for the Earl of Gloucester, our leader, was
not in the fore. He was, instead, directing his knights. His
squires rode to pass orders and to bring up more men from

170

the rear. I saw him look for me. I was not where he thought I would be. I was on his right and close to the enemy. Before me, William of Aumale was rallying his shattered column. His horses blown, he was dismounting his men. The Welsh were also reforming and preparing to advance.

I turned, "Dick, take your archers and harass the left flank of the enemy!"

He waved acknowledgement.

"Form line!"

We had some men who had fallen during the charge and we had a shorter line; however, some of the Welsh knights took it upon themselves to join with us. I raised my sword, "For God and the Empress! Charge!"

We headed obliquely towards the left flank of the huge block of men who were defending Stephen the Usurper. The knights were at the fore and we charged men at arms. Once again we charged shields. Their weapons were in their right hands. If they turned to face us then they would not support Stephen. As we neared, I pulled back on Rolf's reins and his huge hooves rose in the air. As I released him, they clattered and crashed down on the shields of some of the men at arms. I heard their cries and the crack as shields and arms were broken. As a gap was created, I leaned forward to cleave the skull of a knight in the second rank. My knights and men at arms had followed me and we began to make inroads into the side of this enormous column of men. I spied the Earl of Chester as he led his men forward to try to end the battle by killing or capturing Stephen. I had to turn my attention back to the men before me. Rolf's hooves cleared the ground once more and then I felt him tire. His flank was bloody from a sword thrust. Ahead I saw that the enemy soldiers were still in a solid mass. Our horses were tired. I had to do something differently.

I turned and shouted, "Richard!" I slipped my mace into my left hand and shouted, "Dismount!"

As I dismounted, I saw the Earl of Chester as Stephen's axe smashed his sword in two and the Earl was forced to fall back. Richard arrived, "Do you need Lion, lord?"

"No, we fight on foot. Take Rolf back and see to his hurts!"

"We are winning, lord!"

I shook my head. "Not so long as Stephen stands! Now retire!" I turned and shouted, "Stockton! On me!"

Sir William and his men were still mounted as were the Welsh knights. Their horses began to die as the men at arms, on foot, hacked and stabbed at weakened horses. It was time to fight on foot. Sir William began to have his men dismount. Some of the Welsh knights did the same and they joined my band.

"Form a wedge! Gilles, watch my back!"

"Aye, lord!"

There were less than twenty of us but we knew how to fight together. Sir John was on my left and Edgar guarded my right. Sir William and the Welsh saw us and augmented our numbers.

"Forward!"

Holding my shield before me and with my sword touching its top, we stepped together. We marched in time. We had done this before and knew each other's rhythm. I thrust my sword forward and it pierced the eye of a man at arms. As he threw himself back, the sword tore a hole in his face. Sir John brought his sword in a long sweep and hacked into the neck of a second. Günter the Swabian's two handed sword carved death to the right of Edgar. He used both hands to swing the sword and his shield hung loosely from his left arm. My men marched inexorably on. I heard the Welsh leader order his infantry, having rallied to form a mass of warriors behind and to the side of us. We were the cutting edge of a huge band of men. Out of the corner of my eye, I saw more men fleeing back into Lincoln. We were winning but so long as Stephen stood then we did not have the field. Men would die so long as his banner flew and he fought.

I felt a blow hit my shield as Baldwin Fitz Richard struck my shield with his mace. He was one of Stephen's most loyal knights and a worthy adversary. I brought my sword over my head and tried to strike at his neck. He brought up his shield to block the blow but it had such power that I saw him recoil.

Our wedge was now flattened into a line and my men were fighting individually. Only Gilles remained close to me. As Baldwin stepped back, I punched with my shield. In my left hand, I still held the mace and the power of the blow made Baldwin take another step back. He slipped in some entrails and slippery guts which lay behind him. As he struggled to keep his feet, I stabbed forward. He tried to bring his own shield around but he was too late and my sword severed some links in his mail and slid along his side. My sword came away bloody!

He regained his balance and raised his sword to strike me. Blood spurted from the wound I had made as he did so and the strike was weak. I blocked it with my shield and then swung my sword backhand across his middle. He brought his sword down and my blade broke it. "Yield, my lord! Or you will die. You have no sword."

He must have known that his wound would continue to bleed and he was weakening. He dropped to a knee he said, "I yield."

"Gilles, take care of this brave knight."

Stephen was still laying about him with his axe and the bodies of the knights he had slain littered the ground. Enough had died!

"Stockton! On me!"

The men who were close enough joined me and I led six of them towards Stephen. He had been forced backwards so that he was now directly ahead of me. As he slew another young knight, I hacked the head from a man at arms who bravely tried to block my advance. Edgar and Sir John slew a man at arms and wounded a knight who tried to stop me. My surcoat was well known. There were just six men between me and Stephen. "On my men! One more push!" Edgar and Sir John hacked and slashed. Günter still had the strength to swing his long sword in a wide arc. Wilfred and Gurth never tired. The last barrier to our enemy fell and with no more men between us, I shouted, "Stephen! Yield for you are defeated!" It should have been the Earl of Gloucester who made the offer but he was too far back from the fray.

The usurper swung his axe to take the arm from Sir Guillaume D'Aubigny. Stephen lifted his helmet. I could see that his face was drawn and he was tired, "You said it would be between us, Alfraed. I will not relinquish the crown. It is still atop my head."

I nodded, "I knew it would come to this. Then lay on, Stephen the Usurper, and we fight until the crown is finally fallen."

I sheathed my sword for he had an axe and I did not wish to risk blunting it more. I took my mace and advanced. He swung his axe. He had killed so many now that it was little better than a club. Even so, my arm shivered with the blow as it struck my shield. I brought the mace around in an arc. The blow was so powerful that even Stephen took a step back when it hit the top of his shield. He was a skilled warrior and he regained his balance and then swung his axe at me. Instead of blocking it with my shield, I swung my mace and the two weapons crashed together. The axe shattered and fell to the ground. I dropped the mace and drew my short sword. It was sharp. I still had my better sword.

Stephen drew his own sword. It was slightly longer than mine. I think he sensed an advantage for he stepped back as he started to swing. He would use the longer reach he had. It was a mistake for I was quick and I stepped forward and in two strides we were face to face. I rammed the hilt of my sword at his face and punched him. His head reeled as it hit his ventail. He tried to hit my shoulder with the pommel of his sword. I had a plate there and it did no harm. As he stepped back, he swung his sword and I blocked it with mine. He had to get further away to take advantage of his longer sword but the press of men behind him stopped him from doing so. I saw arrows flying overhead to fall amongst those at the rear of this column and knew that Dick was doing his job. If I could finish Stephen then the battle might be won.

Our swords rang together time and time again. When I saw the short sword begin to bend, I took a step back, thrust it into the ground and drew my long sword. The pommel had the blue stone which had been in King Harold's sword. The weapon always filled me with a sense of power and so it was again. Now we had weapons of equal length. We were both as skilled as each other. As I tried to stab him, he countered with his own sword. He tried to swing and take my head but I blocked with my shield. Around us, men died, were wounded or yielded but we fought on. Our swords rang together time and time again. Both our hauberks were torn and links broken. Our surcoats were bloodied and ripped. Our helmets were dented but still, we fought on.

I think it was my belief that I was in the right and that God was on my side and that of the Empress which determined the outcome. I brought the sword from behind me and I put every ounce of strength into the blow. Stephen countered with his own sword but it shattered in two. Before he could do anything more, I dropped my shield and putting my sword to his throat I tore his helmet from his head and shouted, "I have taken the King! Yield!"

Around us, those closest stopped fighting but they did not drop their weapons. It was as though time had stopped still.

I said, quietly so that only he could hear, "I do not wish to kill you for you have fought well but know that I will to avoid further slaughter and death. If you wish to live then surrender now!" I dropped his helmet to the ground.

He nodded and dropping to his knees shouted, "I yield. The field is yours Alfraed, Earl of Cleveland!" Then to me, he added quietly, "The crown has, indeed, fallen!"

Chapter 14

The Earl of Gloucester sent the Earl of Chester and his men to pursue those who had fled. I had Stephen escorted towards the castle by my men at arms. They had earned the right. Their bloodied surcoats and dented helmets told their own story. "Let us go, my lord. You have hurts and injuries. The Countess will have a healer." We marched proudly towards the gate of Lincoln Castle. I was anxious to see both my men and the Countess.

He rose and grimaced as he did so. "You have a powerful arm, Alfraed. I can see why you were so successful in the mêlée."

Richard rode up with our two horses. "Would you care to ride, my lord?"

"Thank you, Alfraed. It is somewhat more dignified than trudging." Stephen was aware of his appearance. A horse would give him some dignity.

We mounted and I led Stephen, the knight who had been King of England, through the gates and into Lincoln Castle. The fact that he rode beneath my banner gave me satisfaction. My men had performed heroically. They had done far more than most of those who had fought that day.

The Countess, flanked by my grinning men, greeted us in the inner bailey. "My husband is alive?"

I nodded, "He pursues the survivors through Lincoln's streets. Have you a healer? This lord is hurt."

She nodded, "If you would care to dismount..." I saw her about to say *'your majesty'* but she changed it at the last moment, "my lord."

176

He had the good grace to bow, "I shall have to get used to that, for a while at least." I dismounted too. "What are your plans for me, Alfraed?"

"I do not command. It is up to the Earl in the short term but, ultimately, the Empress. We will discuss this when the healer has finished with you."

As the Countess and her guards led him off, my men at arms and archers who had garrisoned Lincoln ran up to me, "My lord, we watched from the gate. You were Hercules this day!"

"Thank you, Cedric, but I ache in every muscle of my body! How was it within the walls?"

"The Countess is more like a warrior than many knights I have known, my lord, and yet she is so gentle. She helped the healer with those injured during the siege."

Oswald asked, "Was it our men who destroyed the siege engines?"

Richard said, "Need you to ask, Oswald? Of course, it was!"

Laughing, I said, "You must excuse Master Richard's cockiness, Oswald. He was wounded and now he is a veteran."

Richard flushed, "I am sorry, Oswald, I meant no offence."

Oswald shook his head, "You are a veteran, Master Richard. I can see it in your walk."

It was nighttime by the time the pursuit had finished. The captured knights were all brought into Lincoln so that they could be held until ransomed. I thought better of the Earl of Chester when the first thing he did was to embrace his wife. Robert of Gloucester was, once more, in a good mood.

"That was nobly done, Alfraed. Your charge was timely and your attack on the flank saved the day. I thank you."

It was a genuine gesture and I nodded. "The Usurper fought bravely."

"He did. He slew and wounded many knights before you tamed him. You are still my father's champion even after his death. Where is Stephen?"

"He had wounds. He is with the healer. He is guarded. He asked what was to be done with him."

"I have much to do here. What say you escort him to my sister? That is far from that harpy of a wife of his. Enough of his lords left the field. We still have enemies to deal with but we now hold Lincoln. The country is divided in two."

I looked over to the far corner of the hall where the Countess and her husband were closeted. "And the Earl; is his defection forgiven?"

"Given the result, I think so but we will watch him carefully in the future."

The evening proved to be a strange one. We had been trying to kill each other all morning and yet the former king chatted happily with the Earl of Chester, Robert of Gloucester and me. It was the code by which we lived. The other knights who had been ransomed were also feted. Baldwin Fitz Richard did not seem discomfited that I had wounded him. Sir William had also been wounded. I thought he should have stayed in his chamber but he was keen to be at the feast. He was pale and looked in pain. He had taken a sword thrust to the shoulder. I sat by him. For the young knight, this was an elevated company.

"I hope I did good service, my lord."

"You did, Sir William. The Earl of Chester is lucky to have you as one of his knights."

"I fear he will rid himself of me soon enough."

Dick had been listening, "If you lose his patronage, I would take your men and seek your fortune. Normandy has many opportunities for a landless knight."

Dick was right but I offered him another alternative, "If you need another, lord, I would happily have you as one of my knights. I have no manor yet but Sir John here has none and he seems happy enough."

Sir John said, "Lord, you do have a manor."

"What?"

"Liedeberge."

"Of course, I do. I had forgotten. Would you not wish it?"

"No, lord. I am happy to serve you and live in Stockton. It is my home."

Dick laughed, "Of course, that has nothing to do with Alf's comely daughter who flutters her eyes whenever you pass!"

He reddened and changed the subject. "Liedeberge needs a lord of the manor."

I nodded, "Yet I would not cause a rift between the Earl of Chester and myself. But if you leave his service, Sir William, I can offer you a manor." His face told me his answer. I turned to Sir John, "Have you told Alf of your interest in his daughter?"

"Lord, Dick is teasing. I..."

"A knight does not lie, especially to his lord. Answer me truthfully."

He hung his head and then said, "No, lord."

"Then speak to Alf. It is the honourable thing to do and he will be happy with the match." I smiled, "He will give you a fine dowry!"

Dick nodded, "And you will never need pay for mail or weapons again!" Dick was ever practical.

Three days later Stephen was well enough to travel and it was deemed that we could travel back to Gloucester. The Empress had been informed of the capture of her enemy. Before we left, the Countess of Chester took me to one side. "Thank you, Alfraed, for leaving your men to guard me. They were like rocks. They spoke highly of you. How did you learn to inspire such loyalty?"

"From my father and he learned it from my namesake who fought for King Harold." I held up the sword hilt. "This stone came from his sword. It is this which inspires me. It is a throwback to an earlier time. If I ever become arrogant, I think back to King Harold who lost it all because he did not have the control over his people that he needed. I will not make that mistake. I work hard to keep my people loyal."

"From what your men told me, you have no fears there. Take care, my lord. The Empress needs you more than you can know."

Her husband saw us and joined us. I had spoken little to him while we had been in the castle. I was not certain if he was avoiding me or if it was a coincidence. He put his arm protectively around his wife. "My lord, I am indebted to you. Had you, your men and Sir William not done what you did then the castle might have fallen and my wife held hostage. I am sorry for any offence I may have caused you in the past."

I nodded. "I am unimportant, Ranulf. I fight for the Empress and her son. We are close to victory but until she is crowned and free from attack, I shall not rest. Any offence you may have caused me is immaterial. So long as you are now committed to our cause is all that I ask."

"And I am. I beg you to ask her to confirm my brother as Earl of Lincoln. I pray you will support him."

"I will do so but I hope that you are less high handed with the citizens of these towns. It was they who invited Stephen here."

"I know. I have much to learn and you are a good example." He pointed to Sir William who was chatting to Sir John. "As a gesture of friendship, I understand that Sir William has attached himself to your knights. I do not object. If he can serve you then I am happy."

"Thank you, Earl, I would not have done anything behind your back."

"That is known throughout the land. Your word and your honour are as renowned as your skills with sword and lance. You are still undefeated. I could not come close to Stephen but you despatched him with ease."

That was not true. It had been a hard battle but this was neither the time nor the place for such discussions. "We all lose some time, Earl. My day will come."

The Earl must have spoken with Sir William for, as I left the inner bailey, he was waiting with my men. He looked apprehensive until I said, "The Earl has seen me. We will talk about your future as we ride."

We waited for Stephen to emerge with Robert of Gloucester. They came out with Baldwin Fitz Richard who had recovered somewhat. Stephen mounted his own horse which had been found in the town. His face was grim as was that of the Earl of Gloucester. They had had words. Baldwin said, "My ransom is coming, Earl." There was an implied question.

"Then you may leave when it reaches the Countess." I turned to Maud. "I will fetch it myself, my lady. I may, it seems, be able to return north sooner rather than later."

She nodded, "I pray so, lord, for you work tirelessly."

The journey to Gloucester was a dangerous one. Despite the fact that Stephen had surrendered and would not try to escape, it would not prevent his friends from attempting a rescue. We travelled as though going to war with scouts ranging far ahead. With all of my men back with me, I felt more comfortable. We did the journey in three days. Already warned of our arrival, the Empress had everything ready for us. There were quarters for Stephen and guards to take over our duties. The Empress and her cousin hurried indoors.

Sir John asked, "Is that it, lord? Is it over?"

"I know not. The Empress has yet to be crowned. London is still a supporter of Stephen. Then there is the problem of the Church. Henry of Blois is still an important figure in the clergy. Let us say I will still have Gilles keep my sword sharp."

I did not have the chance to speak with Matilda for some time. The feast which was held was a public place and the Empress and her court celebrated our victory well. She caught my eye a couple of times and smiled but that was all. I rose early, before dawn, and was taking the chill morning air when Judith found me, "My lord, the Empress would speak with you."

I went to her chambers. She embraced me, "Thank you, Alfraed. You have given me the crown. My cousin told me what you did. It speaks well of you that your enemy whom you defeated speaks so highly of you."

"I swore an oath to your father."

"This went beyond a word given to a dead king. You and I know that. And now I make another demand of you."

"Command and I shall obey!"

"No Alfraed, this is not a command. I need you and a small group of your men to escort me secretly to Winchester. There I need to speak to Henry of Blois, the Bishop of Winchester."

"Stephen's brother."

"They had a falling out when we held peace talks. I need the support of the church and Henry is the papal legate now. If he can sway the clergy then I can be crowned."

"When do we leave?"

She laughed, "Would that all of my knights were as steadfast as you, Alfraed! I would leave now before the house is up."

"Then I will choose my men."

They did not ask why they were roused so early; they obeyed. I took Sir John, Dick, Gilles, Theobald, Wilfred and Rafe. The rest I left under the command of Edgar. We left as the sun rose ahead of us. It was a bitterly cold day and the Empress and Margaret were well wrapped in furs. I knew from old that they were both good riders but I had Wilfred and Gilles stay close to them. Rafe ranged ahead.

As we rode I discovered that young Henry had been sent back to Anjou. The Count had asked for him. He wished to train him for war. I had wanted to do that but I took heart from the fact that my son William would be helping to make him into a knight and a warrior. When a flurry of sleet and rain flew into faces, all conversation stopped and we huddled together on the road. The inclement weather meant that we travelled unobserved.

I was unsure of the welcome we might receive from the brother of the man we held prisoner but the Empress seemed confident. Nonetheless, I made sure that our weapons were to hand as we approached the gates of the Bishop's palace in Winchester. We waited outside with the rain still finding its way through layers of clothing. Part of me was excited about being here. This had been Harold Godwinson's capital. My father and namesake had walked these streets. This was my first visit; it had been something I had anticipated since I had arrived in England. I did not think it would be under these circumstances but I took comfort from the fact that no matter how politics and treachery insinuated themselves into our world, in the end, we still remained England. The Normans had come and displaced Harold but I was proof that the English were resilient. It was only the lords who spoke

Norman; all else spoke English. I had to believe in a future which was England.

We were admitted to the hall. Rafe and Wilfred slept in the stable with the horses. They would be content. They had endured worse. We were taken into the hall. Henry of Blois could have been the double of his brother. I had met Theobald but never Henry. Although a man of the church, he was also a political animal. It had been he who had secured the throne for Stephen. He had organised and manipulated the Archbishops and Bishops to anoint the usurper as king. Now I knew why the Empress had come.

He gave a slight bow and smiled. The smile was on his lips and not in his eyes. "My lady and the Earl of Cleveland. I am honoured."

Matilda was not taken in by his false smile, "Your Grace, I seek an urgent conference with you... in private."

The smile left his face and he nodded, "Come with me."

I turned to join my knights when she said, "No, my lord. I need you with me."

As I turned I saw the frown crease the Bishop's face and then he smiled, "As you wish, my lady!"

He led us to a small room. It was guarded and it was comfortably furnished. I guessed this was his meeting place. We sat and he poured some wine. The Empress was about to drink until I put my hand on hers.

The Bishop looked confused and then he nodded. He drank some. "You are cautious, Earl, but you do not think I would stoop to murder, do you?"

I drank some and said, "I was in Durham not long ago where I saw a Bishop murdered by poison. The murderer would be Bishop now."

"That was shocking but Cumin will never be Bishop. Pope Innocent has decreed it so." He shook his head, "First poor Rufus and then Thurstan. We have lost two great leaders."

"And that is why I have come to you, Bishop. You are now the leading churchman in England." He nodded as the Empress spoke and sipped his wine. His eyes never left her face. "Your brother has been defeated and is now a prisoner in my hall. I would be crowned."

"I heard that Stephen was defeated. The word is that it
was the Earl of Cleveland who finally felled him. You are
ever my brother's Nemesis, my lord."

"All that I do is to ensure that King Henry's wishes are
observed. He did not wish Stephen to be king."

"He did not wish civil war either."

The Empress' voice cut through this sparring. "That is the
past, my lords! We speak of the present and the future. Can
you have me anointed as Queen?"

"There are many who would wish my brother to be king
still. It would not be easy."

She nodded, "What would make it easier?"

"Perhaps if one person was given charge of the Church
then a strong hand might guide the bishops to the correct
decision."

"That might work. Who would you suggest? Nigel of
Ely?"

"Nigel is a good man but some might think he was too
closely associated with your cause, my lady. I think we need
someone who is not as close to you."

"Someone like yourself."

He spread his hands. "As the brother of the former king if
I supported your cause then it would give the council more
impartiality."

"It would. If I give you the power over the church in
England, you would support my cause?"

"I am the only one the Pope recognises in the land. There
is no other."

"Then we have an agreement."

"You have made a wise decision, my lady. I will hold a
council before Easter." She nodded. He turned to me. "You
are quiet, my lord, does it not meet with your approval?"

"When the Empress is crowned and my work is done then
I will approve until then I remain suspicious. I have learned
to be so while protecting the Northern Marches."

He looked me in the eye and said, firmly, "I swear that I
will do as I have promised. The Empress will be anointed,
Queen."

It was my turn to smile, "When that is done then I shall be in your debt and I will be able to return to my valley and my people. I prefer their honesty."

"Alfraed!"

"No, my lady, he is right. We have less honesty than ordinary folk. It is the world into which we are born. I envy the Earl. He has managed to avoid such entanglements and political affiliations. He has stayed true to his cause and few others can say that."

We rode back the next day. Stephen had been told that we had been visiting Wallingford and knew nothing about the arrangement which we had made. On the way back the Empress had told me that she was moving Stephen to Bristol which was better placed to house a royal prisoner. The former king did not seem surprised at this and it was my responsibility, once again, to escort him there.

He was in better humour on that short journey than he had been on the journey from Lincoln. I think he had come to accept his position. "You will be glad to get back to your home in the north, eh Earl?"

"I will. The wars in the south have made it a more dangerous place. The Palatinate is now Scottish, as are most of the borderlands. When you gave away Carlisle, it hurt us badly. It did not just drive the Earl of Chester to our side it put a Scottish dagger to our throats." I shook my head, "I know not why you did it, my lord! We had trounced the Scots at Northallerton. They were in disarray. Had I had a larger army then I could have walked in and taken the land as far north as Edinburgh. Men died because of your mistake."

"Those are hard and painful words to hear."

"It is still the truth, my lord, and I only speak from my heart."

"Which you plainly wear on your sleeve. Your loyalty to both the Empress and her father's wishes is extraordinary. I would that I was served by such loyal men." He laughed, "I wish you had stayed in the north. Those lands would be safer and I would have won at Lincoln."

"No, lord, you would not have won."

"I would not have lost and I would not now be in this position."

"On that, we can be agreed."

As we saw Bristol Castle loom up Stephen said, "I looked at this castle four years since with a thought to capture it. I saw then it cannot be taken. Not without a great loss of life." I heard in his voice, resignation. He would not be rescued.

"It is the first time I have seen it and I agree. The Empress said, however, that it is both comfortable and well used for royal prisoners such as yourself."

"And that is a great consolation," he said wryly.

He would have his own servants in the castle and the freedom of the grounds. He was lucky. When I returned to Gloucester, the Earl of Gloucester had arrived. He had serious news. "Queen Matilda, Stephen's wife, is raising an army in the south-east. It seems she is as strong a woman as the Countess of Chester and my sister. What is it about women named Matilda?"

"Then I am not free to return north to my lands, lord?"

"That is for my sister to decide but I would feel more comfortable with you here. Besides, the north is quiet and you have left a large army there."

That was little consolation to me. Now that I had Sir William and his men, I sent Sir John back to Stockton with half of my men at arms and half of my archers. They would take back the ransoms and treasure which awaited us at Lincoln. The Empress might need me but my valley needed my men.

Chapter 15

We hunted when possible and we sheltered indoors when the weather was inclement. I took Sir William to Liedeberge where I established him as my constable. I rode my new manor and I returned to Gloucester. I fretted and grew fractious. As March drew to a close, the Empress sent for me. "My lord, you are like a caged animal. I pray you to ride to Wallingford and see how Fitz Count is. The journey may clear your mind."

I could tell she was worried, "What worries you, Empress?"

"The Archbishop of Canterbury is proving unwilling to attend the conference. He does not support the Bishop of Winchester. They are travelling west to speak with Stephen."

"Then send me, instead, to Bristol. I can report what they say."

"That might be better but I pray you do not inflame the situation. I need to be crowned."

"I will be as ice, my lady."

I took all the men I had left with me. I did not want to intimidate the prelate but I wanted Stephen to be honest. He was surprised at my arrival. "I thought I had seen the last of you, Alfraed. Why are you not back in your valley?"

"The Empress and her brother asked me to stay. I hunt!"

He laughed, "And that sits not well with you. Well, I shall enjoy your company. I grow bored here. Perhaps we might try a bout or two with swords."

"Perhaps. We will ask your gaoler."

"He will not mind."

"Then I will arrange for the practice swords to be made ready. Are your wounds healed?"

"Enough to practise at any rate."

Despite his recent injuries and wounds, we had a good bout. Both of us were sweating by the end. He had, however, failed to strike a blow on me. "Your hands were always the quickest I had ever seen. I thought age might have slowed you down."

"I practise every day with my men at arms. They keep me sharp."

He nodded, "I notice that you do not surround yourself with knights. Why men at arms? Are hired swords better?"

"Mine are not hired; they are oathsworn."

"I have not heard that for many a year."

"It goes back to my father's time. The Saxons held the concept dear. His oathsworn left the service of the Emperor to follow him to England."

"Perhaps I would be better served by those than the ones who fled."

"Your knights did not flee. It was those you had bought; the great and the mighty."

"That is as cruel a blow as any you struck in the battle."

"Yet it remains the truth. You cannot buy men's hearts, you must win them."

The Archbishop, when he arrived with Henry of Blois, looked at me suspiciously. I smiled, "The Empress asked me to come to see things were well done, my lord."

The Archbishop looked to Stephen, "Do you object, your majesty?"

"No, the Earl may stay. He is as honest as men say he is."

There were just the four of us in the antechamber. No cleric recorded the words although all knew of what we spoke later on. The Archbishop began, "The Bishop of Winchester is holding a council at Winchester to ask that we support the claim of Matilda to be the ruler of England. What say you to that?"

Stephen did not appear to bear his brother any animosity. He smiled and spread his arms, "It seems, your grace, I have little choice in the matter. I am the prisoner of my cousin. I was defeated."

"I am afraid that I must press you, your majesty. We swore fealty to you. I cannot in all conscience see how we can swear fealty to another."

Stephen glanced at me and gave me a wry smile. He knew what I was thinking. Many had sworn fealty to Matilda while the king was alive and had reneged on that oath. He said, "Given my present position, I release all from the oath of fealty they took."

"All?"

"All, your grace."

And that was it. The council would confirm that Matilda could be crowned and the nobles could swear an oath to her. It seemed the war was over. I could go home.

When I told the Empress the news, the relief on her face was palpable. The Earl too was delighted. "This insidious war is now a step closer to being over. This is good news. The Council meets at Easter. That means we can have the coronation in June."

"My brother we must move cautiously. Queen Matilda is rallying an army and it is close to London. I will write to Geoffrey de Mandeville and ask for his advice."

I shook my head, "My lady, I would not put anything on parchment. It would be better to send a messenger."

She nodded, "I can see the wisdom in that. Fitz Count would seem a wise choice. He is honest; some say that he could be a priest. I will send to him and ask him to speak with de Mandeville."

"My lady, I beg permission to travel back to Stockton. I will be in London in June for the coronation but I have been away for a long time. The Scots will be becoming restless. In addition, Durham and York are now less secure than they were."

She nodded, "On your way north, I pray you to speak with Fitz Count and ask him to join me here. It will do him good to be free of the chains that bind him to Wallingford."

My men were also pleased to be heading home. Their own beds were rough and ready but they were their beds. We all missed the familiar. We stayed the night with Brian Fitz Count. As we ate in his Great Hall, he confided in me, "My lord, I feel I have done enough in this war. Now that peace looms I have a mind to join a monastery. I have had enough of war and of the petty desires of man. I should spend time contemplating God."

He was older than I was and I could understand his desire for peace but the cloistered world of a monastery did not appeal. As we spoke it became clear that this was not a sudden whim. He had been thinking about it for some time. He was a great warrior but he was kind and had the sort of mind which thinks about his fellow man. Such warriors were rare.

"When the Empress is crowned then it may be the time for all of us to assess our lives. For me, I cannot think of such things so long as the Scots threaten my people. With the war over, Wallingford can return to more peaceful pastimes. This is a green and fertile valley."

"It is, my lord, it is! But my mind is made up. When the Empress is crowned and the land is at peace then I will choose the road to peace and salvation."

As I headed to Lincoln, I found it sad that he should feel that way. I understood him but I had duty running through me like the blood in my veins. Ranulf, Earl of Chester, was in Derby and I spent the night in the castle speaking with the Countess. "I am pleased that this war will soon be over. I know that, thanks to you, we did not suffer as much as we might have but that was bad enough. Your men do you credit."

As I left the next morning I said, "The Empress is beholden to you, as am I. If you ever need my help then send a rider to my castle. I promise that I will come."

She stood on her toes to kiss my cheek, "You are a good man and your wife was lucky. Take care in the north, your war, I fear, is not yet over!"

With Stephen defeated and his allies now concentrating in the southeast, we had an easier journey north. Normally the weather worsened as we headed to our valley but this time it actually improved. I hoped that it boded well for the meeting of church leaders. I knew of the arrangement made by the Empress and Henry of Blois but to those outside, it would have looked as though the issue was in doubt.

We rode through York's gates. I had not done so since before the Battle of the Standards. The Earl of York, William of Aumale, was with Queen Matilda along with his knights. There was just a town watch on the walls. Had I so chosen, I could have taken it with the men I had. I had gold in my saddlebags and there were items I wished to buy. There were many goldsmiths in York and I had a mind to buy something for Alice. She asked for nothing but she made my hall a family home. I also took the opportunity of speaking with some of the merchants and made urgent purchases. When Archbishop Thurstan had been alive, we had been able to trade with the city. Now I intended to subvert whichever Archbishop was appointed to replace him. The merchants knew that we had gold and they would trade with us. With Helmsley in my hands, I arranged to use that as the conduit through which trade goods would come.

After leaving York I travelled to Helmsley to speak with Wulfric. I told him the outcome of the victory; peace. He was aggrieved to have missed the battle. That was his way. "What now, my lord? Would you have me abandon Helmsley and Pickering?"

"No. I would keep hold of them until the coronation. It is only in June. I will travel down to London and attend the ceremony. Then we will truly have peace. However, in the time before I have to leave, I wish to travel north to Durham. I have a message to deliver to Cumin. I would like you and some of your men to accompany me."

"I will and gladly and Sir Gilles?"

"Bring him too. I would make a show of force. It may be that the enemy hears of the peace and decides to grab manors before the Empress can act."

All of us were happy to see Stockton's sturdy walls and we stepped off the ferry with a spring in our step. News of our arrival had preceded us and Dick and those who had brought our treasure back were there to greet us. "So, my lord, we have peace."

"We do, Sir Harold. We will have a week while our horses recover and then I intend to take our men north to Durham. We will deliver an ultimatum to Cumin and then I travel to the New Castle. I wish Prince Henry to know that I have not forgotten the death of Sir Hugh Manningham."

"You have not tired of war then?"

"Of course I tire of it but the moment we stop being vigilant is when our enemies will flood the valley."

I took John and Alice to one side. I gave Alice the necklace I had bought for her. She burst into tears. "It is just a little something to show you that we appreciate all that you do."

"Thank you, my lord."

"I wish a feast in two days' time. I would like Alf and his family to attend along with Father Henry."

"Alf?"

I smiled, "He is the leading man in the town and besides, I have another motive. I wish the wine and beer to flow. The knights who came with me deserve the honour. I wish the same food provided for my archers and men at arms in the warrior hall. They deserve no less." I saw John frown, "Forget the expense. We have just taken more ransom than in all our previous encounters. We have coin, John. Let us reward those who earned it."

"Aye, lord. You are right."

I went to speak with Aiden and his falconers. We walked by the river. "You have ridden my land while I have been gone?"

"Aye, lord."

"And?"

"There are few outlaws living in the forests and the ones who do take but a few animals. They harm not the people. Your men at arms have been scouring the manors. We headed further north and the land is quiet."

"I would have you travel as far north as the New Castle. Speak with those who work the fields and the land. They know if something is afoot." I handed him a bag of coins. They were small ones. "They have just paid their taxes and money will be short. Spread this around and see what you can discover."

"What is it you wish to learn, lord?"

"What are the plans of the Scots."

"We will be back within the week."

"Do not worry about the time. I am back now. I feared that something would occur while I was away. I am content."

Aiden and his men slipped silently from my castle and only I knew that they were gone. After the death of Sir Hugh Manningham and his family and scout, I worried more than I might have but I was confident in Aiden's skills. While in York I had bought more of the cloth I used for surcoats. I needed new ones. Many of my men did too. I had felt somewhat underdressed when in the company of the knights of the west. Alice paid some local women and they made up our new surcoats. When the feast was held, we would look smart. As Henry Fitz Empress had returned to Anjou, I decided to shave my face. To be truthful, it itched. Most of my knights had beards but I had grown up in the east and was used to being clean-shaven. Adela had liked that. When I had bathed and shaved, I felt like a new man.

Before the feast, I took Sir John to one side. "I have not forgotten what I learned from Dick. I have invited Alf and his family this night for a purpose. You will be seated close by our smith; speak with him!"

"But lord!"

"We have one life to live, John. If you wish to be with Alf's daughter then begin that as soon as you can. I regret the months I waited before I married my Adela and she was taken from me too soon. Alice's husband, Tom, was taken from her. We have peace now but who knows how long it will last."

"Very well, lord. You have raised me almost as a son and I will heed your words but I am afraid."

I laughed, "A knight who faced the might of Stephen's army and did not blanch fears speaking with a blacksmith?"

He nodded, "It sounds foolish but it is how I feel."

"Alf is a good man and, believe me, he will be delighted."

Before he had left for his mission, Aiden and his scouts had hunted four fine deer. When time allowed I would hunt the wild boar but the venison would do. John had had many chickens slaughtered. The *'Adela'* had been back in port a number of times while we had been away; she had even docked in the Severn and delivered messages for me. The result was we had plenty of wine and spices. The feast would be worthy of our victory.

I sat at the head of the table. Alice had refused my invitation to join us. But John, my Steward, had accepted my invitation. I sat between Wulfric and Edward. The two old friends bantered back and forth across me. They questioned me about each stroke and action in the battle of Lincoln. From their questions, I deduced that they had spoken with Dick and John and wished confirmation of what they had heard.

"It will be strange to have peace, with Stephen I mean. I know that we still have the Scots to worry about but when the Empress becomes Queen, she can order William of Aumale to aid us. We can recapture Carlisle and the New Castle."

"It will not be as easy as that. There will be much bad feeling. William of Aumale was driven from the field by our men. He will not forgive so easily. However, the ending of hostilities means that we can reduce our garrisons in the south and increase those of Norton, Barnard and Piercebridge. We raised vast sums from ransom. I intend to use that money to build up our forces. In the autumn, I will have Erre travel to Frisia again. Now that the new King of France is trying to take Blois, I fear our source of men from Anjou will shrink."

As the wine and beer flowed and the food stripped from the bones, the noise level grew. I did not mind. They had all deserved it. However, the sudden roar from Alf was so loud that it silenced my hall. I turned and watched as the blacksmith picked up Sir John and almost crushed him, "My daughter is to marry a knight! This is a great day!"

I saw Dick nod towards me, "He just needed a push, my lord."

The celebrations became even louder. Alf's wife, Anne, cried and poor Sir John looked embarrassed. Father Henry said, "This is good, my lord. The town needs a wedding."

"If I am to be there...." I would not promise something I could not deliver. I might be in London.

"This is vital, lord!"

"Then it should be before or after June. I will be needed in London for the Coronation of the Queen."

He frowned, "If the Bishops agree."

I smiled enigmatically, "Oh, they will agree."

He looked puzzled, "Then I will speak with Alf and Sir John."

"I will provide the food. Both Alf and Sir John have done me great service and I would reward them."

He sipped his wine, "It seems to me that you should have some reward, my lord. From what your men tell me, the Empress would not have the crown but for you."

"I have my reward, Father. It is in the faces of each one of those who live in my castle and my manor. I am content."

There were thick heads the next day. Mine was not among them. I left my castle early to walk through my streets. The town was already busy for my people were productive. Alf's forges were silent and unlit but the tanners and wool spinners were at work already. I knew that upstream, just beyond my wall, the mill would be grinding the grain that would make the bread that was already in the ovens. Life went on no matter what happened in the outside world. I passed the fletchers. They already had bundles of arrows ready for Dick. They had defended my walls against the Scots and Stephen the Usurper. They knew how important their job was. As I reached the church, it made me think that the clergy would already be gathering in Winchester to decide the Empress' fate. Here, Father Henry was preparing for his Easter services. The church would be filled with garlands of spring flowers and blossom; the elder and the cow parsley, may and early wild roses.

I knelt in the empty and peaceful church by the grave of my wife and daughter. I prayed for their souls. With eyes closed, I asked my dead wife if I had done as she would have wished. There was silence but it was a comforting silence. After a while, calm and at peace, I left the church and walked along the river. Fishermen were in their boats. Some would head further downstream while others would head to the fish traps upstream. They waved as they passed. My standard, flying from my gates and towers told them that the Earl was returned; I was home.

John had many tasks for me. There were sessions to be held; land disputes to be judged and finances to be decided. The taxes had been collected. Now that the war was over, we would see a return of the queen's tax collectors but that would not be until the next year. I wondered about the coins. With Stephen no longer King, who would mint the coins the people used? Here in the north, I had John's father minting the coins we used in the valley. They were highly regarded for they were of true value. We used no base metal to increase our profits. The coining of the new queen's coins was not my worry; I was a warrior and my care was war.

As John and I worked, the castle came to life. Those who had travelled long distances such as Wulfric and Philip left first. Hugh of Gainford had not travelled. His wife was with child again. I would visit with him. Erre and Edward, along with Sir Richard of Yarm, were the last to leave. They would each be home within an hour of leaving. All knew that we would be campaigning again soon but as I had only taken Dick and Sir John with me, they did not mind, in fact, they relished the opportunity. War was what they did and brought profit for we were successful.

When I had been in York, I had paid old Isaac the Goldsmith to send me any news which reached the city. Four days after Easter a rider arrived with a letter. It brought the news that the church had accepted Matilda as the Lady of England and Normandy. Once she was crowned then my work would be done. The coronation would be in June or July; old Isaac had been unclear on the date. There had been no official proclamation. I would have to wait until Sir William, who was close to the Empress, sent me word.

My thoughts seemed to be prescient for even as Isaac's messenger left and I began to think of my trip to London on the *'Adela'*, Aiden and his men rode through my gates. Their faces told me that they had news.

Chapter 16

I led them up to my hall. Sir Tristan, Sir Harold and Sir John knew of their errand and, along with Dick, they followed to listen to my scouts' news. Aiden began without preamble, "The men who preyed on the people of Durham are no longer there, lord. They are now north of the Tyne. The Scots are ridding themselves of any who do not swear allegiance to King David and his son. We passed whole villages of corpses. The foxes and the crows grow fat and bold."

"And what of Durham?"

"It seems, from what we heard, that King David is no longer a supporter of Cumin. The priest we spoke to said that the Pope had refused to sanction his appointment. He squats, like a toad, within Durham's walls."

"But he does not hurt those who live in the Palatinate?"

"He taxes them and extracts coins as though he was trying to draw blood from a stone. The people are hungry but they live."

"Thank you, you have done well."

"There is one thing more, lord. We travelled to Hexham. All of Sir Hugh's family are now dead. His wife died, it is said, of a broken heart and his sons were hunted down like animals and slain. Many of his men live as outlaws in the wild forests by the wall."

"You met them?"

"We met them. They begged you to bring aid to them."

"When you have rested, I would have you return and tell them that any who wish it can serve with me. When the

Empress becomes the Queen of England, I will lead her armies north to rid the land of this Scottish plague and there will be a lord of the manor at Hexham."

Sir Harold, who had been an outlaw himself, asked, "What do we do now, lord? Do we wait for the coronation and then go with the support of England and her queen?"

Sir Tristan nodded, "That would be the wise thing to do, lord."

"It would be wise and it would only mean a delay of three or four months but I have been tardy by almost a year. Sir Hugh and his family were slain before I went south to aid the Empress. It is the people who suffer. That is what you said, Aiden, is it not?"

"Aye, lord. The ones who prosper are the Scots whom Prince Henry draws into our land."

"Then we do that which is not wise but which is right. We ride with all the knights that I can muster. We take men at arms and we take archers. We show Prince Henry that this land is not his. The tide has turned and will sweep the Scots back across the Tweed where they belong!"

My knights banged the table and made such a racket that Alice and John burst in to see what the commotion concerned.

"Fear not, my knights are just pleased that we ride north. We leave in two days' time, John. Dick, have your men ride to my knights. I want them to gather at Barnard Castle three days from now. I do not want their castle's garrisons. I only want mounted men. We ride swiftly."

The castle became a maelstrom of activity. Alf's forges became white-hot as new weapons were sought and bought by men richer thanks to the battle in Lincoln. Had I wished, I had enough gold from my ransoms to buy three new hauberks. I would wait. My ship arrived the day after Aiden had returned. There were six new men and many goods. I spent an hour with William of Kingston and John, my Steward. I dictated letters for the Empress and my son. Before he returned to his ship I said, "I need you back here by the middle of June so that I can attend the coronation of the Empress."

"I cannot make the winds, lord."

"Then do not go to Anjou. Your priority is to take a message to the Empress. I need her to know what I do."

"I will find her, lord, and I shall be back here by the end of the first week in June. You have my word on that."

I am a man of action and the long days planning our campaign actually gave me energy. It was as though I had a new lease of life. This was not politics and private arrangements made behind sealed doors. This was doing something meaningful; this was giving hope to those who had none. This was doing something which was right. I led a mighty host north. When last I had travelled north, I had led two hundred men. Now the number, when we collected Sir Hugh and Sir Philip, would be nearer three hundred. Although we only had twelve knights and their squires, we had over a hundred men at arms and a hundred and forty archers. For the first time in a long time, I had both Dick and Sir Philip's archers. No matter who we met, they would be my most powerful weapon. Had we had more at Lincoln then the battle would have ended sooner.

We had been at war so long and done this so many times that the preparations seemed simple. They were not but each man knew what they were doing. The servants who had accompanied us to Gloucester had the horses packed and ready to go in no time. We had more sumpters for the arrows we might need; it would not do to run out. We would be close enough to Barnard to resupply our food from there and we took the minimum amount required. The Tyne could be reached in a day from Stockton but I wanted to travel to the upper Tyne from Barnard Castle. I wanted to drive our enemies towards the New Castle from Hexham. I would avenge Sir Hugh first and destroy Hexham Castle. The Scots would not use it nor reap any benefit from Sir Hugh's hard work.

Aiden returned with a message from the men of Hexham. They would join us when the leaves fell. I knew what was in their minds. They could hurt their enemies while summer lasted. They were still Sir Hugh's men. When winter came and made their lives hard then they would join me. I was not

200

offended. I understood. I could not tell them I was coming to their aid but I hoped that they would join me before the autumn.

Sir Hugh and Sir Philip were ready with their men. Sir Philip had brought Father Thomas as a healer. I was glad; we needed someone to care for our men and a priest always made the men feel better about going into battle. I planned on leaving before dawn the next day. The days were lengthening and I would use the daylight.

It was just my knights who dined, that night, in Sir Hugh's Great Hall. They all waited expectantly as I began to speak. "Tomorrow we travel up through forests and the high land towards Hexham. I am not using the Roman Road. I know that is an easier route but I would be hidden from Prince Henry and his men. There are no castles between here and Hexham."

This was the route that Aiden had taken. When he had reported back, he had told me that the villages and farms were largely deserted. It would give us the chance to be invisible.

"We destroy Hexham first. I will not use men's lives to take that which was ours. We shall use fire and arrows. We will take all that we need to make a fire which will destroy the castle. Then we move down the Tyne valley to the New Castle and Prince Henry. By taking Hexham, we cut his lines of communication with Carlisle. He will know we are coming. I want him to bring his forces forth so that we may destroy them in a pitched battle. We cannot reconquer our land with the men we have but I want his grip loosened so that next year when we have the crown of England on the Empress' head, we can lead a mighty army north and drive the Scots hence."

It was what they wished to hear. We had seen at first hand the privations that the people had had to endure. Vengeance was in our hearts. We all went to bed and slept soundly knowing that we were all of one mind and what we did was right.

Sir Philip and his mounted archers rode north and west to lay an ambush on the road which ran along the wall between

Carlisle and the East coast. Dick and his archers headed
directly for Hexham and they blocked the road east. Hexham
was isolated.

I was grimly silent as we rode north. Sir Hugh had been
loyal unto death. He had first built and then held Hexham
against all of our enemies. He had been a rock. Sir Edward
knew me well. "Sir Hugh would not want this, my lord. He
died doing his duty."

"But he did not die in battle with a sword in his hand. That
was denied him. He was tricked and trapped and executed.
That is not the end for a warrior."

"Those days are passed, lord. That was what the pagans
believed."

"It is better to die fighting than to die bound like an
animal waiting for the butcher!" My tone ended the
discussion. I did not want to feel better. I needed to feel
absolved for having left Sir Hugh to his fate.

Despite the hills and the terrain, we made good time. We
were all well mounted. I saw Hexham Castle and the Priory
rise above the other buildings. We had been sighted for our
banners fluttered above us. I knew that the constable would
be bringing all the men he could from the town and manning
the walls. That was to be expected. I would give them a
chance to surrender. That was the honourable thing to do.

As we headed towards the castle, we met villagers fleeing.
They dropped to their knees when they saw us. "Do not harm
us, Warlord! The Earl of Northumbria threatened death if we
did not serve him."

"Go in peace. I do not make war on such as you. The day
of the Scottish invader is coming to an end. When I destroy
the castle then you can return to your homes." They scurried
away. "Sir Edward, send ten of your men at arms to relieve
Dick's archers. Sir Richard, send ten of yours to relieve Sir
Philip. We shall need our archers. Sir Wulfric and Sir Gilles,
take your men and make sure none leave by the north gate."

The gates were barred. Sir Hugh had built them and I
knew that they would be well made. Had the civil war not
begun then he would have made the towers on either side of
stone. As it was, it was a wooden castle. There was a double

ditch and, if they had had any sense, then it would have been well maintained and lined with traps. I had no intention of assaulting it. I rode to the outer ditch and took off my helmet. Richard rode behind me with my standard. I wanted them in no doubt who I was. Faces appeared on the wall.

"I am the Earl of Cleveland, Warlord of the North. This castle was treacherously taken from one of my knights, Sir Hugh Manningham. If you quit it now then you may leave and return to the Earl of Northumbria."

An older warrior with a white beard spoke, "I am Angus of Fife and I refuse your offer. Break your swords against these walls."

"Are there any women and children who have taken shelter within?"

"Aye."

"Then I will give them safe passage for your refusal to quit means that all within these walls will die. I take no prisoners."

He looked left and right. "I see no machines of war! Are you a magician?"

"I repeat, send out any who do not fight and I guarantee them safe passage and their lives."

"I will talk with my people."

Dick and Philip arrived. They went to the horses with the pig's bladders on them and began to prepare for the attack. The specially made arrows lay in bundles tied with red cloth. They had their fires burning and were ready and still, no one had come back to the wall. "Gilles, sound the horn!"

Gilles blew three strident notes on the old Roman buccina we used. The Scottish constable reappeared. "We will take you up on your offer but no tricks, my lord. There are four crossbows aimed at you already."

"I gave you my word. Do not make your death more painful than it needs to be by insulting me! Send them forth!"

I heard the bars being removed and the gates groaned as they were opened. A priest led the women, children and old men who appeared. It seemed that many were the villagers of Hexham and they had taken shelter within. The priest stopped when he drew close. "I pray you to keep your word, my lord." He had a Scottish accent.

"If you Scots kept your word then the world would be a better place. Those whom you lead are English and they know that I keep my word. If I were you then I would pray for the souls of those within for their leader has just signed their death warrant." I could see that he wanted to say more but my face made him think better of it. When he had gone I shouted, "You are brave men for you choose death over life." In answer, a flurry of bolts came my way. I had expected it. They had said they were aiming at me and my shield flicked up. The four bolts hit it. I heard a rush through the air and my archers sent arrows at the walls. Three of the crossbowmen fell dead. I backed Lion towards the safety of the houses behind which my men sheltered.

Just then I heard a cry and then a clamour of weapons to the north of the castle. Sir Harold smiled, "It seems our Scottish friends had fallen foul of Wulfric. He will be in better humour now that he has taken a few heads!"

"Are you ready, Dick?" He nodded, "Sir Philip?"

"Aye, lord."

"Edgar?"

My men at arms were in pairs and Edgar said, "Always, my lord!"

"Then begin!"

First, my archers began to rain arrows on the wall. We had brought plenty and they loosed five in rapid succession. The heads on the walls disappeared. As soon as they did, my men ran forward. One of each pair carried a large shield to protect the two of them while the other carried a pig's bladder filled with warm pig fat and a faggot of kindling. The kindling was bone dry and would fire quickly. They ran to the outer ditch. I had chosen my men because I knew they had the skills for this task. The pig's bladders were hurled and then the faggots. The pig fat was merely warm. It was why we would need the faggots. All of them were thrown at the gates. One or two of the defenders tried to raise their heads and use their weapons. They were slain. As soon as my men were back then half of our archers switched to fire arrows. They were less accurate than ordinary arrows and not all would work. We would be patient. As the first arrows flew, my men at arms picked up more pig's bladders and faggots.

Some of the arrows struck the gate and one or two fell short but the rest all struck home. The defenders must have thought that the arrows had failed for there was no sudden inferno. More arrows were sent and a plume of dense smoke rose. That aided the defenders for it meant my archers could no longer see them. Some threw water to douse the fire below. It made the smoke thicker but my archers released more fire arrows and I saw, in places, that the pig fat was now afire. The water had little effect on the pig fat.

"Edgar!"

My men at arms ran forward. The smoke now helped them for those on the top of the gate could no longer see them. They threw more faggots and pig's bladders. This time there was an inferno when the fat and the wood struck the fire.

"Sir Harold!"

Sir Harold and his men at arms had two wooden bridges we had made. We actually had four but the other two were kept in reserve. Protected by the shields of Sir Hugh's men at arms, they ran forward with the heavy bridges and placed one across the first ditch. The second was not laid over the other ditch for there was a risk that it might burn. It was placed close to the first bridge. My men retreated. We needed to be patient.

A squire galloped around, "My lord, Sir Wulfric says they are trying to escape through the north gate."

"Sir Edward, take your men and go to Sir Wulfric's aid. Sir Richard, go also."

The fire was now out of control. This was summer and it spread to the walls on either side. The gatehouse could not be held. It was a towering inferno. All those who had been there had fled. We could not enter for the fire was too fierce but it would not be long before it would be safe to enter.

"Men at arms, mount."

There was a loud crash as the two gates fell inward. Sparks and flames shot into the air. The gate was open but we could not pass through the fiery towers just yet.

"Sir Harold, the second bridge."

Sir Harold and his men ran over the first bridge and picking up the second advanced to the ditch. The wind swirled the flames and they had to hold their shields before them to stop them from being scorched and burned. As they came back Edgar shouted to James, one of Harold's men at arms. "When you get to hell you will be ready for it, James of the Oxbridge!"

He laughed and said, "Aye, and I dare say that you will be there to greet me!"

I was anxious to get inside the castle but I needed to be patient. When I saw the defenders forming a shield wall within the outer bailey, I knew that it was time. With Sir John, Sir Tristan, Sir Hugh and Sir Harold at my side, we galloped over the bridges. They held and we clattered over in pairs. Sir Harold and I were the first into the bailey and I charged directly at the thin shield wall of Scots. I pulled back my spear and rammed it into the face of the warrior in the middle. Harold's spear took the next one in the shoulder and then the two of us were through the gap we had made. The other three widened it so that by the time my squires and the men at arms had crossed the bridge then the shield wall was no longer a wall.

I jerked Lion's head around and thrust my spear into the side of Angus of Fife. It tore through his mail and into his organs. I twisted as I pulled it out. It looked as though it was being attacked by snakes. He fell to the ground mortally wounded. The spear broke in two as he fell and I drew my sword. As I laid about me, I saw that few of these men wore mail. It was a massacre. We had slain many on the walls and those that had survived our initial charge found themselves surrounded by mailed horsemen who gave no quarter. It ended quickly. We had won. Sir Hugh had been avenged and the Scots would use his castle no more.

"Take the mail and weapons from them and then place the bodies in the hall. Fire the hall when you have searched for anything of Sir Hugh Manningham's."

"Aye, lord."

The fire had died down by late afternoon but by then we had put the bodies in the hall and it was on fire. The rest of the palisade was ignited and soon the air was filled with black acrid smoke and the smell of burning flesh. The Scottish priest came to say words over the funeral pyre. He gave me a baleful look when he had finished.

"I warned them, priest! Get you to the New Castle and tell your Prince Henry that the Earl of Cleveland comes. If he wishes to flee now is the time!"

He turned and ran. The first part of my plan had succeeded, would the second?

Chapter 17

We found supplies in the kitchens before we burned them along with the hall. The beer and the bread we also consumed. My sentries on the road had killed two messengers but two others had fled. That was all part of my plan. I could do little about Carlisle but so long as they thought I had an army abroad, they would sit tight behind their walls. The New Castle was a different matter. It was built of stone and controlled the crossing of the Tyne. I had no intention of storming it. I was prepared for a siege. If I had to miss the coronation because I was reducing the power of the Scots then I would live with that. They would not need me to put a crown on the Empress' head. I had no doubt that Robert of Gloucester would claim that privilege. However, I hoped that I could draw Prince Henry into a battle.

We left early the next morning. I sent Sir Hugh along the southern bank of the river. It was only twenty or so miles to the crossing of the Tyne. There were no castles in our way. It had been why Hexham had been so vital to us. With it destroyed, the Scots would need men to patrol the old Roman Wall and I could raid and attack them at will. I would play the invader in my own land.

As we travelled along the valley, we saw their scouts ahead. What they did not know was that I had sent Dick and his archers, accompanied by Sir Edward and his men, across country, northeast. They would block the road north at Morpeth. I did not need to reduce the castle there. If we blocked the road then they could do little. In many ways, I hoped that the garrison would try to dislodge my men. It would be an expensive foray if they did so.

When we halted, four hundred paces from their city walls, we were close to their west gate and the gatehouse of the castle. I saw the Scottish Prince's standard flying alongside that of Northumbria. I knew that he would be watching. What would he see? He would see a paltry force, albeit mounted, of less than two hundred men. If the priest had reported to him, as I thought he would, then that would tally with the number he had seen. A third of my men had been hidden from him. I guessed that he had the same number of men as I did. Would that tempt him into battle? I hoped so.

We began to set up our camp but I had Sir Philip's archers and men at arms with their bows trained on the walls. If they sallied forth while we were busy, they would get a bloody nose. I rode, with Gilles and Richard, down towards the river. I could see that they had, as I did, a tower and a wall guarding the quay. There were two small vessels there. When night fell I would take the opportunity of firing them. The river was not shallow enough to ford but it mattered not. I saw that Sir Hugh and his men had taken the far end of the bridge across the Tyne. It had yet to be built of stone and my men had taken them by surprise. We could, if we wished, set fire to it. We had Prince Henry trapped in his castle. He could sit out a siege or try to chase us away. I hoped he would chase us away.

I rode back to the gate and sat on Lion just watching. It was a well-built castle. King Henry had begun it. It had a drawbridge and a fine gatehouse. I took off my helmet. I recognised Prince Henry. I had chased him back to Carlisle after the Battle of Northallerton or as it was now called, the Battle of the Standards. I think the name had become popular after the death of Archbishop Thurstan. It was he whom people associated with the victory.

I waited and eventually, the Prince spoke, "So you have taken Hexham. And now you would take this castle of the Tyne. What terms do you offer?"

I shook my head, "The terms are simple. Surrender and give up your title of Earl of Northumbria."

"That is laughable! You have a handful of men and you expect me to surrender!"

"Tell me, Prince, when did I lose to a Scottish army of any size?" There was silence. "Word may not have reached here yet but Stephen of Blois is now in Bristol Castle. He is a prisoner of the Empress. She will be crowned in June. What think you to that? When the ceremonies are over, I shall ask her for an army to come north. We will take back what you have stolen and then see if there are any juicy morsels we might like to take north of the Clyde and the Forth!"

I could see that he knew of the capture of Stephen; it explained why he was willing to discuss terms so quickly but he had not thought through the implications.

"I need time to consider my position. Come back in the morning and I will give you my decision!"

I gave a mock bow. "I am going nowhere!"

I turned as he disappeared, "Sir Tristan, have your men take the first watch. Make sure no one leaves by this gate. Sir Gilles, take your men and watch the river."

Wulfric and my other knights had heard the interchange. "He must be worried, lord. Perhaps he has few men inside the walls. We could assault it."

"No, Wulfric. Too many would die. It is well made. Be patient, we will see what the morning brings."

Gilles and Richard had barely taken off my mail when Sir Gilles galloped up and shouted, "Lord, the two ships are sailing downstream. The Prince has boarded! He has fled."

I had been duped. I should have taken the ships when I first saw them. "Thank you, Sir Gilles. You may have your men join Sir Tristan and watch the gates." He left and I waved over Sir Philip. "It seems the Prince has lied to me. Have your archers pick off as many of their sentries as they can. Tonight I want fire arrows sent over. Have your men work in rotation. I want them to have as little sleep as possible."

Sir Harold said, "A dishonourable trick, my lord."

"I blame myself. I should have expected it. We will prosecute the siege. Have a rider sent to Dick and Sir

Edward. Tell them what happened and warn that they may send a relief force down from Berwick."

"How do you know, lord?"

"There were two ships in the river. Neither was large enough to allow many men to escape. One, I think, was to aid the Prince's escape and the other, more than likely to find help. Berwick is close enough to have men here in a long day."

I had a sour taste in my mouth. I had made my plans and thought them foolproof. I was wrong. I ate sparingly and walked our lines. The camps of my men ringed the town walls to the west and the north. My archers were spread around so that they could annoy the garrison. I wanted the enemy nervous and worried. Wulfric joined me. "You should not berate yourself so, lord. We are in no worse a position than we were. True the Prince has fled but that will make the garrison less keen to fight." I said nothing. "You worry about the coronation, lord. You wish to be there."

"Not for the ceremony, Wulfric. I am not concerned with the pomp and the rituals but until the crown is on the Empress' head, I will not settle."

"Aye, lord. You have been with the Empress since the beginning. There is only Sir Edward who has shared the journey with you."

"And now it is almost done. That is why I wish to be there to see her achieve what her father intended."

"Then if the siege is still in place when you have to leave, just go. Sir Edward can keep the pressure on as well as any."

Wulfric was right. He was just a common soldier but he had the ability to see through complicated problems and create simple solutions. "Very well. We will see what tomorrow brings." Before I retired, I rode with Gilles and Richard around the walls. When I reached the eastern side, I could see all the way to the priory at the mouth of the Tyne. There were one or two small huddles of huts between the town walls and the sea but nothing that suggested reinforcements. If any came they would either come by sea or down the road from Berwick and Bamburgh.

I awoke to good news. Sir Philip's archers had managed to set a couple of the wooden buildings inside the castle on fire. They had put the fires out but the damage had been done and I knew how dispiriting that could be.

"Let us see if they are in a mood to surrender."

I rode, this time, with all of my knights, to the gate. I decided to pretend that I did not know that the Prince had left. "I am here as I promised to speak with the Prince."

An older warrior spoke, "I am Ralph of Ponteland. The Prince has gone and I command the castle now."

"Then my terms are different. Surrender the castle, lay down your arms and you may return to your homes so long as you swear not to bear arms against England again."

"A fair offer, my lord, but I will decline. I gave my word I would defend the castle until the Prince returns. I will keep my word."

I nodded, "I admire your honour but it will end badly for you."

"I pray it does not but I know your lordship's reputation. I prayed last night and our fate is in the hands of God."

I turned my horse and headed back to our lines. Sir Tristan said, "What did he mean 'when the Prince returns'?"

Wulfric said, "He tries to frighten us. In his position, I would do the same." He turned to me. "I had my men count the men on the walls. There are less than eighty in the garrison. I know not how many our archers have slain but we can whittle them down a little more. They cannot defend all the walls. We could attack the west gate of the town. It is the barbican which is stoutly defended."

"Perhaps, but let us wait until we hear from Dick before we assault the walls. Keep up the pressure and let me know if anything changes."

I strode amongst the archers who ringed the wall. Each one chose his own targets. They scanned the battlements and town walls. Each time a head was foolish enough to appear, however briefly, then an arrow sped in their direction.

I stopped next to one, "How goes it, Bertrand?"

"We have hit flesh. I have heard the cries, my lord. Some arrows miss but we have a goodly supply. By the end of the day, they should be weakened so that we can attack the walls."

My archers were confident. They knew, as well as any, the dangers of assault but the fact that the garrison appeared to have few archers and crossbows meant the danger was not as great. I had just reached the west gate when one of Dick's men galloped up. "My lord, a Scottish army marches down the road. Our scouts saw them. Sir Edward is preparing to fall back. Our scouts and archers annoy them with arrows. Sir Edward asks for orders."

This was what I had feared. There was a high and open area just to the north and east of the town. It would suit my horsemen. I would have to abandon the siege and ride to the aid of my men. The archers would work in fours. One would hold the horses while the other three loosed arrows. They would send five flights and then fall back. We had practised the move. They could slow them down and allow me and the rest of my men to join Sir Edward. "Tell him to fall back to the flat ground to the north and east of the town walls. I will join him."

I ran back to the camp. The fact that I was running made men stare. "Alarm! To horse!"

My men were already mailed but it took some time to saddle the horses. "Sir Philip, you command the siege. Keep up the pressure with the arrows. Have a servant signal Sir Hugh to take the bridge." I wanted the garrison occupied rather than wondering where my army had gone.

My other knights looked at me expectantly. "The Scots have sent an army to relieve the siege. Sir Edward and Dick are holding them back. Arm yourselves. We use spears. Keep your banners furled until we attack!"

None asked the numbers and none moaned or whined. It was not their way. We would see the numbers when we drew close and complaining would do nothing. The enemy had been clever. We would have to be cleverer.

"Gilles, ride ahead and try to spy out the numbers. Tell Sir Edward we come. Have him dismount his men. Dick can guard his flanks."

My squire galloped off.

The site I had chosen was not far from the town walls. I had seen it the previous day. It was a flat piece of high ground with fine views of the sea. I saw Gilles reach Sir Edward. My archers were like a cloud of insects further up the road. Beyond them, I could see the banners of the enemy. This was not a battle such as the Standard nor even Lincoln. We would not deploy into lines and face each other. I intended to attack as soon as we were within range. I did not want the Scots to organise. They would be in a line of march. This was the time to hit them. I would use Sir Edward to hold and fix them while we would use the speed and mobility of our horses to attack them. The flat land would allow us to form a long line.

We were trotting up the road and approaching the skirmish rapidly. Gilles galloped up. "My lord, there are two hundred or so of the enemy. Half of them are mounted. The rest are on foot."

"Who leads them?"

"Sir Edward says it looks like the banner of the Mormaer of Berwick."

I had fought the men of Berwick before, at Norham. They knew me.

The ground around us was flatter now and there were no houses. It looked like they used it for winter grazing. "Form line!"

I saw Sir Edward as he and his men dismounted to our right. With just twenty men at arms and fifteen archers, he had a small enough number of men. Dick's twenty-five archers would swell his numbers but the enemy would soon overwhelm them. I had to hope that their eye was on them and not the New Castle. Gilles rode next to me on one side with Edgar on the other. Richard was behind. When I gave the order then my banner would flutter behind me.

I could now see the enemy. Their line of march was already disrupted as their horsemen tried to close with the archers. Dick and his men were too wily to be caught and I watched as Dick ordered them to fall back. I had fought with him enough to know the signals he used.

"Wheel to the right!" I used my sword to bring Wulfric and his men on the extreme left of my line to swing obliquely around. Sir Richard who was on the extreme right held his men until we were aligned. The enemy was over half a mile away and the Mormaer of Berwick was beginning to form his own battle line. Even as I shouted, "Forward!" we were seen. I could see the reaction of those on the right of the Scots as they saw the long line of horsemen approaching. I would not act prematurely. We had to maintain contact with each other. The Scots helped me. They formed an L shaped line. They were slow to do so. Men on horses were intermixed with those on foot. It was not by design, it was by accident.

"Forward!"

I spurred Rolf and we moved a little faster. I saw the arrows from the archers ahead as Dick and Sir Edward used those deadly missiles to slow down the advancing Scots. We were now less than four hundred paces from the enemy. They had a line that had some spears forming a barrier but they had horsemen who were behind those on foot. The Mormaer was making sure his men did not run. Some of those on foot were armed with a round shield and a sword only. We would see if they could face the wall of steel and ash which approached them.

"Charge!"

We were a hundred paces from them when I unleashed my men. I pulled back my spear and aimed it at the mailed knight in the front rank who stood with his spearmen. I knew where to strike. He had an open helmet and he had the flap on his ventail down so that he could shout orders. The thunder of our hooves made the ground vibrate and we were close enough to see the fear on the faces of those who had never faced such a charge before. I punched hard. I was lucky. The knight did not have a spear. My spear crashed into his skull shattering bone and flesh. It went through him and threw him into those behind. My spear shattered and I let it go.

Taking my mace from my cantle, for it was closest to hand, I swung it at the warrior behind the dead knight who stood covered in blood, brains and gore. The mace ended his reverie and his life. All along the line, there was a clatter of metal on wood. The screams of dying men mixed with horses struck by enemy spears. As I looked up, one of the mounted horsemen jabbed his spear at me. He and his mount were stationary. I saw it easily and flicked the head away contemptuously with my shield. Standing in my stirrups I brought my mace across the side of his head. The blow threw him from the saddle and then I was through their lines. I hung my mace from my cantle as I wheeled Rolf around. I drew my sword.

As I turned I saw that my squires were still with me. Gilles' horse had been cut but it was not serious. I stood in my stirrups. "For God, England, and the Empress!" I led my line into the rear of the Scottish horsemen. They tried to turn to face us. My men and Wulfric's had been the only ones to break through their lines but that was enough. The centre and the enemy right were breached and Sir Edward and Dick attacked the enemy left.

I spurred Rolf towards the standard of the Mormaer. He had turned his horse and he and two knights rode towards me. He had a full-face helmet and a long sword but his horse was not as powerful as Rolf. I charged his horse with my shield pulled tightly to my side. I saw that he intended to charge my sword side. Edgar was on my sword side and that decided me. When our horses were less than three paces apart, I jerked my reins to my left and stood in my stirrups. As he tried to control his horse and avoid Edgar's sword, I brought my own blade down hard. He managed to half block the blow with his shield but my blade still bit into the mail of his shoulder. At the same time, Edgar's sword smashed into his right hand and his sword fell. His squire charged Edgar who was forced to turn and face the brave squire. The Mormaer managed to control his horse and use his squire's charge to turn away from me. A second knight struck my shield with his sword. I wheeled Rolf's head around and swung my sword from over the rump of Rolf. I hit the sword of the knight so hard that it shattered. He threw the hilt at me and as I brought up my shield to avoid being struck, he wheeled his horse and followed the Mormaer as he fled.

The head of the squire flew before my face as Edgar slew him but the squire had done his duty. He had bought his master time to escape. Gilles picked up the standard from the squire's dead hands. The enemy broke. They had to try to fight their way through Wulfric and his men. My former sergeant at arms and his men were laying about them and causing great slaughter. His war axe smashed through shields and metal, flesh and bone.

Small pockets of men fought around the bodies of their knight but most fled. I could not afford my men to follow them far and besides, they were broken. They would not relieve the siege of the New Castle. As my men ended the suffering of the dying and collected horses and booty, I led Rolf to Sir Edward and Dick. I saw that Sir Edward's shield was broken and his sword bent. His face was bloody but his grin told me that was the blood of his enemies.

"It is some time since I fought so hard. God's blood but I feel alive."

I gestured to the dead men at arms and archers. "Your men have paid a price."

Dick nodded, "Aye, lord, but the Scots have paid a dearer one."

It was the middle of the afternoon when we returned to the town walls. I had the captured standards planted outside the gates of the castle. Those within would have heard, if not seen, the battle. The captured standards would tell them the result. Sir Philip said, "Sir Hugh has captured the bridge, lord. His men are keeping down the heads of those on the bridge gate."

"Good. Father Thomas, there are men to heal and some to send to God."

"Aye, lord."

"Come, Gilles, let us go and speak with Ralph of Ponteland. Richard, fetch the banner we captured."

We rode to the gate and waited. The constable appeared. His face and helmet were blackened with soot; the result of the fires we had started. I pointed to the banner. "As you can see the Mormaer of Berwick has been defeated. Here is his banner. There is no one coming to your aid. Surrender now and my offer still stands. You may leave and follow your defeated army north."

"A generous offer, my lord, but we stay. I have promised my Prince and I will do my duty."

"It does you great credit but when my men take these walls and take them they will, I cannot guarantee the safety of any within these walls."

He nodded, "We are warriors all. Do your worst, Earl. We shall be ready!"

I rode back to the camp. "Wulfric, have the men make ladders but do so at a distance from the town so that they are neither seen nor heard."

"Aye, lord."

"Sir Richard, have your men begin to build a ram before the gates of the castle but make sure they do it slowly."

He smiled, "You do not intend to attack the barbican then?"

"No, Sir Richard, but I want them to think that we do."

My men needed rest. Sir Philip and his men continued to harass the walls and those of Wulfric's men who were fit enough made ladders. I sat and planned our nighttime assault with my knights and sergeants at arms.

"We spend this day and the next resting and let them think that we intend to use the ram. Tomorrow night we assault the west gate. I will lead the attack. We will then attack the castle from the town. Later today I will row across the river and speak with Sir Hugh."

Wulfric said, "Leading an assault is dangerous, my lord, let one of us do it."

"The day that I allow someone else to lead for me is the day I give up my sword and learn to grow vegetables. I will lead. We will need a bridge making to span the ditch. You had better make it two. I want an attack on a wide front. We outnumber them and I intend to use those numbers."

We had found a small boat upstream and Gilles and Richard rowed me to the southern bank of the Tyne. Sir Hugh had made his camp there. I greeted him warmly, "You have done more than I could have hoped. I pray it did not cost you too many of your men."

He shook his head, "The enemy lost far more for we were cautious."

"Tonight I want you and your men to rest. Tomorrow night, as soon as it is dark I would have you and your men hammer wood as though you are making something to attack the gate. Then have your archers loose fire arrows into the walls. I want them to think that we are attacking this side but do not risk your men. You are putting on a show that is all. We will begin the real attack." I suddenly realised that he knew nothing of our victory and so, while we ate I gave him an account of the battle.

He nodded, "Time draws on, my lord. Will you be able to be there for the coronation?"

"I hope so but this is more important than watching a ritual. It is but half a day to ride to Stockton from here and the *'Adela'* will be waiting for me. Captain William has promised me he can do the voyage in under four days at this time of year. Tomorrow night will decide all."

That evening I walked the camp again. My archers continued to send fire arrows into the town and the castle. Sir Hugh had told me that his men were making it hard for the garrison to fetch water to fight the fire. This constant attack was draining them. When I visited the ram, I saw that they had cleverly constructed the roof first so that the defenders could not see the progress within. Sir Richard was enjoying the deception. "I think my lads will be a little disappointed if they don't get to actually use the damned thing!"

"Tell them that we will be assaulting the walls but not the gate."

"You still intend to scale them, my lord?"

"It is not as hazardous as you might think. I fear boiling oil and boiling water. With the fires we have started, I cannot see them using either. Any water they have is needed to fight our fires. If you had ever seen the walls that the Empire builds then you would know that these are not true obstacles."

The next night we lined up beyond sight of the walls. We had ten ladders and there would be two teams of five men. We would carry our ladders over the two bridges when we heard the attack on the river. Each of my knights insisted on leading eight of the ladders. Edgar and Wilfred would lead men up the other two. I had my sword and my mace. I would not be wearing a cloak. I did not wish to be encumbered.

As we waited in the dark I said, "We must clamber up the ladders quickly. One slip could be disastrous. The first ones on the walls secure it for the others. I intend us to be the first up." I saw them nodding in the dark. Günter the Swabian would be behind me followed by Gilles. I insisted that Richard would be last. He was not happy. He followed Leopold of Durstein who would ensure that my young squire came to no harm. We had all smeared soot on our helmets and mail. We needed to be hidden for as long as possible.

We moved towards the wall as soon as night fell. Dick's archers were close by. They sent arrows at any sentries whose white faces showed above the wall. Philip and his archers continued to send fire into the heart of the castle.

Suddenly I saw, to the south, arrows that appeared to be arcing towards us. It was an illusion. Then I heard a mighty clamour as Sir Hugh began his false attack. The alarm was sounded in the castle and the town. My men picked up our ladder and followed the archers who carried our bridge. They would stand guard close to the walls and pick off any defender they saw. We tried to be silent but as soon as mailed men clattered over the bridge then they knew that we were coming. Leopold and Jean of Angers threw up the ladder and held it there. Holding my shield over my head I climbed up the stairs. I held, in my right hand, a short sword. It would be of more use until we gained the bailey.

I heard shouts above and felt something clatter into my shield. It made me move faster. Then a rock was thrown. Had I not had the shield angled then I might have been thrown from my perch. I used my right hand to pull myself up. I knew how many rungs there were and as I approached the top, I prepared to let go with my right hand. I was still holding on when a war hammer slammed into my shield.

The spike penetrated the leather and wood. I pulled back with my hand. The warrior wielding it was not expecting the movement and he lost his balance. I pressed closely into the ladder as he hit my shield. I yelled, "Ware below!"

As his body and hammer slid from my shield, I took advantage of the fact that there would be no one above me. I clambered up the last two rungs and, thrusting my sword forward, blindly, leapt onto the wooden walkway. Ahead of me, two men were raising rocks to hurl down upon Harold. I ran at them with my sword held out. I just hurled myself into them. One lost his balance and tumbled to the stones below. The other took the full force of my sword in his side. I twisted as I pulled it out. He joined his comrade on the stones below. Without waiting for Sir Harold, I ran towards the door which led into the gatehouse.

Günter had his long sword and he ran next to me. We barely fitted on the walkway but we were a frightening sight to behold. Three men turned from throwing stones at Wulfric to turn and face us. Günter was to my left and he swung his sword two handed in a wide sweep as I stabbed at the man closest to the wall. Günter's sword almost cut one man in two. And the man I had stabbed in the thigh dropped to one knee. The third raised his sword in triumph and then his face showed a look of surprise as Wulfric's axe severed his spine in two.

I could see he was bleeding from a head wound but he was like an injured bear. He roared. Turning to the door he ran at it. The last of those before us had fled within and barred it. He began hacking at it with his axe. Peter Strong Arm joined him and the two set to work as though they were felling trees. It was a matter of a few strokes and a hole appeared. A spear darted out, striking Peter Strong Arm in the leg. He redoubled his efforts. When the next spear came out, I grabbed it and pulled. The hole was bigger now and as the man's head appeared, Peter Strong Arm had his revenge and took the head.

Günter shouted, "Stand back!" He took a run and hurled himself bodily at the door. He was a squat, solid man and the door burst open. His speed took him inside the tower. I followed for I knew he would not be able to use his long sword within the confined space. He was lying on the floor, somewhat stunned. I saw Ralph of Ponteland raise his sword to end his life. As he did so, I rammed the short sword under his raised arm. It came out the other side and was torn from my grip. Looking like Christ on the cross, he fell to the ground and I drew my sword.

I used my shield to barge others out of the way and I ran to the stairs. As I did I held my sword before me. I was lucky, there was no one on them. I ran down. As I turned a corner, I saw that Gilles was with me. When we reached the bottom there were five surprised men guarding the mechanism which lowered the bridge over the ditch. Their surprise worked in our favour. Gilles bravely ran to my right to protect that side. I brought my sword in a long sweep, backhand across my body. An axe and a sword cracked into my already weakened shield. I saw splinters fly. My sword smashed into the coif of a man at arms. I must have broken something for he fell. I punched with my shield at the two men who had attacked me. One fell, stunned but the shield broke in to pieces. I took the mace from my belt and used that to block the blow from the sword. Before he could recover, I had pinned him to the wall with my sword.

Wulfric and Leopold had joined me. "Gilles, get the gate open."

As he did so, I slashed one of the ropes which held the bridge. Günter, looking a little unsteady, joined us and his sword took the other. There was a crash as the bridge slammed down and then Gilles had the gate open. Sir Philip and my archers hurled themselves across the bridge. With swords in hand, they raced into the outer bailey. We had not yet won but it was a matter of time only.

Chapter 18

By dawn, the last of the garrison was either dead or had run through the east gate and fled. We had the New Castle. We had lost men. Sir Richard had lost his right hand. He would never wield a sword again. Father Thomas saved his life but it was a high price to pay for the victory. We had lost many men at arms and all of my knights had a wound to remember the battle by. We spent the next day seeing to the wounded and collecting weapons, mail and treasure.

We ate a frugal meal in the hall. Tristan had to feed the wounded knight. He smiled as he did so. "I never thought to be feeding you!"

"Do not get used to it. I shall have my smith make me a hook. I shall feed myself before too long."

My men were resilient. I spoke to them all at the end of the meal. "Tomorrow I will leave for Stockton. It is a week until the coronation. Wulfric, I leave you in command of this castle. Keep a good garrison. The rest can return home. Sir Edward and Sir Harold, you will accompany me to London for the coronation. I will take Edgar and Wilfred along with my squires. That should be enough. Sir John, you will return and hold Stockton for me until I return. The rest of you must be vigilant. Prince Henry may return to try to retake his castle. Sir Wulfric, do not try to hold the castle against odds that are too great. It is not worth it. After the coronation, we will bring an army north and conquer what was once ours."

We travelled light when we left before dawn. We headed across the bridge and south down the little-used greenway. It had been a busy thoroughfare until the Scots had taken

Durham. Now there was no need for it. There was no trade. I was lost in my thoughts as we headed towards my river. We had done well; we had done better than I could have possibly have hoped. Prince Henry had been dealt a body blow; Sir Hugh had been avenged and we now had a toe hold north of the Tyne. Once peace came again to the south then we could do as I had promised and retake England. I had no doubt that Stephen's wife and her mercenary, William of Ypres, would fight a little while longer but so long as we held the figurehead in Bristol Castle, she could do little to change events. The key had been the battle of Lincoln. In one stroke we had captured the King and ended the war.

As we approached my castle, I saw the masts of my ship in the river. William of Kingston had done as I had asked. Before I had left, we had packed chests with our fine clothes. Normally such things would not be a consideration but I was going to see my Empress crowned. It deserved the best of my clothes. As I changed out of my bloodied surcoat and into a better one Gilles asked, "Do you want me to fetch your spare shield, my lord?"

"No, Gilles. We will not be fighting. We will comb our hair and beards and we will smell of flowers for the women. We go to a church and we go to see a sovereign anointed."

We hurried down to the quay for I was anxious to catch the evening tide. Moments were now precious. Alice looked like a proud mother as Richard and Gilles, dressed in newly tailored surcoats, boarded *'Adela'*. The two of them were as close to her own children as she would ever get. As the sun glinted from the west, it seemed to bathe my castle in a golden glow. Its towers made it look like a crown and I saw the reflection in the river. It was a sign. The crown would soon be on the head of the Empress.

William of Kingston was a good sailor and we made good time. In his hold, he had a cargo for Anjou. None of it was perishable but trade went on and helped us to prosper. "When I have offloaded on the Maine, lord, shall I return to London for you?"

"No, William. I have brought gold. We will buy horses. I have a mind to visit my new manor at Liedeberge. I would see how Sir William fares. Besides, I may be needed by the Earl if Queen Matilda does not accept that the Empress has replaced her. You return to Stockton. I am certain that John will be eager to receive the goods you bring."

I was surprised, as we approached the Tower, that there was not more evidence of the coronation. We had made London with two days to spare and yet I saw no fields filled with tents nor markets taking advantage of the crowds who would attend it. We tied up at the quay next to William's White Tower. The tide was on the turn and as soon as he had offloaded my captain set sail and headed towards the sea.

I noticed that the Empress' standard flew from the Tower along with that of de Mandeville. "Edgar and Wilfred, stay here with the squires. Watch our chests and we will see where we are to stay."

I did not recognise the guards at the gate to the inner ward but they recognised me. "My lord, we expected you days ago. The Empress was most concerned."

"Where is she?"

"She has gone with her ladies and her guards to the Abbey to discuss arrangements for the impending coronation with the Archbishop. The constable is within."

As we entered I saw that the guards were on high alert. Had my livery not been so well known I am not certain we would have been admitted. I had not met the Earl of Essex before but knew that he must be a powerful man if he was given the Tower to guard. The last time I had been here was in the reign of King Henry. He had appointed his most loyal knight to the post. I was admitted, along with my knights, into his chambers.

He gave me a thin smile. He might be an ally of the Empress but that did not mean that he liked me. I had captured his cousin and been an enemy for many years. "The Empress has been fretting about your arrival, lord. She will be pleased you are here."

I nodded, "I had expected more excitement in the city. Where are the merchants who would make money from such events?"

"Queen Matilda and William of Ypres are just south of the city. London is nervous. They have never looked favourably on the Empress. Stephen ensured their loyalty."

I nodded, "He did not tax them as heavily as he might."

"Quite. Still, now that you are here we have the greatest champion in the land. It may sway the people."

"They should not need swaying. The Empress has the right."

"The ordinary folk do not see it that way." He waved over a servant. "Have the Earl's chests brought here." He pointed to a narrow corridor that I knew led to stairs. "The Empress has the floor above. There are rooms for you and your people there."

"Have you horses?"

"Of course."

"Then with your permission, we will saddle them and ride to the Empress. She should have an escort worthy of her position."

"As you wish. The stables are in the outer ward."

My men and chests arrived and after putting them in our rooms, they followed me. As we made our way to the stables, I regretted not bringing my helmet. I had thought this would be a peaceful task. It seemed not. As we headed to the stables Sir Harold asked, "What is amiss, lord?"

"If this was war I would know. It is a feeling that there are enemies waiting in ambush but this is peace and we have a coronation to attend. I know not what the feeling is but it is always better to do something rather than sit and wait. Besides, a ride through the streets of the city will give us the mood of the people."

The horses were palfreys but would suit our purpose. Mailed knights and squires were not a common sight in London and, as we headed west, we were stared at. My livery was recognised. Most people just gave us a wary stare but as we headed through the narrow and to my mind, rather smelly streets, I was accosted by a one armed man. I could see that he was an old soldier. "My lord, it is me, Ralph of Selby!" In case I had forgotten him had added, "I fought

alongside you in the wars against the Welsh with Earl
Robert!"

I halted and dismounted. I did remember him. He had
been a fine man at arms and had been unlucky to have his
horse fall upon him. His arm had to be removed to save his
life. "Of course, I remember you." I saw immediately that
his clothes were thin and threadbare. A pile of rags showed
that this might be his bed too. I was ever honest, even with
my men. "You have fallen on hard times."

"There is little work for a one armed man."

"Why did you not return to the north? Had you come to
my castle, we would have found work for you. We have one
armed swineherds and shepherds. There are many things you
could do."

"I would have, lord, but each report we had was that you
were beset by the Scots. Life is hard enough here in London
but in the north, I did not think I would survive."

I took out ten silver coins. "Here. Take care of these for I
am sure that there are thieves around. I implore you to take
the journey north. Life is not as bad as you might think
there."

He took the money gratefully, "And a word of warning,
my lord. Watch yourself. I have seen men in the streets who
are supporters of the King. You were ever the Empress' man.
Beware."

I was not certain I would ever see him again but I was
glad that I had met him. The coins had been well spent. I
spent the next part of the journey looking out for signs of
danger. Before we left through the Ludgate, I had seen many
groups of roughly armed men. Most had the look of soldiers
who were not wearing mail. More than anything it was the
looks they gave us as we passed which raised my suspicions.
Ralph was right. There were enemies within London's walls.
I turned to Sir Edward. "I like not these men we have seen. It
is as though there is an army hiding in plain view."

"You are right, lord. I recognised some of them or at least
they were familiar from years gone by. They are men at
arms."

Sir Harold said, "If I had not known better, lord, I would have said they were outlaws. They have the leather jerkins and the long dagger that can be used to skin animals."

"Or cut a throat," added Edgar. My men were worldly-wise.

We headed down the river towards the Abbey. I spied the Empress, Judith, Margaret and the four men at arms with her heading east. It was too small an escort.

"I want a ring of us around the ladies and keep your hands close to your swords."

"Surely they would not risk anything here, my lord!"

"I know not, Gilles. Let us treat it as though we are at war and look for enemies."

The Empress' face lit up when she saw me. She turned to Margaret, "Now the sky will be blue and the world a better place. My champion is here."

I reined in next to her. There were few people about but I wanted my words to be private. "I fear for your safety, my lady. There are too many armed men in London City."

She nodded, "When I rode through I felt the danger. Surely I am safe now?"

"I hope so." I turned to the four men at arms. "My men will watch the front and the sides. You four watch our rear. There may be danger!"

"Aye, my lord." The four looked handy enough; time would tell.

The four of them looked to be well equipped and mounted but I had not fought with them. You did not know a man's worth until you had seen him in battle. I took the Empress' reins and pulled her horse next to me. Sir Edward and Sir Harold did the same with Judith and Margaret. With Edgar on one side and Wilfred on the other, the four squires led us back towards the Ludgate.

Although we were admitted back into the city, there was not the warm welcome I would have expected. This was not what I had foreseen on my journey south. I could see that I had frightened the Empress. She needed to be calm. "We have recaptured the New Castle, my lady, and lost few men.

When the time allows, we can take back the rest of your father's kingdom."

"Thank you, Alfraed." She reached over to pat my hand which held her reins still." I had hoped my brother might come but he is busy in the west."

That worried me but I said nothing. If the Earl had brought his army closer to London then Queen Matilda could not threaten the Empress. Was it an accident or something more sinister? As we approached the Billings' Gate, I saw that the mob of soldiers, who had lounged there, had grown. There were about twenty of them. They crowded the narrow street and my squires were forced to move closer together. I did not like it and my hand went to my mace. Suddenly three of them stepped forward and one held the bridle of the Empress' horse.

"Have you got some coins for soldiers who are out of work now, lady?"

I caught Edgar and Wilfred's eyes and nodded as I said, "Take your hand from the lady's horse or lose it."

"My lord, you haven't got your army with you now. This is my town. We rule these streets. You may be lord in the north but here, in civilisation, some of us are better than lords. So I say again..."

He got no further for I had brought my mace across the side of his head. It was not a killing blow but it rendered him unconscious. He fell to the ground. Before his two companions could react, Edgar and Wilfred had their swords at their throats.

"Now for what your friend said I could have him executed." I shrugged, "I still might. All that you two have done is stand close to this piece of vermin and the rest have just watched. So you two need to think about your next actions carefully else my men will run you through and then I," I drew my sword and held it aloft, "will become angry and let my men loose on the rabble who bar our way." I smiled, "What say you?"

They looked at each other and one said, "We will withdraw, lord." They bent down to pick up their friend.

"Leave him where he lies we have been delayed long enough." I pointed my sword at the crowd of men. "Move!" My squires and knights all drew their swords and the mob ran. When the street was clear I said, "Lead on, Gilles." We rode over the unconscious body of the thug. The horses were not dainty. He would be black and blue when he woke.

"I am glad that you were here, Alfraed. Were you not afraid?"

"Of brigands like that? No, my lady, but from now on we only go out with a larger escort than this."

As we saw the Tower ahead she breathed easier. "The Archbishop mentioned something about unrest. Mobs like this have been gathering throughout the city."

"Then I am glad the coronation is the day after tomorrow."

"As am I!"

That evening as we discussed matters with the Constable of the Tower, he concurred with our views. "There have been rumours of crowds gathering and speaking of Stephen as the rightful king," I said nothing.

The Empress looked worried, "I fear it is the army which is gathering in Kent. The people of London are fickle. They will go with the might rather than the right."

I smiled, "And I agree. We just have one day to hold on and then, when you are crowned, we can leave this pestilential hole!"

Geoffrey de Mandeville, whose family was from close to the city said, mildly, "You like not the city, lord?"

"Do not take this the wrong way, my lord, but in all the wars I fought against the French in Normandy, the Welsh in the marches or the Scots in the north, I have never yet fought alongside any lord or man at arms from this city. They are happy to leech off the blood of warriors but seem a little unwilling to shed it themselves."

He looked outraged at my words. The Empress said, "You must forgive my champion, Constable. He has ever been blunt and spoken what was on his mind. It endeared him to my father but I can see how it might offend."

He nodded, "I am unused to such honest comments."

"Then here are more. We cannot stay here in this Tower after the ceremony. It would be as though we were besieged. We have no army to protect us. Tomorrow I will have horses prepared so that on the day after, we can leave the city and head for Oxford. It is a place of safety. D'Oyly is loyal and we are close to the Earl of Gloucester and his men. I would not have the Empress spend a moment longer than necessary here so close to her enemies."

Geoffrey of Mandeville smiled, "And in that, my lord, I think you are right. Choose the best horses which we have."

The next morning we went down to the stables and chose the best horses that we could find. Although none were war horses, that did not matter. I looked for mounts that would have stamina. They would need to outrun any pursuit. I had the squires sharpen their weapons and then I went to find the sergeant at arms of the Empress' guards.

"When we leave here the day after tomorrow, it will be before dawn. I want the men to ride as close along the side of the Empress as they can. Let no one near her. Slay any who approach close enough to do harm."

"We will, my lord, but where will you be?"

"If there is danger before us then I will be in the van and if we are pursued then I shall be the rearguard."

"And to where do we flee, my lord?"

"That I will decide when we leave."

It was not that I did not trust him but he could mention it to one of his men who might speak in the presence of some of the servants. The fewer who knew we were heading for Oxford the better.

In the end, we did not have that luxury. One of the Constable's spies rode in during the middle watch of the night. It was less than an hour to dawn. I was barely asleep and I was summoned, "You had better hear this, my lord."

The man was exhausted; I could see that, "Lord, Queen Matilda is bringing an army led by William of Ypres. They intend to stop the Empress being crowned."

"Where are they now?"

"They are camped twenty miles south of Southwark. If they leave early they will be here by noon."

"Thank you! It is time to put our escape into motion. The coronation cannot take place." I went to rouse my squires and knights. Although we had everything ready, dawn had broken before we mounted. The Constable and four of his men came with us. Before we could make our escape, the guards on the west wall came for us. "Constable! There is a mob clamouring at the city gate. They are armed and they demand that we hand over the Empress to them."

"We have tarried long enough. We leave by the north gate. It means we will have to travel the length of the city wall but there is no other choice."

The sergeant at arms had his men mounted. "Which way, my lord?"

"The north gate!"

"Then you had best beware. There is a postern gate from the city and my men said they saw movements there in the middle watch."

"Then I will lead with my knights." I could now hear the shouts and cries from the west gate. They would not be able to break in but that would prevent us from using the gate. I turned, "Anyone we see with a weapon is an enemy!" I drew my sword. "We will protect you, my lady. Wilfred, Edgar, take the rear and guard our backs."

I nodded to the men at the gate. They opened it and we galloped across the bridge which spanned the ditch. As the sergeant had suspected, there were men waiting for us. A mob of thirty armed with shields, spears and swords raced out to get us. I recognised the man I had hit the previous day. He was their leader. This had been planned. I yelled, "The rest ride on! Stockton! Charge!"

It was the one thing they were not expecting. They thought they had surprise on their side and they did, but seven knights and squires charging them was not the result they expected. I leaned forward and brought my sword over my head. It sliced across the shoulder and chest of one man. As a sword cracked into my leg, I jerked my horse around to bowl over a second and allowed my sword to slice across the throat of a third. My squires were not fighting knights; they were fighting mercenaries and brigands. As I turned my horse, I saw them both laying about themselves with their swords.

The leader was shouting orders; he was screaming, "Kill the bastards! Get the woman! She is worth money to us!"

He was standing at the back with men before him. I rode at them. This was not a warhorse but I knew how to make it one. As I drew near I jerked back on the reins. It reared. Then I slapped its rump with the flat of my sword and it jumped forward. Its hooves caved in the skulls of two men and knocked a third to the ground. I took the head of a fourth. The leader was panicking for he had no one left before him. I spurred my horse towards him. He had an axe. With nowhere left to go, he snarled and leapt at me. I blocked his strike with my sword and then kicked him under the chin. His face was already swollen from the blow of my mace and he reeled. As he did so, I slashed across his chest. I tore it open to the bone. He spun around and fell face forward in the city ditch. It was filled with excrement and dead animals. He landed face down. I did not wait to see if he lived or died. I spun my horse around.

I saw that the Constable and the sergeant at arms had led the Empress north towards the Shore Ditch. This was a long deep ditch that prevented movement from east to west. We would have to ride north until we could cross it. Before then, however, we had to escape the mob which had heard the fighting and flooded through the postern gate. I saw Wilfred and Edgar whirl around, flailing their swords before the mob. The Empress was clear and I shouted, "Fall back! Join me!"

We hurried after the Empress and her guards. I saw that all of my men had wounds. We had been fighting brigands but we had had no shields and we were outnumbered. My worry now was not the mob but Ypres' men. My only hope was that they would think we were heading north for Lincoln. When we reached the ditch, I saw that we could not jump it. "Keep heading north. There must be a bridge!" Eventually, we found a place to cross. It was not a bridge but a cart had fallen in and provided a platform that allowed us to cross. Once we reached the Moorfields, I led us towards

Clerkenwell. There were no castles there but two monasteries. If we were caught we would claim sanctuary. It was not a perfect solution but it might do.

We passed it without incident and I halted at a small stream to allow the horses to rest. I now regretted not bringing archers. They could have kept enemies at bay.

I went over to see the Empress. She looked to be in shock. Her ladies were comforting her. When I approached, she threw her arms around me, "They hate me! How can I be the Queen of England? The people hate me."

"No, my lady. The people are afraid of the army which marches on them. This way they are not harmed. It is what ordinary folk do. I do not like it but I understand it. Now listen, my lady. We are not safe yet. We have another sixty miles to travel. We cannot stop before Oxford. William of Ypres will reach the city about now and he will realise that we have fled. He will send men after us. We only stop for the horses."

She nodded, "I am in your hands now."

"And the hands of God. I pray he helps us!"

We were now exposed for we made a long line as we headed north and west. I had Wilfred and Edgar at the rear and they would let me know of any close pursuit. We had just passed the village of Thame when we saw our pursuers. We were less than ten miles from Oxford. Edgar shouted, "My lord, horsemen!" I slowed down so that I could ride with them. Edgar pointed over his shoulder. I saw them almost two miles away for the road was long and straight. "They will catch us, lord, for they are not mailed."

"Then we will look for an ambush site." I spurred my horse on and reached the head of the column. "Constable, we are going to be caught. I will delay them but you must swear to get the Empress to Oxford."

He was not used to such exertions and was out of breath but he gasped, "I will, my lord."

As I slowed down to join my men, the Empress, who had heard my words, shouted, "Do not throw away your life, my lord!"

"I will not."

It was then I spied, just ahead, a bridge over the River Thames. I held up my hand and shouted, "Knights, we ambush them here!" I stopped. The river was tree-lined. This was no Roman Road and the trees grew close to the road. I pointed to the trees beyond the bridge. "We will hide yonder. Sir Edward, take Sir Harold. You and your squires wait on that side. When we hear them clatter across the bridge, we take them! Hurry!"

I could hear the hooves of the pursuers' horses in the distance. They had been too far away to estimate numbers accurately but if we slowed them down then that would allow the Empress to reach the safety of Oxford. The five of us waited in silence. The short rest would aid our horses which had performed better than I could have hoped. I heard the hooves on the bridge. I counted to five and then shouted, "Now!"

We had been completely hidden by the trees and we burst upon them from two sides. We were attacking from their sword side and they had not seen us. I sliced across the neck of one man and he fell from the saddle. I saw that, in our initial attack, we had cleared the road of six of their men. To our left, there were another ten at least and ahead of us, four more. We had done enough.

"Fall back!"

The ones behind us were in disarray as they tried to negotiate riderless horses and the bodies of the dead and wounded who lay in the road. We charged toward the other four. If we could halt these then the Empress might escape. One was a knight and he recognised me. "I may have lost the Empress but I will have her dog!"

He had a shield and that gave him an advantage. As he charged at me, I switched sides with my horse. He expected me on one side and I went to the other. His blow missed me but bit into the neck of my horse. It began to tumble. I kicked my feet from my stirrups and, as I began to fall forward, I tucked in my head. I was lucky. I hit the rump of one of my enemy's horses and it broke my fall. As I rose to my feet, the knight galloped at me. I held my sword in two hands. He saw that he had me and he raised his sword for the blow which would end the life of the Warlord of the North. I feinted to go to his right. He made the mistake of adjusting his attack and when I jinked to my right, I brought my sword hard across him and took his left leg high up. He fell to the other side and took his horse with him.

The first of those at the bridge had recovered and seeing us, just fifty paces up the road, began to hasten towards us. I pulled on the knight's horse's reins as I pushed his mortally wounded body from the horse. As it rose, I slipped my leg over the cantle and slapped its rump. The horsemen were less than twenty paces from me. I saw my squires turn in their saddles. I waved my sword and shouted, "Ride! Ride!"

I leaned forward over this strange horse and began to speak to it. "Come on, my beauty, show me how you can run!" It seemed to respond. I risked a glance under my arm and saw that they were no longer closing with me. We had five more miles to run. I knew that Oxford was not far ahead but until I saw the gates of its welcoming walls then we were not safe. When my horse began to labour, I knew that he was hurt. The horsemen behind must have sensed it for a couple of them began to gain on me. My next glance showed that the main group was fifty paces from me but two of them were less than ten paces behind and they were closing.

I heard a voice from ahead, "Hurry, my lord! We are almost there!"

There was no point in killing this brave beast. I began to slow. I slipped my dagger into my left hand. I had to time this well. When I felt that they were close, I pulled back hard on the reins and then hacked to the right, blindly with my sword. My horse stopped and my sword struck flesh and bone. My triumph was short-lived as a sword struck my left side. I felt something crack and then the warm flow of blood. The rider had drawn ahead of me and he turned to charge me. I spurred my horse and, standing in the saddle, rammed the dagger into his mouth which was screaming his victory. My dagger was torn from my hand. I looked over my shoulder. The enemy were thirty paces from me. They would soon begin to gain but I could not surrender. It was not in me. I would ride until I died or until they caught me. I dug my heels into the flanks of this brave horse and he responded moving forward towards Oxford.

Ahead of me, I saw that my men had stopped and were turning. "Ride! Ride!" The exertion was too much. I began to feel dizzy. The road itself seemed to be moving. That was impossible I know. Nor could I keep my eyes open. I felt a sudden sharp pain in my side and then I felt blackness envelop me. I knew nothing more.

Epilogue

I was back in Constantinople. I was playing with my first sword and my friend Basil was laughing as I struck the edge against a marble statue knocking off a finger in the process. I heard my father shouting at me to be more careful and I ran after Basil. As I ran into the marble, I fell over and all went black. I heard my father say, sternly, "Alfraed, wake up. Alfraed, wake up."

I did not want to wake up. I did not want to get into trouble and I lay there feigning sleep. And then I smelled rosemary and the voice was not my father's but the Empress and she whispered, in my ear, "Wake up, my love. You cannot leave me alone! We have so much to do."

I opened my eyes and saw that we were in a candlelit chamber. In the doorway stood a priest and Sir Edward. My old friend was grinning, "What happened?"

The Empress shouted, "Praise be to God! He is saved. I owe you much, Father Abelard."

"It was God's will, and this one was strong."

"Fetch food and wine. Tell his squires that he lives. They will worry!"

Sir Edward said, "I will watch the door, my lady."

As he turned his back the Empress kissed me, "I thought you were dead. It has been three days since you were brought in by Sir Richard more dead than alive. You had lost so much blood that I feared you had none left."

I nodded and closed my eyes. Then I opened them and said, "My men?"

"Sir Harold and Edgar have wounds too but they live. We are safe here and my brother is on his way with his army. We will fight again for the throne. At least we still have Stephen secure." I tried to rise. "No, Alfraed, you shall not stir until the priest says you are well. When my brother reaches us then we can make decisions and plan, but you do not move. I thought I had lost you." She stroked my brow and the touch was so tender I felt as though we were one.

"But you have not and I am tougher than I look but you, my Empress, the coronation, you have lost the crown."

"No, Alfraed, it is not lost, it has fallen and with your help, I shall pick it up again. We have not come this far to give up so easily. We will prevail. It will just take a little longer. Now lie back and let me take care of you. Your men will keep us safe; at least until my brother comes."

I nodded and squeezed her hand, "I will be your champion unto death! I am still the Knight of the Empress."

She smiled and kissed me again, "You will always be my champion, my Champion of England," and I was content.

The End

Glossary

Al-Andalus- Spain

Angevin- the people of Anjou, mainly the ruling family

Battle- a formation in war (a modern battalion)

Booth Castle – Bewcastle north of Hadrian's Wall

Butts- targets for archers

Cadge- the frame upon which hunting birds are carried (by a codger- hence the phrase old codger being the old man who carries the frame)

Cadwaladr ap Gruffudd- Son of Gruffudd ap Cynan

Captain- a leader of archers

Chausses - mail leggings. (They were separate- imagine lady's stockings!)

Conroi- A group of knights fighting together. The smallest unit of the period

Demesne- estate

Destrier- war horse

Doxy- prostitute

Fess- a horizontal line in heraldry

Galloglass- Irish mercenaries

Gambeson- a padded tunic worn underneath mail. When worn by an archer they came to the waist. It was more of a quilted jacket but I have used the term freely

Gonfanon- A standard used in Medieval times (Also known as a Gonfalon in Italy)

Gruffudd ap Cynan- King of Gwynedd until 1137

Hartness- the manor which became Hartlepool

Hautwesel- Haltwhistle

Liedeberge- Ledbury

Lusitania- Portugal

Mansio- staging houses along Roman Roads

Maredudd ap Bleddyn- King of Powys

Martinmas- 11th November

Mêlée- a medieval fight between knights

Moravians- the men of Moray

Mormaer- A Scottish lord and leader

Mummer- an actor from a medieval tableau

Musselmen- Muslims
Nithing- A man without honour (Saxon)
Nomismata- a gold coin equivalent to an aureus
Outremer- the kingdoms of the Holy Land
Owain ap Gruffudd- Son of Gruffudd ap Cynan and King of
Gwynedd from 1137
Palfrey- a riding horse
Poitevin- the language of Aquitaine
Pyx- a box containing a holy relic (Shakespeare's Pax from
Henry V)
Refuge- a safe area for squires and captives (tournaments)
Sauve qui peut – Every man for himself (French)
Sergeant-a leader of a company of men at arms
Serengford- Shellingford Oxfordshire
Surcoat- a tunic worn over mail or armour
Sumpter- packhorse
Ventail – a piece of mail that covered the neck and the lower
face.
Wulfestun- Wolviston (Durham)

Maps and Illustrations

Historical note

The book is set during one of the most turbulent and complicated times in British history. Henry I of England and Normandy's eldest son William died. The king named his daughter, Empress Matilda as his heir. When her husband, the Emperor of the Holy Roman Empire died and she remarried. Her new husband was Geoffrey of Anjou and she had children by him. (The future Henry II of England and Normandy- The Lion in Winter!)

Books used in the research:

The Varangian Guard- 988-1453 Raffael D'Amato
Saxon Viking and Norman- Terence Wise
The Walls of Constantinople AD 324-1453-Stephen Turnbull
Byzantine Armies- 886-1118- Ian Heath
The Age of Charlemagne-David Nicolle
The Normans- David Nicolle
Norman Knight AD 950-1204- Christopher Gravett
The Norman Conquest of the North- William A Kappelle
The Knight in History- Francis Gies
The Norman Achievement- Richard F Cassady
Knights- Constance Brittain Bouchard
Knight Templar 1120-1312 -Helen Nicholson

Griff Hosker
June 2016

Other books by Griff Hosker

If you enjoyed reading this book, then why not read
another one by the author?

Ancient History

The Sword of Cartimandua Series
(Germania and Britannia 50 A.D. – 128 A.D.)
Ulpius Felix- Roman Warrior (prequel)
The Sword of Cartimandua
The Horse Warriors
Invasion Caledonia
Roman Retreat
Revolt of the Red Witch
Druid's Gold
Trajan's Hunters
The Last Frontier
Hero of Rome
Roman Hawk
Roman Treachery
Roman Wall
Roman Courage

The Wolf Warrior series
(Britain in the late 6th Century)
Saxon Dawn
Saxon Revenge
Saxon England
Saxon Blood
Saxon Slayer
Saxon Slaughter
Saxon Bane
Saxon Fall: Rise of the Warlord
Saxon Throne
Saxon Sword

23232323232323

Medieval History

The Dragon Heart Series
Viking Slave
Viking Warrior
Viking Jarl
Viking Kingdom
Viking Wolf
Viking War
Viking Sword
Viking Wrath
Viking Raid
Viking Legend
Viking Vengeance
Viking Dragon
Viking Treasure
Viking Enemy
Viking Witch
Viking Blood
Viking Weregeld
Viking Storm
Viking Warband
Viking Shadow
Viking Legacy
Viking Clan
Viking Bravery
The Vengeance Trail

The Norman Genesis Series
Hrolf the Viking
Horseman
The Battle for a Home
Revenge of the Franks
The Land of the Northmen
Ragnvald Hrolfsson
Brothers in Blood
Lord of Rouen
Drekar in the Seine
Duke of Normandy

The Fallen Crown

The Duke and the King

Danelaw
(England and Denmark in the 11th Century)
Dragon Sword
Oathsword
Bloodsword
Danish Sword
The Sword of Cnut

New World Series
Blood on the Blade
Across the Seas
The Savage Wilderness
The Bear and the Wolf
Erik The Navigator
Erik's Clan
The Last Viking

The Vengeance Trail

The Conquest Series
(Normandy and England 1050-1100)
Hastings
Conquest

The Aelfraed Series
(Britain and Byzantium 1050 A.D. - 1085 A.D.)
Housecarl
Outlaw
Varangian

The Reconquista Chronicles
Castilian Knight
El Campeador
The Lord of Valencia

**The Anarchy Series England
1120-1180**

The Fallen Crown

English Knight
Knight of the Empress
Northern Knight
Baron of the North
Earl
King Henry's Champion
The King is Dead
Warlord of the North
Enemy at the Gate
The Fallen Crown
Warlord's War
Kingmaker
Henry II
Crusader
The Welsh Marches
Irish War
Poisonous Plots
The Princes' Revolt
Earl Marshal
The Perfect Knight

Border Knight
1182-1300
Sword for Hire
Return of the Knight
Baron's War
Magna Carta
Welsh Wars
Henry III
The Bloody Border
Baron's Crusade
Sentinel of the North
War in the West
Debt of Honour
The Blood of the Warlord
The Fettered King
de Montfort's Crown
Ripples of Rebellion

247

Sir John Hawkwood Series
France and Italy 1339- 1387
Crécy: The Age of the Archer
Man At Arms
The White Company
Leader of Men
Tuscan Warlord
Condottiere

Lord Edward's Archer
Lord Edward's Archer
King in Waiting
An Archer's Crusade
Targets of Treachery
The Great Cause
Wallace's War
The Hunt

Struggle for a Crown
1360- 1485
Blood on the Crown
To Murder a King
The Throne
King Henry IV
The Road to Agincourt
St Crispin's Day
The Battle for France
The Last Knight
Queen's Knight
The Knight's Tale

Tales from the Sword I
(Short stories from the Medieval period)

Tudor Warrior series
England and Scotland in the late 14th and early 15th century
Tudor Warrior
Tudor Spy

The Fallen Crown

Flodden

Conquistador
England and America in the 16th Century
Conquistador
The English Adventurer

Modern History

The Napoleonic Horseman Series
Chasseur à Cheval
Napoleon's Guard
British Light Dragoon
Soldier Spy
1808: The Road to Coruña
Talavera
The Lines of Torres Vedras
Bloody Badajoz
The Road to France
Waterloo

The Lucky Jack American Civil War series
Rebel Raiders
Confederate Rangers
The Road to Gettysburg

Soldier of the Queen series
Soldier of the Queen
Redcoat's Rifle
Omdurman

The British Ace Series
1914
1915 Fokker Scourge
1916 Angels over the Somme
1917 Eagles Fall
1918 We will remember them
From Arctic Snow to Desert Sand
Wings over Persia

Combined Operations series
1940-1945
Commando
Raider
Behind Enemy Lines
Dieppe
Toehold in Europe
Sword Beach
Breakout
The Battle for Antwerp
King Tiger
Beyond the Rhine
Korea
Korean Winter

Tales from the Sword II
(Short stories from the Modern period)

For more information on all of the books then please visit
the author's website at www.griffhosker.com where there is
a link to contact him or visit his Facebook page: Griff
Hosker at Sword Books